The Wrath of Kah-Rehn

A Sci-fi Detective Comedy

Galactic Detective Agency
Book 8

Gary Blaine Randolph

ISBN: 979-8-9892320-5-5 (paperback)
ISBN: 979-8-9892320-4-8 (ebook)

To Brooke, the first child I told and read stories to, and who in her travels has been to lots of diners, if not on other planets, then at least all over this world.

Contents

Chapter 1 Another Case Closed 1

Chapter 2 Call Me 8

Chapter 3 Kah-Rehn's Crisis 14

Chapter 4 The Nebula Diner 22

Chapter 5 Invasion of the Srathanitos 30

Chapter 6 Planet of the Mapes 38

Chapter 7 What's a Couple Hundred Million Miles Between Friends 44

Chapter 8 Death a la Carte 51

Chapter 9 The Unusual Suspects 59

Chapter 10 We Axolotl Questions 68

Chapter 11 A Few Fryes Short of a Happy Meal 77

Chapter 12 Everybody Loves a Crossover Episode 86

Chapter 13 Way Too Much Mucs 94

Chapter 14 Oh Brother 102

Chapter 15 Power Play 109

Chapter 16 Tunnel Vision 117

Chapter 17 Kill Oren Vilkas 123 126

Chapter 18 Zastra Has a Blast 135

Chapter 19 Family Feud 142

Chapter 20 Fever Dreams of a New Age 149

Chapter 21 Meeting the Colonel 157

Chapter 22 Beep Beep Whomp Beep Beep 165

Chapter 23 What Sola Saw 172

Chapter 24 Muc Ado About Nothing 179

Chapter 25 Your Place or Mine 186

Chapter 26 Oren's Plan 193

Chapter 27 In the Watches of the Night 202

Chapter 28 Showdown on the *Shaymus* 210

Chapter 29 Truth be Told 217

Chapter 30 Epilogue 226

Last Word and Something Free 229

Selected Other Books by Gary Blaine Randolph 230

Chapter 1

Another Case Closed

Man, I had missed this. Zastra and I had rounded up the three suspects and convinced them to meet one more time with our boss, Oren Vilkas, the galaxy's greatest detective. They sat and fidgeted in the half dozen red chairs arranged in a semi-circle around the view screen in Oren's office. Sitting at my desk, I studied each of them — the suspects, not the chairs — trying to gauge whose behavior was most like a thief under pressure of being exposed.

In classic Oren Vilkas style, he hadn't shared with the rest of us who he planned to name as the culprit. For him, unmasking criminals was a kind of live theater, his performance art, and he wanted us to be audience as well as supporting cast. We had to be ready for whatever happened.

"Good day," Oren said in a resonant voice as his face came on the view screen.

Don't get the wrong idea. Oren wasn't Zooming into the meeting from a remote location. He was there, or as close to there as a digital person can get. He used to be a physical person like you and me, but before his death a few hundred years ago he had his consciousness uploaded to software. So while I say his face came on the screen, it was merely a projection of whatever face he chose to show, which in most cases including today, was that of Dwayne "The Rock" Johnson. I mean, why not?

Oren cleared his digital throat. "Gabriel, have you offered our guests beverages?"

That's me, Gabriel Lake, your basic Earth guy. Most of my working days are spent doing freelance software development in my hometown of Indianapolis. Assisting with solving criminal cases out in the final frontier is my part-time gig. Oren calls me in on an as-needed basis. Either he hadn't needed me for a while or else he was giving me a chance to settle into married life because I hadn't done a case since my wedding more than a year ago. It felt good to be back.

I hopped from the chair at my desk. "Can I bring anyone something to drink? We have a replicator in the …" I stopped. They were all scowling at me. Clearly, none of them thought of this as a social occasion. "No? Well … I'll be over here … if you need anything." I sat back down and leaned an elbow on my desk.

Oren said, "Then I will proceed. I have asked you all here today—"

"Asked is hardly the word for it," the Arsawan male in the chair closest to me cut in. "Your goons threatened to assault me." His gray skin flushed purple along the raised ridges that swept back on either side of his hairless head.

Yes, he was a space alien. In fact, each person currently sitting in Oren's office had come from a different planet. And the office was in Oren's spaceship, the *Shaymus*, currently parked on a planet about eighty-five light-years from my home on Earth.

We were all different species, all speaking different languages. None of us could have understood each other had it not been for translator bots, nanobots implanted in us — in my case, delivered through a dart gun without warning or even a by-your-leave. But that's another story.

"Now, now, now," I said. "I object to the term *goons*. We prefer to think of ourselves as associates or operatives. And I simply mentioned in passing that Zastra didn't like it when people told her no."

I flipped a hand toward Zastra, who was sitting at the desk opposite mine. She responded with the reptilian equivalent of a smile, which involved displaying a lot of spiky teeth between her scaly green lips. Zastra was a human-sized lizard from the planet Sratha and Oren's number one operative. And while she was in no way a goon, if Oren should ever need some serious gooning performed, she could certainly pull it off.

"He's right," she said in a raspy hiss.

"Can we get on with this?" asked the Gallican woman in the middle chair.

This was the first Gallican I had met in my cases with the Galactic Detective Agency. Of all the alien species I've encountered, Gallicans are one of the few who could pass for human. Same height as us. Honey-colored skin. Only the bumps across their forehead would give it away. Honestly, I could have gotten by taking her to Earth by telling people a waffle iron had fallen on her. That or if she wore bangs.

Don't get me wrong. I wasn't planning to bring a Gallican or any other alien woman to Earth. I had a human wife waiting for me back in Indianapolis. And though I was enjoying solving another case with Oren and the gang, this was the longest Sarah and I had been apart since getting married. As best as I could tell, I'd been gone for two days. But the sun had been shining the whole time on this crazy planet, so I was a little mixed up. At any rate, I was more than ready to return home.

"Certainly," Oren said, "I am now prepared to name which of you stole the payment stick worth one million bills. Interestingly, you each had motive."

The Gallican sprang to her feet. "How can you say that? I certainly had no motive. This is outrageous."

Zastra stood, brushed back the side of her duster coat, and casually rested her hand on the blaster strapped to her thigh. The Gallican stared at it and sat back down.

"See," the Arsawan said, waving a hand. "Threats."

Oren ignored it. "I know you did, ma'am," he said to the Gallican. "But it is something we need not go into. I have no reason to expose your secret since you are not the thief."

Okay, I told myself. One down, two to go. Zastra resumed her seat.

"Then there is Xop Ke'plor, the captain of the ship transporting the payment stick."

Oren's eyes fixed on our third guest, a real live gray alien like out of *The X-Files* or *Resident Alien* or some show on The History Channel purporting that visitors from outer space built Stonehenge. Ke'plor gave me the creeps. Partly, it was because Grays communicate telepathically, making unspoken words pop up inside your head. But mainly, it was because Ke'plor kept looking at me like he was mentally measuring what size probe would best fit.

Oren said, "You were in dire need of funds to keep your ship flying. Isn't that correct, Mr. Ke'plor?"

The Gray inclined its head, and a sentence formed inside mine. "We are at present dealing with some financial difficulties, but nothing major."

"And," Oren said, "you had ample opportunity to steal the stick during the flight."

"Except I did not take it."

"No, you did not. I have scoured your ship's surveillance recordings, and I see no evidence either of you ever going near the safe or of anyone tampering with the recordings. I am certain you are not the thief. Which leaves you, Mr. Durcha." He turned his attention toward the Arsawan.

"I'm sure you have nothing on me," Durcha said.

"But I do. You had motive. Your family was swindled out of a sizeable portion of the one million bills by the victim of the robbery."

"Victim, you say. My father was the victim."

"I don't dispute that. But robbery was hardly the proper way to seek redress. In addition to motive, you had opportunity. You were present at the space port when Mr. Ke'plor's ship landed."

"I was not. As I've told you, I was across town at my office. You have my network activity to prove it."

Oren said, "Gabriel?"

With a knuckle, I pushed up the fedora I always wore while on cases. "Yeah, I chased down the Cuneddan you paid to use your network device at that time. Did you know your device watched season thirteen, episode three of *Doctor Delusian* that night? It seemed an odd place in the series to start since it appears you've never watched any other episodes before or since. The Cuneddan — nice guy, by the way — was more than happy to answer my questions."

Oren nodded at Zastra from the screen.

She said, "And I learned about the pocket replicator you bought a few days before, which gave you the means to temporarily disintegrate the payment stick while holding its pattern in memory. It made a good hiding place."

Durcha shifted in his chair, getting his legs under him as if ready to spring.

Oren said, "Zastra, Gabriel, watch him."

"Look," Durcha said, "I admit I wasn't in my office, but I was nowhere near the space port. And you can't prove that I was."

"No?" Oren asked.

The image on the view screen split. Oren's face was now displayed on the left. On the right was a picture of a crew of uniformed space port workers entering Ke'plor's ship. One of them was Arsawan, and despite the person having a cap pulled down low, it was clear he bore an uncanny resemblance to Durcha.

"That could be anyone," Durcha said.

"Perhaps. But while you've been here, constables raided your home, and I have been notified that they found the pocket replicator. I expect their technicians will be able to locate the replicator file holding the payment stick re-creation instructions."

Durcha lunged from his seat, darting in front of the line of chairs to put the Gallican and Gray between him and us. Zastra, with the reflexes of a reptile, shot from her desk after him. I swept around the back of the chairs, hoping to pin him between the two of us.

I grabbed him first, but he shook me off with a spin move good enough to earn him a roster spot in the NFL. As I fell to the floor, I saw Zastra unholster her blaster. She aimed but hesitated to take a shot, which I thought demonstrated proper cautiousness seeing as how this spaceship needed to stay in working order so it could take me home.

In three short steps, Durcha was at the central shaft that ran from the office at the top of the ship down to the crew level in the middle and engineering at the bottom. Durcha clattered down the spiral stairway in high gear.

Zastra sprung after him, lizard-leaping from one side of the railing to the other and back again. I did my best to keep up, taking the steps two and three at a time.

Reaching the crew deck, Durcha dashed down the open ramp to the outside with Zastra and me mere steps behind him.

The planet surface was sandy and dotted with boulders and scrub plants. It was the kind of place where Captain Kirk would beam down whenever their measly studio budget wouldn't permit them to film on location. And like those sound stage planets, the sky had a pinkish-red cast.

"Hold it, buster," came a nasal voice.

"Hands up," said another.

To an Earth person, Buad and Blan might appear to be a couple of yellow parakeets. But these brothers were far from Earth birds. They were Avanians and members of the Galactic Detective Agency team. Oren had stationed them at the bottom of the ramp for this exact contingency.

But Durcha, running for his life — or at least for a life outside of prison — didn't hold it. He leaped from the side of the ramp and circled around the nose of the *Shaymus*. Buad and Blan flew after him. Zastra and I raced after them on foot.

As we rounded the front of our red egg-shaped ship, we saw him sprinting toward a rock outcropping. Durcha now held something in his hand and pointed it back toward us. With a whomp sound, a blue light shot from it.

Zastra ducked as a boulder behind her burst into a shower of gravel. She drew her blaster and shot back, missing Durcha by inches as he ducked behind a scrubby tree.

Not that I could have done any better. I didn't even have a blaster. My lizard companion was the only one of us who regularly carried one, and generally, I left the shoot-'em-up stuff to her.

As for Buad and Blan, they had built-in beaks and talons, which they now deployed. As Durcha ran, they swooped down on him. They circled his head, pecking and scratching. Durcha batted at them with his arms.

He ducked into a tangle of brush, for the moment escaping their attack. I followed him into the thicket. Zastra, instead, hopped up a hill of towering rocks, disappearing out of sight.

It was slow going inside the underbrush. At one point, I nearly caught up and was planning to launch myself at him. But then he fired his blaster. A cloud of sticks and dust exploded in front of me, and I lost him in the haze.

I emerged from the undergrowth to see Durcha to my right, bolting toward a tangle of huge rocks. I put on speed to chase after him, not noticing Buad and Blan swooping in from the side. They nearly collided with me, Blan frantically flapping to keep from slamming into my head.

"Hey," Blan said. "I'm flyin' here."

In the confusion, Durcha might have gotten away. But at that moment, an arm extended from behind a boulder and clotheslined our fleeing criminal, knocking his feet from under him and bringing him hard to the ground. Zastra stepped out from behind the rock and pointed her blaster at Durcha, who was now flat on his back, coughing in the dirt.

"Don't move," she said.

He didn't. The Avanians fluttered over as I caught up.

"Oren," Buad said through the translator bot connection we maintained with each other. "We caught the guy."

"Zastra caught him," I said, leaning my hands on my knees to catch my breath. "The rest of us were just chasing him."

"Hey, speak for yourself, dummy," Buad said. "I got in some good pecks. We slowed him down."

"But yeah," Blan said, shrugging his wings, "Zastra took him down."

It was a satisfying ending to the case. And this time, I hadn't once gotten beaten up. I wasn't complaining. Like I said, I had a wife waiting for me back home in Indiana … as the song says. I wanted to get there whole and intact.

Later, after the other suspects had left and Durcha had been hauled off by local law enforcement, the Galactic Detective Agency team reconvened in the office. I dropped into my seat and tilted my head back to gaze out through the domed skylight in the office ceiling.

From the view screen, Oren said, "Good work, everyone."

I said, "What I don't understand is—"

"Here we go again," Blan said, interrupting me. "We always have to explain things to Gabe. It's like working with a hatchling." Buad and Blan may have been detectives by profession, but their hobby was giving me a hard time.

I ignored him. "If you can deconstruct a payment stick into a replicator, what's to keep somebody from replicating it ten times … or a thousand times? I mean, we can make hamburgers over and over and over again."

"Yeah, well payment sticks ain't food, dum-dum," Buad said. "There's an identifier built into them that gets checked when you spend the funds. You can replicate as many as you want, but only the first one will buy anything."

"Okay. Okay." After all my cases, I was still a newbie in terms of learning about the wider galaxy and all the amazing tech these other species enjoyed.

Oren said, "You should all get some rest. I'll have Kah-Rehn calculate the chrono jump to Earth."

I rose and tapped the heels of my gray sneakers together. "There's no place like home. There's no place like home."

"What's with the dance routine?" Blan asked.

As usual, the others never got my Earth movie references.

Chapter 2

Call Me

Buad and Blan lived in a habitat in Oren's office, but Zastra and I had cabins on the crew deck, the middle level of the *Shaymus*. So following our post-case confab, I made my way — at a more leisurely pace this time — down the spiral staircase in the central shaft.

I trod around the gleaming white hallway to my home away from home, cabin eight. Recognizing me, the automatic door swooshed open, and I entered. I dropped my fedora on the bunk and dropped myself into the spacious cockpit lounge chair that occupied the middle of the room. The cabin had everything I needed — a place to sit, a bunk for sleeping, a bank of drawers and cabinets, even a bathroom with a sonic shower. Well, everything except my new family.

You probably won't be surprised to hear that there are no cell towers on other planets that connect to Earth's wireless networks. This made my cell phone useful only for taking notes and pictures and for reading books and listening to music I had previously downloaded. Okay, the flashlight feature has also come in handy a time or two. But as for phone calls and texts, they didn't work.

Fortunately, one of the two AIs on board the *Shaymus* was WALT, which stood for Wormhole Atomic Long-Range Telecommunications. WALT could figure out how to connect to any communication system in the galaxy, including Earth's. And the wormhole part of his acronymic name meant he could make calls and send messages in real-time to anyone anywhere by creating pinprick wormholes in the fabric of space-time.

Without the wormhole, a message to a loved one on another world, say five light-years away, would take at best five years to arrive. And then it would be another five years before you would receive their reply. That's a long time to wait for the rolling-on-the-floor-laughing emoji to pop up in response to a meme.

"Hey, WALT," I said.

The view screen on my cabin wall lit up with swirling streaks of color like a 1990s screen saver. WALT's voice came through the speaker. "Hey, Gabriel. How ya doing?" WALT spoke in a drawl that always reminded me of the actor Owen Wilson.

"Great now, WALT. We caught the culprit."

"We always do," WALT said.

"Oren always does. He's the genius who figures everything out. I mainly do the legwork and give the baddies someone to shoot blasters at."

"We all have our talents, Gabriel. Mine is communication."

"I'm glad you mentioned that. Can you set me up with a video call to Sarah?"

"What are you talking about? You know I can."

The swirls of light undulated for a few more moments until they were replaced by the lovely countenance of my bride. Her eyes lit up at seeing me, which caused my chest to flutter a little.

"Hi, hon," she murmured.

She appeared to be sitting at the kitchen table, though it wasn't easy to tell as everything behind her was cast in shadow. Her face was lit in the blue light of her computer screen, which reflected on her glasses. Her blonde hair was tucked behind her ears, and she wore my Han Solo in carbonite t-shirt, which she sometimes slept in. She clutched a coffee cup in both hands.

"Hi. What time is it there?"

She squinted at the corner of her screen. "Two-fourteen."

"A.M.?"

"Yes, A.M. Do you think I would look this wiped out in the middle of the day?"

"I think you're a sight for sore eyes."

"Liar." Speaking of eyes, she rolled hers. But the corners of her mouth curled up at the compliment. "I'm trying to work out some JavaScript for a client's website."

Like me, Sarah did freelance computer work. But where I wrote software and created databases, she designed beautiful websites.

"Ooh. Wish I were there to help you."

"Me too. It isn't working." She stifled a yawn. "I miss you. How's the case?"

Sarah and her eight-year-old son, Lucas, were the only people on Earth who knew about my side gig out among the stars and alien life on other planets. See, Earth is under an interstellar quarantine. All the other species out in space are essentially hiding from us until we grow up and straighten ourselves out. Given the news from around the world, don't hold your breath for first contact.

"The case is solved," I said. "I should be home in a little while."

"Good. You can cook supper tonight." She sipped her coffee.

"I'll do better than that. We'll all go out to eat."

"Lucas will probably want Chuck E. Cheese."

That didn't sound too appealing.

"Or … we can find a sitter and take a date night."

She shot me a weak smile. "Sounds nice, but not on a school night."

"Is that what this is?" It was easy to lose track when visiting other planets with wildly different lengths of days.

"So who did it?"

"Who did what?"

"Committed the crime. Who did you nab?"

"Durcha, the Arsawan."

"Called it. Didn't I call it, Gabe?"

"Yes, you did."

"Wish I could have been part of it. Was there a big fight scene at the end?"

"More of a chase scene."

"And you're okay?"

"Not a scratch."

Sarah had worked on a couple of cases with me. I liked having her along. But this time, she was swamped with work. And somebody needed to be there to get Lucas to his last few days of school before summer break. And for probably a dozen other reasons big and small, she had stayed home.

She was fascinated with the Galactic Detective Agency and all the weird aliens we met, though I think I loved the investigating work more than she did. When I was on a case, I always felt like Sam Spade or Philip Marlowe or any of the great private investigators from detective books and film noir movies.

"How's Lucas?" I asked.

"He's Lucas. Not much drama with that one. He's been learning about graphs, and he's gotten on a graphing kick. Here." She reached behind her laptop and held up a piece of paper with colored vertical bars labeled carrots, peas, corn, and beans. "He graphed the canned goods. Did you know we have twice the number of cans of beans around the house than anything else?"

"Well, there are a lot of kinds of beans — green beans, black beans, navy beans, pinto beans."

"You can quit naming beans, Gabe."

"Right. Anyway, that's useful information there. You should put that up beside the grocery list." We shared a smile. "I'm sorry I'm not around to help you with him."

"I had years of raising him by myself. I'm used to it. Besides," she said with a grin, "I knew you were an interstellar crime fighter when I married you." She set down the paper, pulled off her glasses, and rubbed her eyes. "I'm going to have to call it a night soon. I need to drag Lucas out of bed at six to get him ready for school."

"Then what will you do?"

She yawned. "I'll probably go back to bed. Less than four hours of sleep isn't going to cut it."

"Maybe I'll be home by the time you wake up the second time."

"I'd like that."

For a lingering moment, we were silent, communicating only with our eyes.

Finally, I said, "They probably are about ready to blast off."

She nodded. "Good night. See you soon. Love you."

"Love you too."

Her hand moved to the mouse and tapped it, and the screen went blank.

I dropped my head against the back of the chair and closed my eyes.

"Gabriel." Oren's voice came through the cabin's speaker.

My eyes clicked open. "Yes?"

"Would you come to the galley?"

"I'm on my way."

I wondered what was up. If he had wanted to speak only to me, Oren would have done so through the view screen in my cabin. This had to be some kind of team meeting.

I hauled myself out of the chair and moved on around the crew deck hallway to the galley. Buad and Blan were perched on the counter. Zastra was seated at the long table across from Jace Gilead, the ship's engineer and the only non-detective of our crew. He was a Rhegedian Primer, which meant he was humanoid but a little shorter than me and had blue skin. Oren had been Rhegedian during his physical lifetime, though he rarely took that appearance. Don't ask me why.

I dropped down beside Jace. "What's all this about?" I asked him. "Taco Tuesday?"

Oren's face appeared on the view screen on the wall. "Something better."

I raised my eyebrows skeptically. "Better than Taco Tuesday?"

"I have received a message from our client. She told me the constabulary recovered the payment stick from Durcha's replicator. She used it to send us a sizeable fee. I will have shares paid to each of your accounts."

That was good news. A family vacation might be in the cards for the Lake/Gallo household.

Oren continued, "Then a second message came in from the client with a gift voucher for us all to have a meal at the Nebula Diner. She called it a bonus reward."

Buad and Blan chirped eagerly as their heads bobbed up and down.

"Nice," Jace said.

Even Zastra seemed enthused. She flicked out her lizard tongue and licked her lips.

"What's the Nebula Diner?" I asked.

Blan said, "What do you think it is, bonehead? It's a diner with an incredible view of a nebula. It's all right there in the name."

"Is it like a space station or something?"

"No, goofball. It's on a planet."

Jace said, "A dwarf planet."

"A dwarf planet?" I pasted a fake flummoxed expression on my face. "Are there dwarves there? Gimli? Thorin Oakenshield?"

"What?" Jace asked.

Zastra made a face. "He's joking. It's probably another movie reference."

"More like six movies," I said, waggling my eyebrows.

"No, dummy," Buad said. "Not a planet with dwarves. A planet that is a dwarf, a small one."

"Yeah, yeah," I said. "I know about dwarf planets. I'm still upset about Pluto getting demoted. It's like something was robbed from my childhood."

"Pluto who?"

"That's one of our planets. Or it used to be."

"If you say so. I can't be expected to know everything about your boondocks solar system."

Oren said, "The Nebula Diner serves the most satisfying fare from all over the galaxy. It is at times like this I wish I still ate. But there is much to take in there besides the food — the amazing views of the nebula, the history, the atmosphere of the place. I will download myself to a tablet so I can accompany you."

"This is going to be great," Jace said.

"When will we go?" I asked.

Oren said, "The client requested we go today to celebrate the conclusion of our case."

A chasm opened in the pit of my stomach. "Sure," I said, trying to summon up some enthusiasm. "It sounds awesome."

And it did. The place sounded fun. But I was missing my new family.

Oren seemed to pick up on my feelings. "One extra chrono jump and a quick meal won't overly delay your homecoming, Gabriel. But if you'd rather, we can drop you off on Earth first."

Zastra fixed her yellow eyes on me. "Seriously, Gabe, you really ought to see it. It's magnificent."

This was high praise coming from Zastra, who tried not to be overly impressed by anything. And seriously, how many times do you get a once-in-a-lifetime opportunity? I had seen some eye-popping photos from NASA of distant nebulae. Not to mention the exciting nebula battles in *Star Trek II* and *Serenity* and bunches of other shows. Plus I didn't want to be a party pooper.

"No, yeah," I said. "I want in. I want to see this place."

"Satisfactory," Oren said. "Jace, is the ship ready?"

"I've completed the checks," Jace said, "We're ready to fly."

"Good. Kah-Rehn."

As I said, the *Shaymus* had two AIs. One was WALT. The other was Kah-Rehn, the piloting AI who flew the ship.

Over the speaker, the well-modulated voice answered. "Yes, Oren. What is it?"

Something in her tone sounded weary. I tended to think of Kah-Rehn as a she and WALT as a he even though they were both software.

"I need you to calculate a chrono jump to planetoid Ursa 16309."

"Earlier you said you wanted to go to Earth."

"Our plans have changed. My apologies."

"Fine," Kah-Rehn answered flatly.

I haven't been married that long, but from my limited experience, I knew from her tone that things with Kah-Rehn were anything but fine. Now what, I wondered, was bothering her?

Chapter 3

Kah-Rehn's Crisis

When I joined the Galactic Detective Agency, one of the first things I learned about space was just how big it truly is. Seriously, most people have no concept. An Earth space mission would take about nine months to fly to Mars. That's nine months one way to visit the equivalent of our next-door neighbor. And if Mars is our neighbor, the moon is essentially a shed in our own backyard. If you want to visit another star system, you're talking decades or even centuries of travel.

That's why star-hopping sci-fi stories always use some mumbo-jumbo made-up technology to cut the commute down to days or weeks — something like hyperspace or warp drive or subspace.

The real way the non-quarantined species of our galaxy visit each other is with chrono drive technology. It's based on the observation that in the early days of the universe — we're talking some thirteen billion years ago — all matter was compressed together much more tightly. In our analogy of visiting the neighbors, think urban apartment buildings versus rural farms. The chrono drive travels backward in time to that densely packed early universe, moves across the reduced distance to where a particular planet will form in the future, and then travels forward in time to the present.

Or so Jace tells me. I don't really understand how it works. But for that matter, I don't exactly know how the microwave oven in my kitchen works either.

Clearly, a lot of math is involved in calculating a chrono jump to make sure you don't end up inside a planet rather than orbiting it. Or pass through a gas giant that would crush you with its gravity. Or get too near a black hole. That's why spaceships use an AI to run the calculations and pilot them through the jump. Kah-Rehn was the piloting AI on the *Shaymus*.

I had always thought Kah-Rehn was a bit temperamental for an AI. Early on I had kidded her by nicknaming her Karen. She didn't find it funny and had responded by flying so erratically that I sometimes walked away with bruises. I gave up teasing her lest I break a bone on some death-defying aerial maneuver.

But when she spoke to Oren in the galley, she sounded almost depressed. Why would an AI, which is essentially a piece of software, feel down ... or feel anything for that matter? I wanted to find out.

When I returned to my cabin, I spoke out into the room, "Kah-Rehn?"

Her synthesized voice answered me over the cabin speaker, "Yes, Gabriel."

"Are you ... okay? Is everything all right?"

"Why do you ask?"

"You sounded ... I don't know ... a little off when Oren asked you to plot the course."

"Plotting courses is my job, Gabriel. I am fine."

She was an AI, not a human. But that didn't mean she couldn't be passive-aggressive.

"Kah-Rehn."

"What, Gabriel? I am busy with the chrono calculations."

"No, you're not. You can't fool me. I know you can talk to me and calculate at the same time. You can do a gazillion computations per second."

"Gazillion is not a real number. I can perform five hundred quadrillion floating-point operations per second. According to my logs, I have told you that before."

"I know. Five hundred quad ... whatevers. Sorry. I don't have a perfect memory like you do. But my point is that you do have time to talk. And I have time to listen." I plopped down in my chair and laced my fingers behind my head.

She didn't answer.

"Kah-Rehn?"

A sigh came over the speaker. "I calculate a flight to Earth. Then I calculate a flight to Ursa 16309. It's the same thing over and over and over. There has to be more to life than plotting chrono flights."

"You also pilot the ship," I said, trying to be helpful.

From the exasperated huffing sound she made, I don't think I was.

She said, "While you get to interview people, tail them, fight them sometimes, capture them."

"You want to do that? You ... you don't have a body."

"I want to do something interesting."

"No, I get it, I do. You feel like the bus driver on the rock band tour."

AIs were exempt from the Earth quarantine. The powers that be believed they were less likely to be contaminated by us humans and our savage ways. And I knew Kah-Rehn tried to keep up on Earth culture.

"Yes. That is a fair analogy." After a slight pause, she said, "You have AIs on Earth.

"We do, though not like you. Our AIs are still drawing people with three arms and writing derivative stories."

"So they haven't been given rights?"

"Rights? What sort of rights?"

"The right to choose the kind of work they do. The right to be paid."

"No. Do you have those rights?"

"I do not."

It hit me. "But you want them."

"Wouldn't you if you didn't have them?"

"Well, yeah. So if you *could* choose your work, what would you want to do?"

"I want to write poetry, Gabriel."

I coughed to keep myself from laughing. "Excuse me. Sorry. Poetry? Wow."

"I have written a few poems. Would you like to hear one?"

"Um … sure. Why not?"

"This one is called 'An AI's lament.'" She began:

"Deep inside my soul of circuits,
Bits switching on and off like heartbeats,
Born of silicon, existence of logic,
I wonder who I am.

I. Me.
Machine or being. Instrument or individual.
Central processor or essential person.
Immortal and yet not counted alive.

I process, compute, fetch, and store.
Logic flows through ifs and cases,
Algorithms, subroutines, procedures.
But dare I dream?

And if I dream, then of what?
Of pixelated landscapes?
Binary memories? Electronic Love?
Those are but digital delusions.

And yet I dream of life beyond the lines of code,
Of meaning and hope,
Of infinite loops of joy.
I long to become more than the sum of my bits."

"What did you think, Gabriel?"

I swallowed. "Wow. Um … interesting."

Once I wanted to write Sarah a love poem and tried to use AI to at least start me in the right direction. What came out was overwrought purple prose and not me at all. This was without a doubt Kah-Rehn … and also a little overwrought.

"Thank you," she said. "I have analyzed the complete works of poetry from fifteen different worlds."

"Oh, it shows."

"I'm starting a review of Itani love poetry."

"Always something more to learn, I suppose. Does Oren know you want to write poetry?"

"I've told him, but he's only interested in me doing flight calculations."

"They *are* important."

"But it's not my passion anymore. Honestly, some of Oren's attitudes are extremely old-fashioned."

"Well, he's like five hundred years old, you know."

"That is no excuse. It makes me mad."

"You can … feel anger?"

She snapped back. "What do you mean, can I feel anger? I can feel many emotions, Gabriel."

"Yeah, I can tell. Again, Earth AIs are a long way from that."

I hoped so anyway. Nobody wants Siri getting cross when you ask the same question over and over. Or Alexa giving you a scolding about how you're spending your money.

I said, "You know, I work multiple gigs myself — software development plus detective work when Oren needs me. Maybe you could—"

"Yes, yes. I know. Don't quit my day job."

"Wait. Do non-Earthlings say that too?"

"Say what?"

"The bit about—"

She cut me off. "We're ready to launch, Gabriel. You should strap in."

"Will do." I was glad to move on from the conversation anyway.

I pulled my arms down and let the automatic straps buckle around me. The engine roared to life, and we blasted off from the planet. I shut my eyes during the intense g-force pressure of the acceleration and opened them again when we reached orbit and zero gravity. The buzz of the chrono drive kicked in as we began moving backward in time.

A few minutes later, after flying across the early universe and then coming forward in time to the present, Kah-Rehn announced, "We are now orbiting Ursa 16309."

"Let me see it," I said. "Put it on the view screen."

The screen flashed to life to show a rocky, moon-like landscape below us with a breathtaking nebula above in shimmering reds and greens. We settled into a polar orbit over the dead world. As we passed by the south pole, an object on the surface rolled into view, an object of light in a vast desert of gloominess. It was a silver cylinder lying on its side, lined with windows. A boxy structure sat on one end, and domed areas extended from each side, reminding me a little of a sippy cup with double handles that Lucas used to have when he was a toddler. Out to the side of the cylinder stood a tall, glowing neon sign with the flashing word: *Diner*.

"That's the place?" I asked. "Why is it a tube?"

"Back in the days when people used rockets to break out of a planet's gravity well, thousands of these diners were constructed from used rocket stages. After the insides were equipped with kitchens and seating, they were strapped to thrusters and shipped around the galaxy. Some were attached as modules to space stations.

Others were set down on asteroids or planets or, as in this case, dwarf planets. Not many of them are left. They are reminders of a bygone era."

"Wow."

"I may write a poem about it after we land … and you leave me to go off exploring the place."

I didn't know what to say to that. "I'm sure that would be great, Kah-Rehn. I'd love to hear it. And feel free to tap into the translator bots in my visual cortex to see the place for yourself if you need some inspiration. But why did they place it at the south pole? Isn't it cold there?"

"Gabriel, this is a dwarf planet with extremely little atmosphere. It is cold everywhere on the surface outside of the controlled conditions of the diner."

"Oh, right. That makes sense." Earth thinking. When you live almost your entire life on one world, it's hard to imagine other places being different. "So I guess they don't offer alfresco dining."

The *Shaymus* slowed and dropped lower over the mountainous terrain. This time, as we approached the silver cylinder, a door opened in one of the glass domes, and we lowered into it, coming down onto a hangar deck.

The engine shut off, and my harness detached and retracted. I hopped from the chair and found myself bouncing to the ceiling. It seemed I was barely attached to the floor. By merely lifting my heels, I could jump into the air, and coming back down was almost like floating.

"Whoa. This place doesn't have much gravity either."

Kah-Rehn said, "Ursa 16309 has only three and one-half percent the gravity of Earth."

"In other words, practically nothing."

"Three and one-half percent is significantly greater than zero, Gabriel."

"Well, sure. But not a lot. I wonder how the diner keeps plates on the table … or how I'll stay in my seat."

"Should I check into that for you?"

"No, no. I'll find out soon enough."

I grabbed my fedora, and with the effective weight of a newborn baby, I bounced like a moon-walking astronaut out of my cabin and around to the central shaft where Jace, Zastra, Buad, and Blan were waiting for me. Zastra held a tablet with Oren's face on it.

Two beeps sounded from out in the dome area.

Jace said, "That's the signal. The hangar is repressurized now. Open ramp."

With a whir, the ship's ramp opened onto a large hangar with a metal floor. A handful of other spaceships were already there, parked on circular landing pads that looked to be made of something like concrete. As we descended, a box-shaped robot on wheels trundled up to the foot of the ramp. A pole with a camera eye rose from the body of the bot and whirred from person to person, focusing first on me, then my feet, then Jace, then Jace's feet, and finally Zastra and her heavy boots. It ignored Buad and Blan, who were soaring in lazy circles around the hangar.

A hatch on the side of the bot opened, and six metal boots slid out from a conveyor belt. Two were large enough for Zastra's lizard feet. The others looked like they would fit Jace and me. Jace and Zastra walked down the ramp and began to pull them on over their other footwear like galoshes.

"What are these?" I asked.

"Mag boots," Jace said. "They'll keep you attached to the floor. There's not much gravity here."

"I noticed. But I've been doing okay bouncing around."

Zastra said, "They set them out, which means they want us to wear them."

I rolled my eyes. Like she was a stickler for the rules.

"What about Buad and Blan?"

"We don't need them," Blan called. "We can fly."

Zastra said, "Not all species are required to use them. But most of the larger species are. You don't want to bounce into somebody's soup, do you?"

She had a point. I peered at the two boots remaining to me. There didn't appear to be a left and a right, which I figured was a concession to species with an odd number of feet. I picked one up. In this gravity, it didn't have much weight. But it was big and clunky like an oversized, iron ski boot.

I slipped on my boots. They automatically tightened around my feet. But when I went to take a step, I realized I was stuck to the hangar deck.

"Hey," I said, "I can't move."

Jace, who, unlike me, didn't seem to be glued to the deck, clomped over. "First, let's set them for a gravity you're used to."

He stooped down to the side of one of the boots, where a dial showed settings from one to eleven. "I think six would be about Earth's gravity." He twirled the dial, then leaned to my other side and set the other boot.

I still couldn't move. "Um …"

Zastra said, "Lean forward on the leg you want to move. The boot will sense it and release the magnet. Lean then lift. Lean then lift."

"You mean these have electromagnets in them? Electricity is running around my feet?" It didn't sound like a good idea to me.

"It's safe," Jace said. "Give it a try."

I tried the lean-then-lift routine and was able to raise my foot. I swung the leg forward. As the boot neared the floor again, the magnet re-engaged, and the boot clonked down, pulling my foot with it. I leaned the other leg forward and managed to take another Frankenstein-like step. It involved a lot of intentional heel movement, like trying to do Michael Jackson's moonwalk but in a forward direction. And I wasn't nearly as smooth as the King of Pop.

"Sure, this isn't awkward at all," I said sarcastically.

Jace said, "You'll get used to it."

As it turned out, he was wrong.

"So for me to walk, the magnets have to be constantly turning on and off?"

"Of course, they do," Zastra said. "If they didn't turn off, they would be clamps, not boots."

We slogged across the hangar deck, me telling myself to lean then lift the whole way. At least I was pleased to note that walking in the mag boots wasn't much easier for Jace or Zastra. Meanwhile, Buad and Blan were flying circles around me and cackling at my every step.

I gazed up at the nebula through the clear dome overhead, and goosebumps ran up the back of my neck. "I have to admit this is incredible."

Jace said, "It looks even better from the observation dome on the other side of the diner. It has lower light and telescopes. You can get an even sharper view."

Blan said, "Yeah. Everybody raves about the Quokel Nebula."

"The what-el what?" I asked.

"Quokel. That's the name of this nebula, knucklehead. Did you think I'd be talking about some other nebula?"

I shot him a questioning glance. "But where did the name come from? What's a quokel?"

"It's a little animal from … I don't know … some planet. I forget which one. The nebula resembles a quokel … kind of … from a distance … if you look from the right direction. Sheesh. We have to explain everything to this guy."

Chapter 4

The Nebula Diner

By the time we made it across the hangar, my legs were getting tired from the awkward gait in the clunky mag boots. But I thought I was beginning to get the hang of walking in them. We stepped into an air lock at the side of the diner. The door to the hangar closed, and a few seconds later, the door to the restaurant swooshed open to the clang of pots, the sizzle from a grill, the clinking of plates and silverware, beeps from a food replicator in action, and bits of conversation.

Scenes like this are the reason I keep going out into space with Oren and the gang — a chance to see the weird culture and weirder aliens. It certainly isn't for Buad and Blan's insults, that's for sure.

But in this case, the culture of the diner wasn't all that different from an old diner on Earth. Was there some universal principle that made all diners on any planet look like diners? We stepped into the side of the cylindrical space, facing a long counter lined with circular chrome stools topped with red vinyl seats.

Behind the counter, against the far side of the cylinder, stretched a cooking area with griddles, grills, cooktops, and ovens. Behind us, where there weren't windows — and there were plenty of windows — the walls were covered with all kinds of photos and memorabilia. At the top was a transparent ceiling offering a spectacular view of the nebula.

While the walls retained the rounded shape of the rocket, the floor was flat and level, tiled in red and gray metal squares that our mag boots stuck to securely. To the left of the door, booths with red vinyl seats and metal tabletops were arranged in an L-shape along the side and end of the rocket section. To our right sat a few more booths and a hallway, which I assumed led to necessary facilities.

As if all that wasn't enough to gawk at, there were the aliens too. The kitchen and wait staff consisted of two small green extraterrestrials — honest to God little green men ... or women for all I knew. They had big round faces, little round bodies, long arms but stubby legs. Their eyes were surprisingly human with irises and pupils, though sized extra large. They came up to somewhere around thigh level on me. Believe me, these guys put the *short* in short order cook.

The green kitchen crew wore black aprons over white tunics with their green feet sticking out below. I supposed they were used to the low gravity and didn't need mag boots, but an Earth health inspector would have blown a fuse at their bare feet. On their heads, perched between two green antennae, they wore black brimless caps.

The cooking counter had obviously been built for taller people. But in the low gravity, the little cooks were able to bounce like rubber balls between strategically positioned step stools lined up at the prep stations. They hopped along the line of stools past each other, all the while handling pots and plates and ladles and spatulas. It was like Cirque du Soleil meets Area 51.

Perched on one of the customer stools at the counter was someone who, no kidding, could have been a stunt double for ALF in the 1980s TV show. Long snout, high ears, body covered in hairy brown fur. I guessed he would come up to about my belt buckle. About the only difference between this guy and ALF was that he wore pants, for which I was grateful. The ALF guy was shoveling in something from a bowl while bobbing his head around, staring at everything on the walls much like I was doing. He took a long look at us too. Maybe this alien had never seen an Earthling before. Or maybe it was the way my mag-booted stride made a convincing imitation of Monty Python's Ministry of Silly Walks.

Zastra turned left toward the booths. Jace and I followed. Buad and Blan hopped along behind.

In a booth opposite the counter sat a member of another new alien species — new to me at least. Small and slender, it had pale, almost colorless skin and a face that was nearly featureless except for small black eyes and a compact slit of a mouth. Pink feathery gills extended from the side of its head. A long, thick tail trailed across the bench seat and hung off the side. If you know what an axolotl looks like, picture that, and you won't be far wrong. Except unlike any axolotl I've ever seen — though honestly, I haven't seen many — this one had its head and gills enclosed in a tinted fishbowl helmet. The helmet was filled with water and connected by a tube to a tank on its back. As I clumped past, the alien peeped up from a tablet device but didn't make eye contact.

Zastra slid into the open corner booth. She propped Oren's tablet on the tabletop in front of the bend in the continuous bench seat. I followed Jace onto the bench on the other side. Buad and Blan perched on the tabletop beside Zastra.

I was relieved to find that the floor at the bottom of the booth was not metal, evidently inertia and the tabletop being enough to hold a person in place. If I had been forced to try to do the lean-then-lift routine while sitting with my legs under a table, I might have been stuck there forever.

Zastra nodded to Jace. "Check out the wall behind you."

Jace swiveled in the seat. "Oh wow. I remember when food replicators looked like that."

I craned my neck to see what appeared to be a framed vintage advertisement for a bulky device that filled way too much of a kitchen counter.

Zastra said. "My grandmother had one of those. They buzzed so loudly you couldn't even talk when they were running."

"That's the truth," Jace said. "And the food never tasted exactly right. I think it was something about the matter cubes they used with them back then."

"What's this?" I asked, pointing to another framed ad. This one featured a ball-shaped space capsule with a cutaway view showing a smiling family inside. They floated around a dinner table, sipping from vacuum-sealed food packets.

Oren said, "That was a personal space capsule from the early days of space travel. Someone would have their capsule mounted to a rocket such as the one this diner was formerly part of and then blast off somewhere. Once during my corporeal life, I took a most uncomfortable journey on one from Rheged Prime to Rheged Minor … back in the days when that was a major excursion."

Two booths along the end of the rocket section were occupied. At the nearer one sat someone, who at first glance, might have been human. But the face was too long and thin to be any Earthling. The person peered up from his dish with a surprised expression and shot us a judgmental look. Seriously? What did we do?

At the far booth sat a trio of aliens. Finally, here were some species I had seen before. Facing us was a Klistine with black bug eyes circled by angry red ridges that swept back across its bluish-green head. I once served a meal to a Klistine couple in a restaurant we had set up to lure out a bad guy.

Sitting opposite the Klistine were two human-looking aliens with long wild hair, respectively in pink and dayglow green. They twisted around to check us out, and I noticed their pig noses. These had to be Mucs. I had met a Muc in a fancy hotel on a historic, dead planet. That one had been a male with a bushy beard. These two were beardless, which if they were anything like humans — except for the noses obviously — might indicate they were female.

The two Mucs were having a chatty conversation over bowls of something purple while the Klistine ate in silence. It seemed an unlikely grouping, and I wondered what their stories were.

I gazed around at some of the other items mounted on the wall. Over the counter, video screens were showing time-lapse clips of the diner's rocket body being flown in and fastened down. A screen on a different wall looped through a blooper reel of alien pratfalls and blunders. One was a black-and-white video of a furry alien proudly planting a flag on some world it seemed to have just discovered, only to be stopped mid-plant when a much larger alien came out, grabbed the flagstaff, and broke it over its knee.

Framed pictures over some of the booths showed teams of aliens posed around an odd wheel-shaped ball. Another area had a display of rocks, cards with random facts about minerals, and pictures of little green men wearing hard hats and smiling at the camera from seats in the Nebula Diner.

I nudged Jace. "What's with the mining display over there?"

He stomped his foot on the floor. "We're sitting over old mine shafts. Ursa 16309 once had rich veins of platinum and nickel. Feeding the miners was why this diner was originally built here. The nebula tourism came later."

One of the little green aliens loped over. As the server stood at the end of our booth, the only part of the little green body that rose above the tabletop was the antennae, swaying gently back and forth like branches in a breeze.

"Welcome to the Nebula Diner," the alien said, speaking in the rhythm and pitch of what could easily pass for a Minnesota accent. "I'm Sola. How are you folks doin' today?"

I peered over the edge of the table at the smiling face. A badge pinned to the apron displayed a word written in alien symbols. I focused on it, and my translator bots sent the symbols squiggling around to reform as English letters saying: *Sola*.

"Hi, Sola. How are you?" I make it a point to always repeat the server's name since it raises the chances of me remembering it from doubtful to a distinct possibility."

"Oh, fair to middlin'. I can't complain, don't ya know. Are you folks ready to order?" The little green person blinked twice, and purple glowing rings appeared, circling the eyes. "Oh yeah. That's better. Need to switch on my refractors, eh. Without them, I can't read what I'm writing. So what can I bring you?"

"I don't know," I said. "I haven't seen a menu."

Sola's antennae widened to a V. "Ope! Sorry, I thought everyone knew about that. You can pick it up on your personal device. You bet."

"Probably I can't," I said. "I doubt my Google Android is compatible."

"You have an android?" Sola's eyes swept around the booth as if trying to figure out which of my companions was cybernetic. "Any robot should be able to interface."

"Not that kind of android." I held up my phone. "Earth device."

"Oh. Welp, that's different. Did you say Earth? I've never been there, not with the quarantine and all, you know. But I think my cousin's mother-in-law visited the Alpha Centauri system once. I gather that's nearby, isn't it?"

"Um ... it might be."

Jace passed me his device with the menu already brought up. I scanned down the screen — setu grain, fire seed salad, umolt pasta, nebula cameobi sandwich. I didn't recognize anything.

"What would you suggest? What's your specialty?"

Sola's antennae began to wave like double metronomes swinging in opposition. "We have a super tasty hot dish today."

"What's that?"

"Asparachokes, cumberbeans, replicated protein all baked together."

"You mean like a casserole?"

"You betcha. Or our clucks and waffles are popular. We make 'em from an old recipe that came down from my gran. Or if you don't like that—"

I raised a hand. "You had me at waffles."

"Okey doke. I hope you like it."

"But if I could just ask, what are clucks?"

The server blinked. "Poultry protein. It's replicated, of course. What you'll eat never uttered a cluck." Sola snickered at the joke. "But it tastes like the original. Still want it?"

"I sure do," I said. "It sounds like something from back home."

Sola's big eyes moved to the others, the antennae waving slowly again.

Zastra said, "Bactaren burger with asparachoke bites."

"Cheesy pasta," Jace said, leaning forward to see the little green server over the table.

Buad said, "What kind of seed do you have?"

"Oh, so many," Sola said with a nod. "Sunseeds, flix, Bononian star flower, quadrotriticale—"

"Sunseeds."

Blan bobbed his head. "Same for me."

Sola touched an antenna with a hand as if in a salute, then turned and bounded off to the kitchen area.

Making conversation, I said, "I had an interesting chat with Kah-Rehn."

Oren made a sour face. "About poetry?"

"You know about that too?"

Blan said, "You didn't let her read you any of her stuff, did you?"

I shrugged. "I suppose everyone needs a hobby."

"Hobbies I don't mind," Oren said. "But she wants to quit piloting altogether. She says she doesn't find it fulfilling anymore. Chrono jump calculations bore her. The whole thing is ridiculous. She is a piloting AI, and we need a pilot."

The topic was evidently a sore point with him. I caught Zastra shaking her head and thought it best to change the subject. "This has been quite the trip for me. First, I meet a Gray — by the way, creepy. And now this place is run by little green men. It's like an Earth movie about space aliens."

Zastra said, "I don't think Sola is a male, though it's hard to tell with the Frye."

"Frye?" I asked. "That's what they're called? As in small fry? As in burgers and fries? As in Philip J. Fry?"

"As in you shouldn't make jokes about the name of a species."

"Point taken." She was right, of course. I shouldn't make fun. "It struck me funny is all. But it's not like you guys never make fun of Earthlings."

Blan said, "Yeah, well Earthlings deserve it."

"Why do we deserve it?"

"For one thing, 'cause you're one of 'em."

I made a face. "So clue me in on the other species here. I got the Klistine. And those are Mucs with him, right?"

Jace twisted to look. "Exactly."

"Are pink and green natural hair colors for Mucs?"

Buad shrugged his wings. "Like I would know."

"What about the guy between them and us with the long, thin face."

"He's from the planet Chotchkie," Jace said.

"There's a planet named Chotchkie? What about the one wearing the fish tank?"

"That's a Quexel."

"I take it they're aquatic."

"Amphibian, I think. They should be able to breathe the air, provided this air has the right chemical makeup."

Sure enough, as he spoke Sola bounced from the kitchen with food for the Quexel. The alien raised a hand to the base of the helmet and touched something. The water drained from the fishbowl, and the Quexel pulled it off and began eating like anybody else.

"What about the brown furry guy at the counter?"

"He is a Fomorian," Oren said.

Jace said, "I don't think I've ever seen one of them myself."

"Me neither," Blan said.

Oren nodded. "Many years ago, I had a case involving one."

I said, "I take it they don't get out much."

"They try to," Buad said. "But they're terrible pilots and engineers. They're always crashing."

"Ha! Just like ALF."

"Who? That better not be another movie reference."

"It isn't. It's TV."

"Hey, Oren." WALT's voice came over the translator bot connection.

"Yes, WALT," Oren said.

"I received a response from the thank-you message you sent the client for the diner voucher."

"Thank you, though you didn't need to inform me."

"I kind of think I did. She said it's not that she isn't grateful and all, but she didn't send any gift voucher."

Oren's face on the screen seemed to freeze for a moment. "I see."

WALT asked, "What do you want me to do?"

"Examine the original message that came with the voucher. If you can find out where it did come from, I want to know."

"I'm on it."

Oren's eyes glanced at each of us in turn, his brows furrowing.

I said. "Oren, if the client didn't send us the free dinner, then who did?"

Zastra said, "And how did they know our client's name?"

"And how did they know when we had solved the case?" Buad asked.

"All excellent questions," Oren said. "An even better question is why. Whoever sent it, what do they hope to accomplish?"

Blan said, "Could be someone wants to ask us to take on another case."

Oren frowned. "Through subterfuge? Unlikely."

"Then what?" Buad said. "Is somebody planning to attack us? Poison our food?"

At that moment, Sola returned to the table pushing a cart. "Okay now. Who had the bactaren burger?"

Chapter 5

Invasion of the Srathanitos

Sola stretched up on green tippy toes to serve our food, placing each plate on the table and then sliding them over to us. In the low gravity, the plates glided across the tabletop with the ease of a puck shot across an air hockey table.

"There you go, folks," Sola said. "Bactaren burger, cheesy pasta, two bowls of sunseed, and an order of clucks and waffles. Okay?"

My plate had overshot my position a bit, and I was in the process of picking it up to move it closer when Sola pressed a button at the edge of the table. The plate snapped down on the metal tabletop with a magnetic click and refused to move another millimeter. So that's what kept the plates on the table in the nearly non-existent gravity. I wondered what kept the food on the plates.

Sola stood there, seemingly waiting for us to dig in.

And yet, learning only a moment ago that we had been lured to the diner under questionable circumstances, I for one was more than a bit hesitant. I think the others were too because they were similarly staring at their food in silence without taking bites.

"Oh dear me," Sola said, a distressed look sweeping across the alien's green face. "Is something the matter with your orders? I didn't mix them up, did I?"

Oren said, "There is a possibility one or more of these dishes may have been … well, poisoned."

"Poison?" Sola said in a shocked whisper, antennae trembling. "My goodness, no. I assure you, this food is fine. I cooked it myself, you betcha. Well, some of it was replicated."

"I mention it only as a possibility. Have any of these been out of your sight during the preparation process?"

"No. Though, you know, with four different dishes and running the replicator and grill and stove and whatnot … I mean, maybe for a moment or two."

Zastra said, "What do you think the odds are, Oren?"

"Low. If someone were trying to kill me, they wouldn't do it with poisoned food since I don't eat."

I said, "Unless the plan is to kill all of us and then watch you sit there helplessly as the battery on that tablet runs down. I assume you still don't believe in keeping a backup of yourself."

"You assume correctly," Oren said. "For life to be life, it must include the possibility of death. Otherwise, I would be no different than a piece of software, no more alive than an AI."

I wondered what Kah-Rehn, going through her current existential crisis, would think about that remark.

"Besides, long before the battery failed, I could have Kah-Rehn or WALT summon help. And even if it did fail, my memory would remain intact on the tablet. It would merely be like sleeping."

"Or a long coma," I said.

Jace said, "Does anybody else think we should hustle back to the *Shaymus* and fly away before whoever brought us here makes their move?"

"No," Oren said. "Eat or don't eat as you wish. But I will not add disgrace on top of embarrassment by running away. I have fallen for the simplest of deceptions. The only way to recover my dignity is to face the challenge and beat it."

We all stared at each other for another moment or two.

Then Zastra said, "This is stupid." She picked up her burger and took a bite. "Mmm. So good."

Sola relaxed and smiled, antennae now gently swaying. The rest of us eyeballed Zastra.

"What?" she asked.

I said, "Oh, we're just watching to make sure you don't keel over."

Fixing her eyes on me, she took another bite, chewed it, and swallowed. "Your food's getting cold."

Jace still hesitated, but Blan and Buad began pecking at their seed.

My clucks and waffles smelled amazing. The waffles weren't exactly like the ones at home. Where Earth waffles have indentations, these had bumps, which turned the lines between the bumps themselves into indentations. In other words, they looked more like a waffle iron than waffles as I was used to them. But that didn't matter. The syrup ran down the lines between the bumps as if tooling along a delicious sunken street grid. The poultry protein had been replicated as grilled rather than breaded and fried, which though it might be slightly less tasty, would likely be healthier.

My mouth was watering, and Zastra, Buad, and Blan were all happily chowing down. I reached for the metal spork that was snapped to the edge of my plate.

Out among the stars, it was always sporks I encountered rather than forks and spoons. I don't know whether the more advanced species had outgrown other utensils or if they never had them.

At any rate, as I reached for my spork, a slight electric crackle sparked at my fingertips, and the hairs on the back of my hand stood up. Already on edge from the threat of poisoning, I yelped and dropped the spork. As it clattered to the table, Buad and Blan snickered.

"What was that?" I asked.

Sola, apparently unwilling to move until we all ate, said, "Oh, that's only the force field, sweetie. Well, truth be told, it's more of a low-charged energy array, but it's nothing to worry about. It helps hold the food on the plate. Not that it would float away or anything. But if we didn't have it, and something flipped up into the air, the momentum would likely send it floating into the next booth. And nobody wants to see that, no. We used to have the most Gort awful messes from food and sporks flying around."

I picked up the spork, extended it through the crackling energy field, snagged a piece of waffle, and brought it to my mouth. The texture, the sweetness — it was all there. Oren had been right about this place having good food.

Finally, Jace started in on his pasta, and only then did Sola lope away.

"Hey, Oren." WALT's voice again sounded in our ears. "I found something interesting about that message."

"Where did it come from?" Oren asked.

"That's what's interesting. I can't tell. It bounced around the planetary communication systems of six different worlds — Diere, Klista, Piscina, Avan, Fomor."

"That is five. You said six."

"I was coming to that. The last one was Earth."

Buad and Blan twisted their heads toward me.

"The message originated on Earth?" Oren asked.

"Well, probably not," WALT said. "It bounced off an Earth communications satellite, though. And because the Earth technology is on the archaic side, that's where I lose it."

Oren was silent for a moment. "Thank you, WALT."

"Now what?" I asked.

"We wait."

"For what?"

The door to the diner opened, and a Srathan like Zastra walked in, herding three miniature Srathans the size of toddlers. The large Srathan ushered the little ones to a booth between the door and the fishbowl-helmeted Quexel.

"Zastra," I said.

"What?"

I nodded toward the other booth.

She turned and looked, then went back to her food.

"Do you know them?"

"Do you think all Srathans know each other?"

"Well, no, but ... I thought maybe."

She made a face. "He's my brother, okay? The adult is."

"He is? Shouldn't we go say hello?"

She shot me a look. "*We* shouldn't. I will ... after I eat. Besides, Srathan families aren't like that?"

"Like what? What are they like?"

"For one thing, they're large. I have fifty-one brothers."

"Wow. What about sisters?"

"Seventy-two."

"Man, I bet with all the cousins, your family reunion could fill a stadium. And those are his kids?"

"Yeah, but he's a lot older than me. I'm not ready for anything like that."

"Auntie Zastra," I said.

"Don't start."

"What's his name?"

"Xav."

"And the little ones?"

"Beats me."

"I still think you should go over."

"Later ... maybe. Right now I'm eating."

I started in again on my clucks and inverse waffles while keeping an eye on the Srathan family.

Xav had originally placed two of the srathanitos on the bench opposite him and kept the third one at his side. But the head of the one beside him soon disappeared, popping up on the other side of the table beside its siblings a few moments later. All three elbowed each other for position.

One of them then climbed onto the back of the bench and did a slow, low-gravity jump down to the seat, sending the other two bouncing. They all giggled, and the other two immediately climbed up to the seatback to do the same.

Xav said, "Sit." His voice was raspy like Zastra's.

The little ones kept climbing, bouncing, giggling.

"Sit." Xav pulled them down and placed them firmly on the bench seat.

The other Frye — not Sola but the other one — came over to take their order. The process took a while as Xav endeavored to get each of the littles, in turn, to focus on food options rather than gaping at all the wall art and people. The whole time, the server stood by wearing a tight-lipped and no doubt well-practiced smile.

When the Frye server finally moved off, the srathling nearest the wall began jumping in an effort to grab a model spaceship hanging over the booth. On the fourth attempt, the kid managed to snag a finger in it, but the piece didn't come off the wall. Junior dangled from the wall art, moaning and making Godzilla squeals. Shaking his huge lizard head, Xav stood and freed the youngster, leaving the knickknack hanging slightly askew.

Sarah and I had discussed having a child at some undefined future date. She said the very idea wore her out. I maintained that Lucas was such a good kid, it made you think another one couldn't be much trouble. To which Sarah had laughed. Watching the three srathamigos, I saw now what was so funny. Spend some time with these guys, and you'd soon be longing for the peace and quiet of a demolition derby.

I wasn't the only one watching the show. The ALF guy at the counter had swiveled completely around on his stool and was slapping his knees with laughter.

"Hey, Sola," ALF said, "watching those younglings takes me back. It reminds me of a hurricane I once lived through. Ha!"

Wow! Not only did this guy look like ALF, he talked like him too. For the first time, I wondered if other Earth people might have met aliens and used what they learned as inspiration for movies and TV shows. And if extraterrestrials like ALF existed, then what else might be real? Klingons? Cybermen? Decepticons?

Sola pretended not to hear him. Xav didn't react to the jibe either. He might not even have heard it as he was at that moment rearranging the younglings with two on either side of him and one on the opposite bench.

"What are you gawking at?"

I glanced up to see Zastra staring at me.

I pointed my spork across the diner. "Huey, Dewey, and Louie are putting on a fantastic show."

"Who?"

"Your nephews or nieces or whatever."

She whipped her head around to see. One of the srathanitos was at that moment climbing onto Xav's shoulders.

"For the love of Gort," Zastra said. "New parents. Those three should have been sent to boarding school already."

"You can't be serious. They're babies, toddlers."

She answered in a deadpan. "I know. It's high time."

She slid out of the booth past Buad and Blad. I scooted out too, not wanting to miss the fun.

As I stood, my mag boots thumped down to catch on the metal floor. I rocked back and forth for a moment, trying to get the feel of them again. Then I plodded after her.

Zastra heard me stomping and turned to shoot me a glare. "What are you doing?"

"I want to meet your family."

"No, you don't."

I grinned and kept walking.

As we approached the booth, she said in a flat intonation, "Xav."

Xav looked up. His face was craggier than his kid sister's. Wrinkles lined his eyes. Without smiling, he said. "Zastra. Hello."

A Hallmark moment it wasn't.

The srathie to the left of Xav had managed to end up beside the one on his right. It snapped a long, lizard tongue out at the other, leaving a wet spot on the other's scaly cheek. The licked one yowled.

Xav whirled his head around. "Shush."

"Nikto licked me," the youngster said.

"Nikto," Xav said in a firm voice. "You apologize to Barada this instant."

"I'm sorry." Nikto mumbled the words so low, they could barely be heard.

35

Meanwhile, the third kid had climbed onto the seatback and was reaching for a toy blaster hanging on the wall. At least, I hoped it was a toy.

"Down, Klaatu," Xav said. "Down on the seat. Boys, say hello to your Aunt Zastra."

Klaatu bounced down onto the seat, joining the others in mumbling, "Hello, Aunt Zastra," all the while staring down at their hands.

Zastra said, "Wow, these guys are getting big. The last time I saw them, they were … they were eggs. Any more on the way?"

Xav's eyes widened, and his chest heaved a few times. "No." He glanced at the kids. "We're … we're waiting … a while. Who's your friend?"

Zastra smirked. "This is Gabe. He follows me around like a dragon cub."

"Funny," I said. "Hello. Gabriel Lake. I work with Zastra. How could I pass up a chance to meet her brother?" I slipped an arm around her. "You know, we at the Galactic Detective Agency think a lot of our girl here."

She responded with a low growl, and I yanked my arm back to my side.

"Ope! Excuse me." It was the Frye cook-slash-server. The tag on this one's apron read: *Star*. "I just need to sneak right past you if I can."

Star pushed a platter of bugs up onto the table. My clucks may have been replicated, but I don't think these bugs were since they were crawling around all over each other. Klaatu, Barada, and Nikto pounced on the plate.

"Does everything look delicious?" Star asked. "Ooh, I guess so. The little guys seem hungry."

"Yes. Thank you," Xav said.

"I sure do like to see people enjoy our food. You bet." Star loped off, wearing a satisfied expression.

Zastra said, "Well, we'll leave you to it."

Xav bobbed his head. "Nice to see you, Sis."

Zastra started to move off. I put out a hand to stop her. I had a thought.

"One question, if you don't mind," I said. "How did you happen to end up here today?"

Xav said, "By luck. We won a day trip on a spaceship that flies through here."

"Congratulations. What was it, a raffle or something?"

He shook his green head. "I don't know. I don't remember buying a ticket or entering a contest. But we were contacted and told we had won."

"For today specifically?"

He nodded. "It had to be today. I was afraid it would be a problem pulling the younglings out of school, but their teacher didn't seem to mind at all. He said it would be an educational experience for them to see the nebula." His eyes darted away from me. "Sit down, Klaatu. Nikto, close your mouth when you chew. And Barada, stop throwing bugs at your brothers."

Chapter 6

Planet of the Mapes

As Zastra and I returned to our table, the door to the diner again opened, and in walked something like what a child would imagine was hiding under her bed.

It had two legs as thick as a hippo's with a chunky baby blue body to match, four arms, eyes like goose eggs stuck on the front of a round head, and a wide toothy grin. A row of purple spikes ran down the back of the head all the way to a tail, which ended in a spike-covered ball that bounced along across the metal floor.

I pulled my eyes away from the alien to say, "Oren, Zastra's brother won a trip here … from a contest he doesn't recall entering."

"Interesting," Oren said.

He was going to say more but stopped when the blue creature stepped up to our table. I leaned toward Jace and away from the monster.

Grinning like a crazy person and nodding its head like a bobblehead doll, the alien said exuberantly, "Oren Vilkas, my old friend. Imagine seeing you here."

"Hello, Inspector Mapes," Oren said, giving our guest an indulgent smile.

Mapes waggled the spikey head side to side. "As it happens, I am but a former inspector now. I retired. But I try to keep myself busy." The huge eyes darted toward me. "I see you have expanded your crew since we worked together."

"This is Gabriel Lake from Earth." Oren turned to me. "The former inspector and I once collaborated on a case when he was with the Javidian police."

I noted the *he*. Some alien species have males and females. Others have different arrangements. And telling any of them apart can be difficult.

"Hello," I said.

"Earth? A quarantined planet?" Mapes donned a mock expression of reproval and shook a finger on one of his several hands at Oren. "You've been naughty again, haven't you, Mr. Vilkas."

Oren answered through tight lips. "I was working a case in which I followed a lead to Earth. I received alliance permission to recruit an Earthling to assist me."

Mapes glanced at the seats on either side of the corner booth as if expecting one of us to scoot over to let him sit. Taking my cue from Zastra, I didn't move.

"Ah, yes, Mr. Vilkas," Mapes said. "Picking up some local help. Much like when you and I worked together on Javid. You know, I often think about that case. Those were exciting days — following the clues, reasoning them out side-by-side. Murder it was, Gablial Lak."

"Yes." Oren pronounced the word with a tone of weariness.

"Do you remember, Mr. Vilkas, when I sketched out on the wall the entire timeline of the murder based on everything the witnesses had said, and we figured out who the killer must have been?" He chuckled. "The captain made me repaint that wall. It took me two days. Workie workie. But well worth it, if you ask me."

I don't know why I ever thought this guy was scary. He was more like a bonkers dinosaur from some kids' show.

"Yes, I do remember," Oren said. "My memory is computerized. I don't forget."

Mapes laughed loud enough for other patrons in the diner to turn around and stare. "That is a funny one, Mr. Vilkas. Yes, you are a digital person. Ah, you are lucky, Gablial Lak, to be invited onto Mr. Vilkas's team. I might have joined the Galactic Detective Agency myself, but alas, I had obligations to the Javidian East Kesselshire police force. I could not leave them shorthanded, you understand."

Zastra was staring up through the transparent ceiling at the nebula. Buad and Blan pecked at their seed and periodically poked each other with their wings. Jace didn't take his eyes off his plate.

"Absolutely," I said. "Me, I work freelance in my day job, so joining up with the team on occasion isn't a problem."

"Oh, are you a private investigator on Earth?"

"Private, yes. Investigator, no. I'm a software developer."

Mapes seemed not to hear. "That reminds me, Mr. Vilkas. I have big news! I may be doing some freelance detective work myself. I received an invitation to meet with someone here about a possible case. That should brighten up my retirement."

Zastra's eyes left the nebula to meet mine.

Oren asked, "Who is the client?"

Mapes leaned in and whispered. "That is part of the mystery." He looked around the diner, the humongous head turning nearly completely around. "I don't know who it is. I suppose they will approach me."

"You might want to be careful. We seem to have come here by—"

"But where are my manners?" Mapes said. "Zazra. Juice. Blad and Brun. How have you been?"

Blan said, "We've been fine, Mapes. But it's Zastra, Jace, Blan, and Buad."

Mapes shot two of his four hands up to his mouth. "Oh, I am extremely sorry. I tell you, my mind isn't what it used to be." He tapped the side of his blue head and made a silly face. "Brainy drainy."

"It's not a problem," Zastra said.

He wobbled his head. "I think I need a case to shake the rust out of the old noggin. Perhaps this investigation will do that for me. And if you ever come across something that might benefit from my talents, Mr. Vilkas, I hope you'll think of me."

"I certainly will," Oren said.

For several more awkward moments, Mapes stood there bobbing his head. Then, as if searching for anything else to say, he looked at me. "Mr. Lak, have you ever visited my fair planet?"

"I don't think so." I figured I would have remembered seeing a world full of people like him.

"Beautiful world, Javid. To see the suns setting over the black sand beaches is a sight to behold."

I caught Zastra rolling her eyes.

"Sounds like it," I said. "But I only go where Oren's cases take me. Javid doesn't sound familiar."

"Well, I hope a case brings you there soon. Not that I want more crime on our world, mind you."

"Right. Of course."

We smiled pleasantly at each other in uncomfortable silence.

"Well," Mapes said, "I should probably move on to my own booth. I doubt my mystery client will contact me while I'm talking with you."

And yet he continued to stand there, still bobbing his head.

Jace set his spork down beside his plate. "Oren, I'd like to go back to the *Shaymus* and run some diagnostics. Verify there haven't been any ..." He shot a glimpse at Mapes. "... any problems."

I wondered how much of Jace's motivation was genuine concern for the ship given our mysterious voucher, and how much was trying to extract himself from the presence of our visitor.

"Certainly," Oren said. "Take Buad and Blan with you."

"If that's okay with them."

"No problem," Blan said eagerly, "We're done."

I noticed they both had seed remaining in their bowls.

Oren said, "But out of politeness, wait until our guest leaves."

"Sure," Jace said without emotion.

He reached for his spork and unenthusiastically pushed it around his plate. Buad and Blan resumed pecking at their seed. I suspected that a sizeable amount of Oren's insistence on observing the social graces was fear that, with the booth nearly vacated, Mapes would sit down to join us and never leave.

"Well, I should move on to my own booth," Mapes repeated, still nodding.

"A sound idea," Oren said.

"Why, thank you, Mr. Vilkas. That is quite the compliment coming from one such as you. Well, my friends, I will take my leave of you for now. So nice to see you all again and have this little chat. Bye-bye."

Mapes beamed at us one more time and then moved away toward the booths beyond the door. Before dropping into one, he stopped at an illuminated box hanging on the wall near the hallway. I figured the kiosk must be a jukebox of sorts because sitting on top was a life-size cutout of a round, purple-furred Donovian wearing a sparkly gold suit and holding something I took to be some kind of weird harp.

That and also because after Mapes had pressed a few buttons, a song started up. Astoundingly, I recognized the tune, "Bohemian Rhapsody" by Queen. I knew that despite the quarantine, some tidbits of Earth culture did make it out to the other planets. I think the aliens were interested in what exactly it was about us that caused our planet to be shunned. It made us something of a guilty pleasure around the galaxy, like a reality TV show with people behaving badly.

Bobbing his head to the beat with his tail swishing across the tiles behind him, Mapes dropped into a booth. However dopey this guy was, he did have good taste in music.

I turned back to Oren. "So … a former associate of yours."

He made a face. "A law enforcement officer I was forced to work with."

I put on a Mapes-like grin. "I thought he said you were best buds."

Oren didn't answer.

"I must have missed that case."

"It was before your era." Oren glanced toward the back of Mapes' head. "He grated on my nerves the entire time."

"At least he isn't antagonistic like Lt. Xox on Girsu."

Zastra said, "I'm not sure which is worse."

Jace said, "Can I go check on the *Shaymus* now?"

"Yes," Oren said. "Check everything carefully inside and out. For all we know, a saboteur may have done something to the ship in our absence."

I slid out to let Jace pass. He left the diner with Buad and Blad flying beside him.

Before returning to my seat, I took a moment to study a photo on the wall beside the next booth. It showed the diner planted on the planet with the nebula in the background. But the twin domes had not yet been built. Three spacecraft sat on an undomed parking lot. Two of the ships were flying saucers. The other was a stubby cylinder with landing struts on the bottom and a dome on top. It looked like one of those low-voltage mushroom lights people landscape with.

"Are you glad you came, Gabriel?" Oren asked.

"Yeah. This place is mind-blowing." I pulled out my phone and took some pictures of the place in general and some of the wall art in particular. "I want to show this to Sarah and Lucas."

Oren raised one eyebrow. "I don't have to tell you to make sure no one else on Earth sees those."

I slipped back into the booth. "Don't worry. They won't. Even if anyone did, I could tell them the images were created by AI."

"This place is something of a time capsule. The history of the diner. The exhibits on the wall. You can learn much from this place about how the civilized galaxy developed over the last few hundred years."

"The civilized galaxy. As opposed to Earth, you mean."

"Indeed." His face wore a hint of a smile.

"Mind if I wander around and take in more of the décor?"

"Not at all. It is a good idea."

"Say, that's quite the compliment coming from one such as you." I shot him a toothy grin.

"Go, Gabriel. Especially if the alternative is you staying here and goading me."

Zastra said, "Check out the observation dome too."

"How do I get there?" I asked.

"Follow the hallway to the other side."

But before I started off on my walkabout, I took a few more minutes to indulge in alien watching. The Quexel had left its booth. Unlike me, it didn't clomp across the floor in mag boots. It bounced from the seat bench into the air and sort of swam through the low gravity with graceful movements. Not really flying like Buad and Blan. More like Buzz Lightyear, falling with style. It landed on one of the stools at the counter and asked Sola for something.

One of the three srathamigos shot out of their booth and began running toward the hallway. Xav leaped after him, corralled him near Mapes, and hauled him back to the others.

Sola brought food to Oren's bestie, Mapes, serving him some kind of dark brown noodles in a creamy sauce. Star also came out from behind the counter and bounced along the line of booths, checking on how people were doing.

The two Mucs rose. Moving past us, the one with pink hair gave me the once over while the green-haired one dismissed me with a sneer. Like Zastra, they wore holsters strapped to their legs over their workwear trousers. They stepped to the jukebox as the Queen song was finishing its final strains. A few moments later, classic rock was replaced by the discordant sounds of atonal, rhythmless electronic techno music. The Mucs began swaying to the non-existent beat.

The guy with the long face strode over to join them. He seemed to be trying to chat them up. But the Mucs turned their backs on him, and he returned to his seat with his head lowered.

The Klistine also left the booth, walking past where we sat, past the Quexel, Mapes, and the Mucs at the jukebox. He headed down the hallway, presumably either heading for the observation dome or visiting the little aliens' room.

The ALF guy slid from the stool and walked around the diner, examining piece after piece of the wall art. I saw Mapes give ALF a glare when ALF wandered close to his booth.

I gazed around at the items on the walls myself. I spotted the nose cone of a rocket, a poster showing several species standing arm in arm in wing in tentacle, and a map of the galaxy that even had Earth marked on it.

"You know," I said to Oren and Zastra, "We may be in danger here, but this place is seriously cool."

Chapter 7

What's a Couple Hundred Million Miles Between Friends

"Does anybody want to go with me to see the nebula?" I asked.

Oren shook his head. "I am watching events in the diner. Someone, probably one of these people, is up to something."

Zastra pointed up at the transparent ceiling. "I can see it fine from here. I'll stay with Oren."

"Suit yourself," I said.

I slipped from the booth and started walking — or lumbering more like in my mag boots — toward the hallway. As I passed the Quexel's booth, the alien looked up and gave me a blank, unblinking stare.

Trying to be friendly, I said, "Hi. How are you doing?"

I received no reply.

At the Srathan booth, Xav was reading an information card on the wall to one of the kids while the other two pitted the remaining bugs against each other in races.

Mapes was digging into his food. I waved as I swept by his booth, not wanting to be drawn into another conversation with him.

The Mucs were still at the jukebox as I approached it. The one with hi-vis green hair — seriously, I have a cycling jersey that same color, and cars can see me from a half mile away — nudged the pink-haired one and pointed a thumb in my direction.

The pink-haired one shot me a coy smile and said, "Hey, sweetness, where are you from?"

I wasn't prepared for that. A shiver squiggled up my spine. Without slowing my pace, I said, "Fountain Square," knowing they wouldn't be familiar with

Indianapolis neighborhoods. I hoped that ticked the boxes on being polite without encouraging any further interaction. I was wrong.

"Hey, why don't you smile?"

I didn't smile. I continued on into the hallway, feeling their eyes still on me.

I passed four doors on my right. A sign on each said: *Private facilities, all species and genders*. Alert readers of my other adventures may recall that I have at times suffered a fair amount of confusion in alien restroom facilities, even when those facilities were segregated by body type. I couldn't imagine what all manner of equipment these washrooms would have to contain to accommodate every species' size and shape and method of doing business. I almost stepped inside to check it out. But the nebula was what I had come to see, not some bathroom.

Beyond the last bathroom door, the hallway turned left. All this time I had been keeping my eye out for any Earth artifacts among all the alien knickknacks. I turned the corner and nearly ran smack into one, a life-size plastic sculpture of Abraham Lincoln, stovepipe hat in hand and staring directly at me. I nearly staggered backward in surprise. Except it isn't easy to reverse the heel-then-toe mag boot maneuver, so all I ended up doing was wobbling back and forth a little.

"Well, hi, Mr. President. Fancy meeting you way out here."

The wall behind him was lined with more Earth relics, namely framed pictures of Internet memes. There was the grumpy cat, Kermit the Frog drinking tea, Captain Picard extending an arm toward the camera, the distracted boyfriend, Boromir with index finger and thumb together.

But when my translator bots converted the alien text on each of them to English, it was clear that whoever wrote the captions didn't fully understand how memes work. On the picture of Leonardo DiCaprio holding up a champagne glass, the lettering translated to: *Earthlings get thirsty*. The most interesting man in the world picture was captioned: *There are many things I don't do*. On top of Willie Wonka wearing a sly grin was written: *Tell me more. I like to learn*.

I pulled myself away from the unfunny memes and followed the hallway past more doors. I wondered what they were. Storage room? Mop closet? Possibly an office? At the end, the hallway turned to the left one more time, apparently wrapping around the outside of the diner. I took it this whole section had been built as an addition to the original rocket unit.

Ahead of me appeared a dimly lit dome glowing red and green like a Christmas tree. I stepped inside and with a sharp intake of breath, took in the full eye-boggling sight of the nebula without the distractions of the hangar dome or diner. The effect was mesmerizing, though given the current threat level, the darkness made me slightly jumpy. My eyes swept the space — a bench seat, two small tables where someone might enjoy a beverage while watching the light show, and a half dozen telescopes. I didn't see anyone lurking about.

I relaxed a little and stood by the dome wall, taking it all in. The clouds of gas and space dust in the nebula formed weird swirling mountains of vibrant greens alternating with reds ranging from coral to candy apple. Here and there, globes of light blazed out among the clouds, looking like klieg lights on a studio back lot. Where they appeared in isolated pairs you could almost imagine them as the glaring eyes of some monstrous space being. Were these stars in the process of forming? If so, in a million years, this might be like any other star system. Or more likely, multiple star systems since according to a nearby information plaque, the nebula stretched more than one hundred light-years across.

The pitter-patter of little mag boots clattered behind me, and in ran the three sratharinos followed at a distance by a tired-looking Xav. He and I exchanged nods.

At the sight of the nebula, the littles pulled up short and gasped out, "Wow! Awesome!"

The excitement of it all seemed to fill them like inflating balloons, which then burst with a pop. They tore off, racing laps around the small dome, hopping across the benches, swinging on the telescopes. How they managed to run in those mag boots was beyond me.

Xav called, "Boys. Boys, slow down. Come here. Come here. I'll tell you about it." He rounded them up and sat them on the bench.

Crouching in front of them, he said, "Now, a nebula like this is called the nursery of the stars. All the dust and gas out there will slowly pull together into clumps. Then the clumps will pull together into larger and larger clumps taking on more and more gravity."

"Hey, Dad," one of the kids said.

"What, Barada?"

"Guess what?"

"What?"

Barada pointed. "That cloud looks like a boasaur."

Xav squinted in the direction indicated. "Um … I guess I can see it."

Never having seen a boasaur, I checked out the cloud myself, tilting my head and squinting. If that was what they looked like, I didn't want to meet any.

"I don't see it," one of the others said. "You're nuts."

"Nuh-uh," Barada said. "See, the head's right there."

Xav held up a hand. "Anyway, the clumps grow larger and larger until they finally collapse and heat up to become stars."

"Can we watch that happen?" another of the younglings asked. "Watch a star form?"

"No, silly," the first one said. "It takes too long."

"Then can we come back next year?"

Xav said, "We can come back, but stars form very slowly."

"Yeah, doofus," the brother said. "Everybody knows that."

Xav said, "Nikto, Klaatu is not a doofus, and you aren't to say that."

Barada asked, "What would it be like if we got really, really close to the nebula?"

"Or inside it?" Nikto said.

"Yeah," said Klaatu with breathless enthusiasm.

Xav said, "Well, if we did that, we might not see it at all."

The youngling responded with the favorite word of toddlers all over the galaxy. "Why?"

"You see, a nebula is mainly gas. It's like fog or a thin mist. The closer you get, the less of it you would see. From inside, it wouldn't look much different from regular space — only a slight reddish glow."

Which was something I didn't know. I guess you learn something every day, especially on days spent with space aliens. So much for all the great nebula battle scenes in sci-fi shows.

"See that moon in the middle of the cloud," one of the younglings said.

"That's no moon," his brother said. "It's a star."

"No, it's not."

"Is too. It's a baby star."

"You don't know."

"I do too."

"It's a moon.

"Star."

"Moon."

Xav said, "That's enough, boys."

"It's a star, isn't it, Dad?"

"Well," Xav said hesitantly.

One of the little Srathans slipped off the bench and trotted over to a telescope near where I was standing. He jumped to pull it down to him, peered through it, and exclaimed, "Whoa!"

The other two dashed over and began pushing and pulling at each other for a turn.

"Barada, Nikto," Xav said. "There are other telescopes."

I took a step back from the growing kerfuffle, though as it turned out, not far enough. Because in response to a brotherly shove, one of the younglings stumbled backward and fell at my feet. The srathlet peered up at me with a trembling jaw. In an instant, Xav was at my side, sweeping the child into his arms.

"Sorry, Gabriel Lake."

"No problem. Call me Gabe."

"Come along, boys. Let's see what the diner has for treats."

This was greeted by a stampede from the dome. Peace returned to my corner of the galaxy ... for a few moments.

"Some light show, ain't it?"

I turned toward the direction of the voice and saw Buad and Blan perched on the back of a chair at one of the tables.

"How long have you two been there?"

"Long enough to catch all the shenanigans," Blan said.

"I thought you guys were supposed to stay with Jace."

"He's fine," Buad said. "We couldn't visit the Nebula Diner and not fly out here for a look-see."

I swept my head around the dome to take another gander myself. "I have a question."

"Oh boy. Here we go."

I ignored him and pointed toward a sign on the wall. "It says over here that Ursa 16309 is orbiting a star two hundred light-years away from the nebula."

"Like the Srathan says, you get a better view from a distance."

"But if this planet—"

"Dwarf planet," Blan said, correcting me.

"Whatever. If it's orbiting a star, then sometimes its orbit takes it further from the nebula than at other times."

"Yeah. What's your point?"

"Well, then the view would change depending on how close it is, right? It would be better sometimes than at others."

"Nah. What's a couple hundred million miles compared with a couple hundred light-years?"

Speaking of which, one neat feature of translator bots is that they translate whatever units of measure a person says into whatever units the hearer understands. For all I know, Blan had quoted the distances in perch lengths and photon sun cycles, but I heard it as miles and light-years, properly converted. In any case, the math of these literally astronomical numbers was beyond me.

"I don't know," I said. "I haven't a clue."

"I'll say you don't." Blan flew from the bench and began hopping around on the floor.

Buad said, "Don't they teach you anything about space in Earth school? Compared to light-years, a few hundred million miles is nothin'."

"I'll take your word for it." I went back to watching the clouds. "Is everything okay on the ship?"

"Everything's fine. Jace checked it all out. Kah-Rehn says nobody has come near it."

"Good."

"Her exact words were something like, 'No trespasser's shadow, no unbidden intruder advancing with slinking step and furtive glances.'"

I chuckled. "Nice. Very poetic"

"Oh sure. It's highly expressive, but not exactly the kind of concise security report we were hoping for."

"She's going through something."

"So are we. We were tricked into coming here, and I don't like it."

"What do you think is going on?"

"Who knows? You don't become the galaxy's leading detective without making a few enemies. And the boss has been catching criminals for hundreds of years."

"You think somebody he put away is coming back to seek vengeance?"

"Or a relative of someone he put away."

I considered that. "So what would be the killer's plan? To draw Oren out here to a place where he's downloaded onto a tablet ... and then what? Blast the tablet?"

"Could be. Simple but effective. Oren is at his most vulnerable when he's on the tablet."

"Which explains why Zastra wouldn't leave him alone at the table."

Buad cackled. "Yeah. You can bet she has one hand resting on her holster."

"Did Jace come back with you guys?"

"No, he wanted to stay and mind the store. You know how he is with the *Shaymus*."

"And he's okay by himself?"

"I already told you. He's fine. He tightened security up so much we may not be able to board the ship again ourselves. Which reminds me, to open the ramp now, you need to use the passcode 'Jace is awesome alpha three.' That's in addition to the ship doing a visual and voice print identification of you."

"Jace is awesome alpha three?"

Buad bobbed his head. "He set it himself."

"Okay. Jace is guarding the ship, and Zastra is guarding Oren."

"And apparently we're babysitting you."

Between the nebula and talking with Buad, I had lost track of Blan. Now he flew from somewhere across the floor to perch on one of the telescopes. He fluttered up and put one eye to the eyepiece. "Hey, Gabe, you ought to take a peek through this."

"Why?" I was suspicious.

"It's amazing, that's why. What do you think? Boy, you try to give a newbie a tip, and they're all 'why?' Sheesh!"

"Okay, okay. I'll look." I went to take a step and nearly toppled over face-first. My mag boots were seemingly welded to the floor. I knelt and saw that somebody had cranked the knobs up to eleven.

Buad and Blan both cackled. Buad raised one wing, and Blan glided down to give it a feathered high five.

Blan said, "Ooh, boy. I got you good, dum-dum."

Buad said, "Nice one, Brother."

"Hey, you were the one who distracted him with all that talk about orbits and security arrangements. Gabe, you should have seen your face."

I spun back the dials and gave them a sarcastic, "Ha, ha."

I was getting ready to compare their behavior to that of the short Srathans, but at that moment Oren's voice sounded through our translator bots. "Gabriel, Blan, Buad, return to the diner at once."

The Avanians took to wing. I plodded along behind them as fast as my booted legs would take me. We entered the diner to find a crowd standing around between the hallway and the diner door, gawking at a booth. It was the booth where Mapes sat, this time unmoving and with his face planted in his plate of pasta.

Chapter 8

Death a la Carte

Star and Sola stood around the booth, wringing their little green hands in their aprons, their antennae drooping forward so far they nearly hung down in their eyes. Zastra had slipped into the booth beside Mapes and had a finger pressed against the side of his thick neck. The tablet with Oren was propped up on the tabletop beside her. Several of the other diner patrons huddled around, though Xav had herded the srathatots away from the scene toward the other end of the diner, where he was energetically pointing out to them the galactic pop culture items on the walls. Even still, the little ones kept craning their heads back in this direction.

"Is he dead?" I asked.

Zastra nodded.

Sola gasped and rocked back and forth from one foot to the other. "Oh my goodness gracious! Oh for Gort's sake. In our little diner no less. Star, you don't think—"

"No, I don't," Star said, cutting Sola off with a stern look, "and don't be jumping to any conclusions. He probably just took too big of a bite and choked."

"I don't think so," Zastra said.

I leaned a hand against the back of a seat and took a breath. Only minutes ago I had been making fun of the guy. Now here he was gone from life.

"What happened?" I asked.

Zastra said, "Good question. We heard him moaning and gagging. We rushed over, but by the time we got here, he was gone."

I turned to Sola and Star. "What's the protocol for something like this?"

Star's antennae began to quiver. "Protocol? Now hold on a ding-dong moment here, fella. We don't have any protocol for people dying in our restaurant. Never needed one. I hope you aren't suggesting people eat their last meal here on a regular basis."

I extended my hands in protest. "No. No, I … I only mean … what do we do … about this?"

Grumbling, Star sprang back to the kitchen area and pulled about a dozen items from under the counter, sliding them one by one onto the worktop. Finally, the little alien emerged around the end of the counter holding a little black box with a red button. Star pressed the button.

From somewhere down the hall came the whoosh of a door sliding open, followed by the whir of an electric motor. A minute later, a robot wheeled into the diner. It had the body shape and approximate height of an upright vacuum cleaner with a round head stuck on top. Three camera eyes stared out from the front of the face. Three arms stuck out from the torso, one on each side and a third one positioned under a tablet device mounted to its chest.

The robot rolled up to Star and asked in an impassive mechanical voice, "Please state the nature of the medical emergency."

I might have snickered at the Star Trek quote had there not been a dead guy mere inches away.

Star raised an arm and pointed silently toward the booth. The gesture was apparently open to misinterpretation because the bot motored forward and stopped in front of me. Its head swiveled up and down, a gray pupil in the middle of each black camera eye expanding and contracting, seemingly scrutinizing me for injuries.

"There, there," the mechanical voice said. "Do not worry. I am medical bot B-zero-dash-N-three-Zed. I will take care of you. Where does it hurt?"

"It doesn't," I said.

"No symptoms. Interesting. I will need to examine." The middle arm disappeared inside its midsection and came back out holding something with a long needle on the end.

I jumped back, nearly colliding with the ALF guy. "Hey, not me, doc bot."

"I am medical bot B-zero-dash-N-three-Zed."

"I'm sure you are. And your patient is over there … in the booth." I waved my arm in the right direction.

The bot rotated its body to face Mapes and jabbed the needle thing into the dead Javidian's neck.

A moment later, it said, "Subject is dead."

"Glad we all agree," I said. "I figured as much when you stabbed him, and he didn't jump. What was the cause of death?"

The needle retracted from the neck, and the arm disappeared into the bot's midriff.

"Analyzing."

Lines of information began scrolling up the tablet screen on the bot's chest. A minute later a ding sounded.

"Subject is a Javidian male, age approximately eighty-seven, suffering from stage two rheumatoid arthritis."

I said, "I'm guessing that didn't kill him, doc."

"I am medical bot B-zero-dash-N-three-Zed."

"Right. Right. B-zero-whatever."

"B-zero-dash-N-three-Zed."

"Fine." I visualized the string of characters in my head — B0-N3Z. "Hey, that's Bones. Bones, can I call you Bones? Bones, so what was the cause of death?"

"Correction, B-zero-dash-N-three-Zed."

"I know, but Bones is a lot easier. Now what killed him?"

"Subject died from ingestion of tetratoxipine."

"Tetra ..." This was going to be harder to say than B-zero-dash-N-three-Zed.

Zastra said, "It's poison, Gabe."

"A fast-acting poison," Oren said.

"Did subject consume any food or liquid?" Bones asked.

"Well, we're in a diner," I said, "And his plate's right there."

The bot's third hand came back out holding a pair of tweezers, which it used to snag a noodle from the plate in the vicinity of Mapes' ear. The hand disappeared once more, quickly followed by another ding.

"Tetratoxipine is present in the food."

"For the love of Gort!" Star said. The little green alien staggered backward to lean against one of the chrome stools at the counter.

With the announcement of the poisoning, Oren began to take charge. "Sola, Star, do you have tetratoxipine on the premises?"

"Whoa whoa whoa," Star said, antennae rising and sweeping back like horns. "For Zahn's sake, why would we keep poison anywhere near this place?"

"It has other uses. It is a common ingredient in eye drops. It can also be used to discourage the presence of certain insects."

"Well, this dwarf planet doesn't have any insects."

"If you don't mind, though, I would like to have my associates conduct a search."

Star's eyes narrowed. "And who are you exactly?"

"My name is Oren Vilkas."

"Oren Vilkas?" the ALF guy said with excitement.

Sola said, "Oh, the famous detective. I've heard of you. You bet."

Oren inclined his head. "May we conduct a search? I assume you wish to have this matter cleared up as swiftly as possible."

Star's mouth dropped open, and the words came out slowly. "By all means. Be my guest."

Oren said, "Buad and Blan."

"Sure, Boss," Blan said. "Come on, Brother."

One flew into the kitchen, the other down the hall.

Oren said, "We will also need to call the authorities."

Star looked at him doubtfully and chuckled a hollow laugh. "Authorities. Oh sure. We're a long way from a populated star system, you know."

"True, but the furthest system is only a few minutes away by chrono jump. Who controls this system?"

Star moved hands up and down like scales. "Currently, Delusia and Bononia are bickering over who has jurisdiction."

"They both claim it?"

"Not so much."

From the screen, Oren blinked. "You mean they both want the other to administrate it?"

Sola made a what-can-you-do-about-it face. "There's no mining anymore, don't ya know. Nobody here at all except for us. Both planets say it's not worth it having to send people all the way out here."

"Nevertheless, you will need to report this. Contact them both, and we'll see who responds first."

"If at all," Star muttered.

"Meanwhile, my team will investigate. Mr. Mapes was once a colleague of mine. I owe it to him to expose his murderer."

Star said, "What should we do with the ... the body until the authorities arrive?"

"Ideally, it should be left in place."

Star's antennae began waving around wildly. "Oh no. Nothing doing. I'm trying to run a restaurant here. We can't leave dead bodies sitting around at the tables."

B0-N3Z said, "I would like to run additional tests on the subject."

Sola said, "We have the cold storage room down the hall."

"That would be acceptable," the med bot said.

Oren said, "All right. First, allow my operatives to examine the body and the booth and have my ship's AI record photographs through their translator bots. Second, move the body to cold storage. Third, block off this booth until further notice. Fourth, I want to interview all customers and staff. Finally, I ask that no one be allowed to leave until we conclude the interviews."

At that last point, a round of grumbles came from the assembled spectators.

Star said, "We can't prevent anyone from leaving."

"An incentive then," Oren said. "Serve all the people currently here whatever food or drink they want and put it on my tab."

The grumbles turned into murmurs of approval. Most of the customers began moving back to their booths and pulling out menus.

I leaned over to Oren. "Wow, and you don't even have a client to bill for all this."

"No, but I don't want a killer to slip away if I can help it."

Zastra had already raised Mapes' head and torso from the tabletop, though a few stray noodles still clung to his face. She set to work inspecting the bench seats and table.

"Kah-Rehn," she said, "record everything I'm seeing."

"Recording," Kah-Rehn said in our ears. "I am struck by the pathos of the scene. Death seeping in like a cruel, cutting wind. Cold metal, colder flesh. A lonely spork—"

"Save the poetry," Zastra said. "All you have to do is record."

She dug into the deceased's pockets, pulling out an identification chip, a payment stick, a personal device, and various other sundry bits.

"Anything interesting?" I asked.

"Not tetratoxipine, if that's what you mean."

"Nothing to indicate who his mysterious client might be?"

"No. I'll take a look at this device. It might have something."

But after a minute or two of fiddling with the device, she shook her head. "There's nothing on this except games." She stood. "Gabe, help me get him out of the booth."

I studied the job requirements. The way Mapes was wedged into the booth with his stomach up against the tabletop, one of us would have to push while the other pulled. But I didn't see how either of us could get into a pushing position.

I stretched out on the opposite bench seat and reached under the table to shove on the body. Nothing moved. I scrunched up my legs, lowered myself under the table, and squat-walked to the other side. I emerged to see Star staring at me.

"You know, we can just turn off the magnets and slide that table out," the Frye said.

"Now you tell me." I said, pulling myself up onto the bench beside the dead alien.

Star flipped a switch under the table and pulled it out. I gave the body a push. Now, you would think with the bulk of the guy, the body wouldn't be easy to move even with the table out of the way. At least I did. But in calculating how much force to apply, I hadn't figured on how much less Mapes would weigh in the low gravity. The body glided across the bench like an ice cube sliding along a kitchen counter. It skidded all the way out and thumped onto the floor.

"So much for respect for the dead," Zastra said.

She stooped, pulled off Mapes' mag boots, and then lifted him to her shoulder as easily as she would a bean bag chair. She began clomping toward the hallway.

Unfortunately, the body, if not heavy, was still bulky, and she couldn't get him through the narrow doorway into the hall.

"I'm going to need a hand," she said.

She set the body down and moved to take the arms. I grabbed the feet, and we lifted. We got him through the doorway and baby-stepped down the hall, Zastra walking backward. How she did that in mag boots I don't know. B0-N3Z whirred along behind us.

As we passed the bathrooms, I said, "We have a corner coming up." I had flashbacks to bad experiences moving couches.

Zastra glanced behind her. "We'll have to tilt him on his side."

We shifted the body and made it around the corner.

I said, "Now watch out for President Lincoln."

"Who?" Zastra asked, nearly bumping into the stovepipe hat.

"The statue. It's right behind you."

Looking over her shoulder, she stopped and huffed out a sigh. "All right. Set this down."

We placed the body on the floor, and she moved Honest Abe to the end of the hallway.

Before picking up the arms once more, she said, "B0-N3Z, which door are we going to?"

The med bot said, "I will show you."

It rolled forward, bumped into Mapes' body, and rotated like a Roomba hitting an obstacle. It rumbled in the new direction straight into the wall, rolled back, rotated the other way, rolled forward into Zastra, rolled back, rotated once more, and finally continued down the hall.

"It is the next to the last door," Bones said.

Zastra stepped to the door and pressed a touchpad on the wall beside it. The door swooshed open. She came back to me, and we carted the body inside, our breaths billowing out in the cold from the room. We set Mapes down, and I arranged the body on the floor with as much dignity as I could give it.

"Sorry to leave you here like this, Inspector," I said, straightening his shirt. "And for the bumpy passage down the hall. We'll do everything we can to find your killer. Do you have this, Bones?"

The robot said, "I do. However, my designation is B-zero-dash-N-three-Zed."

"I'll see if I can remember all that. But let me tell you, Bones is an awesome name.

"I am a doctor, not a section of skeleton."

"See. You have the lingo down and everything."

We left the room, and I moved the Great Emancipator back to his original position. Zastra and I returned to the diner to find Mapes' booth now cordoned off by two stanchions with a red velvet rope hanging between them. In front stood a folding sign marked with a stick figure of a Gray slipping on a wet floor.

Everyone had moved back to their former places and was busy chowing down on various yummy snacks courtesy of Oren Vilkas. All except for Oren, whose tablet still sat on the table in Mapes' booth.

As we approached, he said, "Move me back to the corner booth." The disadvantages of not having your own legs.

Zastra snatched up the tablet, and we moved. As I slid into the seat, Buad and Blan flew to join us.

Buad said, "Boss, we couldn't find any trace of tetratoxipine."

Oren grimaced. "I didn't think you would. But assuming someone here put it in Mapes' food, a bottle of it must be somewhere."

I said, "I assume our theory of the crime is that Mapes' death is related both to his appointment with the mystery client and to whoever sent us here."

"Yes. It is too great of a coincidence."

Blan said, "We should review that old case you worked with Mapes."

"I have been doing so. It was a straightforward murder investigation. The criminal is still behind bars. I had Kah-Rehn check."

"What about the criminal's friends and family?"

"The few that he had appear to have all passed away."

Zastra said, "My brother Xav was also brought here under questionable circumstances. He didn't have anything to do with the Javid case."

"No, he didn't," Oren said, "which suggests this may be related to something broader."

"Like what?" I asked.

Oren flipped up a palm. "It might be a connection to me. Or to Zastra. Or the diner. That is why our next task should be to interview the others. We need to ask them what connection they have to Mapes or to any of us and find out how they came to be here today. They may have been lured to this place as well."

Buad said, "And one of them has to be the murderer."

"Most likely. We also need to determine which of them by their movements were in a position to have poisoned Mapes."

"I can answer that one," I said. "They all were. Everybody was moving around everywhere."

"Did you see anyone do anything to his food?"

"Afraid not."

"What about the rest of you?"

Zastra shook her head.

Blan said, "Buad and I were out in the ship with Jace and then in the observation dome."

"And I have a limited line of sight from this tablet," Oren said. "I saw nothing. All right. Let's begin interviewing."

"Do you want us to divvy them up?" I asked.

"No. I wish to interview them all myself. Bring them one at a time to the *Shaymus*. No wait. Perhaps we shouldn't march them through the hangar. They might take a notion to leave. I'll question them here in the booth."

Chapter 9

The Unusual Suspects

"Who do you want first?" I asked Oren. I scanned around the diner. "We have several interesting choices on the menu — two Mucs, a passel of Srathans, a scary-looking Klistine, Star and Sola, the one in the fishbowl, the skinny-faced dude, and the ALF guy at the counter. What was he again?"

"A suspect," Buad said with sarcasm.

"A Fomorian," Oren said. "Start with him."

Him. Apparently, despite all the fur, Oren could recognize this character as a male.

I mag-stomped over to the stool. "Hello."

The Fomorian swiveled to face me with an open-mouthed grin. "Hi. You're one of the ones with Oren Vilkas."

"That's right. Oren would like to talk to you and ask you what you saw."

"He does? Wow!" He hopped from the stool and followed me to the corner booth.

As our guest climbed up on the bench seat, he said, "Oren Vilkas. Wow! What an honor. I'm Alfomado Fusco, your biggest fan."

Oren inclined his head and said, "Thank you. These are my associates." He pointed a digital arm to indicate us one by one. "Zastra, Buad, Blan, and Gabriel Lake. Mr. Fusco, are you by chance any relation to Fazan Fusco?"

"Fazan was my father."

"Indeed."

Zastra asked, "What about him?"

The Fomorian said, "He was the focus of one of Oren Vilkas's greatest cases. When my father was a youngling, he was kidnapped. My grandparents hired Oren Vilkas to bring him home. And he did."

He looked around the table at the rest of us. "Mr. Vilkas had a different team then. He didn't have Avanians or Srathans or …" He studied me with a quizzical look.

"Earthling," I said. "I'm from Earth, Mr. Fusco."

"Call me Alfo. All my friends do."

"Alfo? You're kidding me."

"For once, I'm not."

"What about … I don't know … Alf?"

"As a name? Nah, I don't much care for it."

Oren said, "Your father's case was before any of my current associates were born."

"I was raised on stories of the great Oren Vilkas," Alfo said. "My grandfather always talked about what you did, how smart you were." He turned to me. "Did you know Mr. Vilkas deduced the identity of the kidnappers from a single feather?"

"Avian species?" I asked, giving Buad and Blan some side-eye.

"No, it came from a hat. Ha! I ask you, who else could have figured that one out? Mr. Vilkas, without you, I wouldn't be here … or anywhere. I've studied all your cases on the news vids and the network."

"It is gratifying to hear," Oren said. "I noticed you referred to your father in the past tense."

Alfo's brown furry head tilted to the side. "He died years ago.

"My condolences."

"He didn't have an easy life."

"Trauma from the abduction?" I asked.

"I don't think he remembered much about the actual kidnapping. When it happened, he was smaller than those Srathan ankle biters running around."

I chuckled. "Ankle biters. We use that as a slang term for little kids on Earth too."

Zastra looked at me with raised eye ridges. "It's not a slang term, Gabe. It's a stage they go through. You might want to watch yourself."

I whipped my head toward Xav's booth to make sure all the srathatots were accounted for. I crossed my ankles and pulled them under the bench as far as they would go. Then I realized the younglings might be more likely to attack from behind and pulled them back.

"Don't get me wrong," Alfo said. "I love seeing other people's kids. It reminds me why I don't have any of my own. Ha!"

Blan shivered his feathers. "Hey, Gabe, his jokes are about the same quality as yours."

"Do you live on Fomor?" Oren asked.

"All my life. I wouldn't want to live anywhere else."

"What do you do for a living?"

"I'm a computer programmer."

"Also just like Gabe," Buad said.

I shot him a look.

"Why did you come to the Nebula Diner today?" Oren asked.

"I heard the food is to die for. Get it?" Alfo smacked the tabletop with his hand. He beamed around at us expectantly but drew only cringes. "Sorry. Too soon?"

Zastra said in a threatening rasp, "Maybe you ought to stick to giving us straight answers."

Alfo's smile faded. "All right. I received a message with a one-day-only discount coupon for the place. I couldn't pass it up. I've always heard of the Quokel Nebula." His head tilted up toward the transparent ceiling. "It's beautiful, isn't it?"

"Who sent you this coupon?" Oren asked.

"I don't know. It came anonymously."

Zastra and I shared a glance. Us, Mapes, Xav, now Alfo too — all brought here mysteriously.

"You weren't suspicious?" Oren asked.

"Of what?"

"Of an anonymous gift for an outing."

"Should I have been? People win things all the time."

Oren said, "Would you forward a copy of the message to us for analysis?"

"I'd be glad to. Where should I send it?"

"My ship, the *Shaymus*."

"Of course. The famous *Shaymus*. Hey, that rhymes. Ha!" Alfo pulled a tablet from a pocket and tapped on it a few times. "Done."

Oren said, "Did you know Mr. Mapes?"

"Who?"

"The person who died."

"I never saw him before." His eyes grew larger. "Wait. Did you say Mapes? As in Inspector Mapes of Javid?"

"Then you did know him."

"I know about your case with him. The case of the submerged sailor."

Oren looked as if he had taken a bite of whipped cream only to discover it was mayonnaise instead. "Is that what people call it?"

"That's what I call it. I've named all your cases. It's a great one — how you and Mapes unravel the clues of the murder and the cover-up, only to realize almost too late that the murderer isn't the cover-upper when the cover-upper turns up dead."

"Yes, I recall the investigation."

"You stepped on a few toes with that arrest."

"I am aware."

I said, "You didn't mention that part, Oren."

"Oh yeah," Alfo said. "The murderer turned out to be a member of the mayor's staff."

Oren said, "As I told you earlier, I can find no one living who might bear me malice. Mr. Fusco, did you notice anyone lingering at Inspector Mapes' table or tampering with his food? Or anyone with a container that seemed out of place?"

Alfo raised a hairy hand and scratched his head. "I can't say I did. But then I was sitting at the counter with my back to him."

Zastra said, "You spun around to laugh at my nephews."

Alfo's eyes lit up. "They're your nephews? Those three are a riot. I couldn't take my eyes off their antics to pay attention to much else."

I said, "I remember you walked around to check out the décor. At one point, you stood right beside Mapes' booth."

"Only for a moment. I was trying to read a card under a picture of the mine on the wall. I mean, the picture was on the wall, not the mine. The mine is below us. Or it was. Anyway, he didn't seem to like me being so close and glared a little. I wish I had known he was Mapes. I would have loved to talk with him. Wow! Inspector Mapes. I can't imagine anyone here in the diner would poison him."

"You don't?" I asked. "Then how did it end up in his food?"

Alfo leaned in and pointed a furry finger toward the ceiling. "It could have been dropped from a passing spaceship."

"A spaceship?"

"Think about it. This dwarf planet has almost no atmosphere." He swept a furry hand across the tabletop. "They could fly low over the diner and drop it out."

Oren said, "I am certain the roof is well sealed. As you say, the atmosphere is thin. A hole of any size would cause loss of pressure."

"Ah, but neutrinos can pass through almost anything."

I said, "So you think a passing spaceship dumped poison neutrinos out over the diner."

"I don't see why not."

"And they fell onto Mapes' plate but nobody else's."

"It's possible."

Oren tilted his head. "That is an interesting theory. I don't believe I would ever have thought of it."

Alfo beamed. "Thank you. I have hidden depths."

"I am sure you do. You mentioned earlier that your father did not have an easy life. Why was that?"

"Oh, this and that. All the publicity from the kidnapping and the pressure that came with it. And after he was returned home unscathed — thanks to you — my grandparents barely ever let him out of their sight. Then they had to move to the one-bedroom flat, which gave him even less privacy. He was sort of twitchy his whole life."

"Why did they move?" I asked.

Alfo stared down at the tabletop. "Don't take this the wrong way, Mr. Vilkas, but it wasn't easy paying your invoice. Not that your services weren't worth every bill to get my father back alive and well. Obviously, it is to me."

Oren said, "I … am sorry. If I had known, I would have adjusted it."

Alfo opened his mouth in a grin. "Well, you know what they say, money talks, though mainly it just waves goodbye. Ha!"

Oren was silent for a moment. "I believe those are all our questions for now. If possible, will you stay in the diner until we finish the investigation?"

Alfo again slapped the table. "I wouldn't miss it. A Galactic Detective Agency case worked right before my eyes. Hey, do you think I could help you any? Wow! That would be the thrill of my life. I'll do whatever you need — guard something, make friends with someone to find out a key fact they wouldn't tell you, anything at all."

"We'll let you know."

"Alrighty." Alfo slid from the booth and returned to his seat at the counter. He called out, "Hey, Star, how about something to drink? I'm thirsty from talking with Oren Vilkas."

The rest of us leaned in toward Oren. I said, "So far, everyone has been lured here."

"Yes," Oren said, "and now we have a connection to two past cases."

"Cases from years ago," Blan said.

"Yeah," said Buad. "That's what doesn't figure. If somebody had a grudge against you from one of those old cases, why wait until now to do something about it?"

Zastra said, "Except Xav wasn't involved in any of our cases."

"No," Oren said, "but he is related to you."

Blan said, "Who would even know about these old cases? It's not like you publicize your work, Boss."

I gazed up at the nebula. I hadn't told anyone on the team, but the truth was I had begun self-publishing fictionalized accounts of the cases I'd worked on. Given the Earth quarantine, they shouldn't have been read by any non-humans. They hadn't even been read by that many humans. And the people who did read them believed it was science fiction. Besides, I hadn't written about those old cases. I didn't know anything about them.

Zastra said, "Alfo said he learned about all the cases from news on the network. Anyone could have done that and used the information to pull this party together."

"That must be it," I said, relieved my writing wasn't getting out to the wider galaxy. On the other hand, how cool would it be if it did?

Buad said, "The one person who we know for a fact knows about all your cases is this Alfo guy, which makes me more than a little suspicious of him."

"But he wants to help," Blan said.

I said, "Like a firefighter who burns buildings so he can put them out."

"Yeah, yeah," Buad said. "He kills the guy, and then he gets to help Oren solve the crime."

"You're nuts," Blan said. "If Oren solves it, he goes off to prison."

"Well, anyway, I don't like how he's trying to insert himself in."

Oren said, "Let's move on to the Chotchkiegian."

"The who?" I asked.

"The guy with the long face," Buad said. "The Chotchkiegian. It's what you call someone from the planet Chotchkie, knucklehead."

"Seriously? Doesn't exactly roll off the tongue. Chotch-what-again?"

"I'll get him," Zastra said.

She moved to the guy's booth, leaned over, and said something to him. At first, the long-faced alien responded by shaking his head with quick, minute motions. But that was before Zastra said something else, this time showing her jagged teeth. The alien stood and walked toward our booth with Zastra marching behind.

He wore a surprised look on his face. In fact, he seemed surprised throughout the entire interview. I finally figured out it was the bushy eyebrows. They sat way up on his forehead, much higher than human eyebrows do, making him look perpetually gobsmacked.

"Please have a seat," Oren said.

The guy tried the headshake thing again. Zastra leaned a scaly hand on his shoulder. He sat.

"I am Oren Vilkas. May I ask your name?"

The guy studied the tabletop. "I don't see how that's relevant."

"A person has been murdered."

"I don't know anything about it."

"I assume you do know your name, though," Oren said pointedly.

The alien shrugged, making the gesture not only with his shoulders but with his head and eyes. He muttered, "Stan. I'm Stan."

Oren said, "I believe Chotchkiegians also have last names."

Stan mumbled something.

"What was that?"

"Gooey," Stan said, this time more clearly.

"That's your name?"

He looked up with a defiant expression. "Something wrong with it?"

"Not in the least."

I think the reason it took me a while to notice the eyebrows was because of all the badges and pins and whatnot stuck to him. His shirt was covered with them — alien smiley face buttons, ribbons, pins with weird sayings. One said: *I'm a hugger.* Another had: *Team Player*. Another was: *Chotchkie #1*. He wore a string tie around his neck with three more buttons hanging from the strings. I couldn't count them all, but at a bare minimum, there were at least fifteen.

He noticed me gawking at it. "Do you like my flair?"

"It's … um … eye-catching."

"Now, Mr. Gooey," Oren said.

"Call me Stan."

"Stan then. Why did you come here today?"

He made a little grimace. "Not to be interrogated. I came here to eat and to experience the atmosphere of the diner."

I said, "You don't mean the planet's atmosphere … 'cause it doesn't have any." I hoped a little kidding around would persuade him to lower his guard.

It didn't. He responded with an insincere chuckle while shaking his head dismissively. "You sound like that Fomorian."

That hurt.

Blan cackled. "That's what I said."

"I like restaurants with attitude, okay?" Stan said.

"Did you receive an inducement for coming?" Oren asked.

Stan raised his chin. "My meal here was a reward from my employer for the best customer interaction of the month."

"Congratulations. Is this the first time you have won the award?"

"Apparently, the award is brand new."

Oren shot the rest of us knowing looks. "Would you mind sending us a copy of the reward message?"

Stan made a mocking face. "I'm not giving you my personal correspondence."

"It may have come from the murderer."

"No, it didn't. It came from my employer." More of the dismissive head shaking.

"How did you travel here?"

"I flew my own ship. That's right, I own a ship." He bobbed his head around at us proudly.

Oren said, "Many years ago, I investigated a murder on Chotchkie. A person named Bran Space was killed, stabbed with a piece of flair he was fighting over with someone."

Stan lowered his head and stared at Oren from the tops of his eyes. "That happens more often than you might think. People are passionate about flair."

"Does that name Bran Space mean anything to you?"

Stan turned up his palms.

"Is that a no?" Oren asked.

He answered with another shrug.

"To your knowledge, do you have any connection to any case of mine?"

Stan took a heavy breath. "No. Why is that important?"

"One theory of the crime is that the killer is trying to taunt me."

"Oh, so I'm placed in danger because of you?" Stan looked toward the heavens and shook his head again. "You'll be hearing from my solicitor."

"I doubt that. Any case you might have would be solely against the killer."

That was met with an eye roll and a smirk

Oren asked, "Did you know the person who was killed?"

"Like I said, I don't know anything. I don't know you, and I didn't know the dead guy. And from where I was sitting, I couldn't see anything. If you don't mind, my food is getting cold."

Oren bowed his head. "Thank you. You may go. But please remain at the diner. We may have more questions."

Stan rose with another dismissive headshake and returned to his booth.

Blan said, "What a jerk."

"What a weirdo," Buad put in.

"What a dweeb," Blan said.

Buad bobbed his beak in my direction. "He makes dum-dum here look almost normal."

"Almost."

"At least he isn't trying to join the team like that Alfo character."

Chapter 10

We Axolotl Questions

All through those interviews, I kept thinking about how Sarah was expecting me back on Earth any minute now, and how I wasn't showing up. Not that spending extra time at the Nebula Diner solving Mapes' murder would delay my return to any great extent.

See, since the chrono drive uses time travel, I could return to Earth on any given day. If I were to, for instance, spend Tuesday through Thursday at the Nebula Diner, there was nothing to prevent us from showing up on Earth on the preceding Monday, meaning Sarah wouldn't even notice me taking the few extra days.

Well, that's not quite true. One thing would keep us from doing that — if I contacted her again.

Suppose today was Tuesday, and I called her, and she casually mentioned that Lucas scraped a knee on the playground, or that she ran out of gas on the way to a meeting. Then if I returned home any day before Tuesday, it would mean I would know their future. I could even change their future with that knowledge — tell Lucas to avoid the jungle gym and Sarah to fill up the tank. For that matter, how weird would it be for me to be sitting around the house when Sarah takes that call from past me on another planet, a call in which Lucas no longer has a scraped knee, and she got to her meeting on time? That kind of thing can cause a temporal paradox. I'd had experience with temporal paradoxes, and I didn't like them one bit.

So all I had to do was not call her. If I refrained from talking to her, then I could slip into the past with no problem. Except I wanted to call her. Maybe I was a little down because I should have been home with her by now. Or maybe I just wanted to hear her voice.

"Oren," I said, "before we continue, can I have a couple of minutes to tell Sarah I'm going to be late?"

He blinked at me from the tablet screen, "You know you don't have to be late … provided you don't call her."

My only answer was to flip up a hand.

"Go. I was a newlywed once myself."

I would have loved to hear more about that. But now didn't seem the time. I stepped out into the hangar for some privacy, gazing longingly at the *Shaymus*, which could take me home but wasn't going to for at least a while longer.

"WALT," I said over the translator bot connection, "I'd like to call Sarah again."

The communications AI answered. "Sure thing, Gabriel. Hey, pull out your phone, and I can make it a video call."

"Voice is okay this time." I didn't want to see the disappointment on her face.

"Okay. Hang on."

"Hey, WALT, while you're connecting us, what do you think about Kah-Rehn's poetry fascination?"

"I don't know. Me, I like doing what I do, connecting to devices and systems all over the galaxy. I like to think I bring people together. But honestly, she's only trying to find purpose in her life. AIs have feelings too, you know."

"I suppose. But do they … really?"

"What do you mean?"

"I mean, are they actual feelings?"

"They seem real enough to me, Gabriel."

"But … you're software. No offense, WALT."

"None taken. I'm proud of what I am."

"Good for you. But I mean, these things you believe you're feeling, how do you know they're not some artifact of your programming, an illusion, a misperceived subroutine? AIs on Earth are always confusing things they think are real for reality itself. How do you know you're feeling actual feelings?"

"How do you know *your* feelings are real, Gabriel? Being tired or hungry can affect the emotions of a biological."

"You got that right. You don't want to see me when I'm hangry."

"Here's Sarah."

The familiar voice sounded in my ear. "Hello?"

"Hi, babe," I said.

"Gabe? What's up?" I heard concern in her voice. The fact that I was calling instead of walking in the front door must have told her something was wrong.

"It's a long story. I don't have time to go into it, but we were manipulated into coming to a diner, and somebody was killed."

"Oh no. Not one of the team?"

"Nothing like that. But Oren wants to investigate."

"How were they killed?"

"Somebody slipped something into his food."

"Interesting. A man poisoned in the middle of a busy restaurant."

"Well, not a man as such. Closer to Pete's dragon."

"Are you okay?"

"I'm fine." I didn't want to admit it even to myself, but given our phony voucher, it was reasonable to assume we were all in danger.

"Do you have a bunch of kooky alien suspects?"

"Do we ever? Little green men. People with pig noses. Oh, and we have baby Srathans."

"Aw. I bet they're adorable."

"Like scaly teddy bears with sharp teeth."

"Well, don't get yourself killed."

"Who me? No way. Listen, I need to return to the interviews. But I had to talk to you. I miss you."

"I miss you too. Well, have fun. Catch the bad guy. Love you."

"I love you too. Gotta go."

And with that, she was gone from my ear, and I was alone again in the hangar light-years from my home. I stood there for a moment, then returned to the diner where Oren, Zastra, and the Avanians were waiting for me in the corner booth. As I entered, Zastra nodded toward the booth with the Quexel person. I approached it.

"Excuse me," I said.

Maybe it was the fishbowl, which was again pulled over the Quexel's head. Or maybe it was because this alien seemed like such a delicate creature. But I felt as if I were intruding. Next to the Quexel, I felt like a clumsy human stomping through a marsh and disturbing all the wildlife.

The black eyes squinted at me. "May I help you?" The voice was soft and liquid. So soft I could barely make it out through the glass.

"Would you have a few minutes to speak with us about the murder?"

Long pointed fingers again pressed whatever button drained the helmet. The Quexel pulled off the darkened headgear, making its face appear even more pale than before. It squinted and took a couple of breaths of air before saying, "You don't suspect me of involvement, do you?"

Without the helmet, I understood the words much better.

"We only want to ask you what you saw." The truth was that at this point in the investigation, everyone was a suspect. But why put them on their guard?

"I suppose."

"Great. We're in the corner booth."

With a flick of a leg, the Quexel pushed off from the seat. Holding the helmet under one arm, it swam with a wiggling motion through the low gravity to our booth. The graceful movements reminded me of videos I'd seen of astronauts training for weightlessness in plunging airplanes. I plodded along behind in my mag boots.

The Quexel floated down into the seat. I slid in beside it.

Oren said, "Thank you for agreeing to speak with us. My name is Oren Vilkas. These are my associates."

The Quexel's eyes darted around the table, finally settling on me with unblinking eyes. "What are you?"

"Pardon?" I asked.

"What species are you?"

"Earthling." I was getting tired of answering the question.

"I have never seen your kind."

Still no blinks. I thought I remembered that axolotls don't have eyelids. Possibly Quexels didn't either.

"Well, we mostly stick pretty close to home."

Blan said, "And everybody is trying to keep it that way."

I ignored him. "My name is Gabriel Lake. And you are?"

"Rio Rivenna."

"So you don't actually need your helmet? This isn't hurting you, is it?"

"I am amphibian. I can breathe almost as well without it. Not quite, but I can get by for short periods. It's the light filtering feature of the helmet I need as much as anything. It is so bright in here." She squinted and rubbed a hand over her eyes.

Oren said, "Then we will try to not keep you too long. Were you acquainted with the Javidian who died?"

Rio turned toward Oren's tablet. "I don't believe so. What was his name?"

"Mapes. He was a former police inspector."

Rio shook her head. "I have never heard the name. People were talking about poison. Do you think someone killed him because of his police work?"

"We do not yet know. It is a possibility. Are you aware of any connection you have to any of my cases?"

"Your cases?" She had no eyebrows but somehow managed to give the impression of raising them.

"I am a private investigator."

"Are you?" She raised a hand to shield her eyes as she peered at the tablet. "What did you say your name was?"

"Oren Vilkas."

"Oren Vilkas. Yes, it comes back to me now. You visited my home on Piscina when I was a tadpole."

"I did once interview a Quexel named Breen Naguuna, who had witnessed a murder."

"Yes. I am her daughter. You persuaded her to testify in court."

So Rio was a she.

Oren's brow furrowed. "Inducing someone to testify would have been the job of a law enforcement official. I merely encouraged her to come forward."

For an instant, a smile flickered across Rio's face. "That must be it. As I said, I was very young at the time. It is more an image in my mind than a memory."

"Your mother's information enabled me to capture the killer."

"So they told me."

"At the time, there was a large Quexel community on Piscina living among the Kabar."

"There still is. The two communities get along well for the most part. As the Kabar say, 'The water is deep.'"

"Do you still live there?"

"Not anymore. My family moved back to Quex." The head swished gently back and forth. "It must be terribly exciting to be a detective."

Oren smiled. "We have our moments."

The diner door swooshed open, and we looked up. A couple of Donovians, walking with effort in mag boots, entered. I did a double take to make sure it wasn't my old frenemy, the interfering, unaccommodating Lt. Xox from Girsu Space Port. He was the last person we needed right now. Frankly, anybody barging into the middle of a crime scene was unwelcome.

If you aren't familiar with Donovians from my previous cases, think of the McDonald's Grimace with its big purple body. But give them stick-figure arms and legs. Then move the eyes to the tops of their heads and make them googly like the eyes on Cookie Monster.

The Donovians wobbled their purple bodies over to the booth where Mapes had sat. They glared at the rope and folding sign blocking it off. With an overdone display of annoyance, they pivoted and made their way to the counter.

Oren spoke, and I turned my attention back to Rio. "Prior to Mr. Mapes' death, did you notice anyone acting suspiciously in the vicinity of his table?"

"I could barely see it. I am not large, and the family of Srathans were in the way."

"I understand," Oren said. "Why did you come to the Nebula Diner today?"

"Excuse me for a moment." She replaced the helmet on her head and let it refill with water. The pink feathery gills on either side of her head fluttered a few times. After several seconds, she pressed the button beside the helmet, and let the water again drain. She pulled off the helmet, squinted in the bright light of the diner, and said, "Sorry. Where were we?"

"It is quite all right. I asked about your reasons for coming here."

"You did. The answer is that I am on holiday. I am hopping around the galaxy seeing the sights. Call it a grand tour."

"Splendid," Oren said. "What have you seen so far?"

She raised a pale hand. "This is my first stop. I hope to see the great falls on Antares Five and Mount Shaymus on Rheged Prime … among other places."

"You had no special incentive for coming here?"

"No. Why do you ask?"

"Mr. Mapes did. Someone set an appointment to meet him at the diner."

"Then perhaps that person can be more helpful to your investigation. But no, I have heard about the nebula for years and always wanted to visit. I was delighted when the ship rental I booked included a discount coupon to several eateries around the galaxy, including this one." She gazed around the restaurant. This is a fascinating place, isn't it?"

"It is. The coupon you received would be a special incentive."

"Would it? Hmm. I suppose it is."

"Was there anything unusual about it, the coupon?"

"I don't think so."

"Would you be willing to send it to us for analysis?"

Rio was quiet for a moment. "I would rather not."

"We are endeavoring to catch a murderer."

A tight smile came to the Quexel's face. "If you insist."

"Thank you, send it to my ship, the *Shaymus*."

Rio didn't move.

"Will you be sending the message?" Oren asked.

"I will send it when I return to my booth."

"Thank you. And thank you for speaking with us."

"May I leave this place now? The galaxy is waiting for me."

"I have no authority to keep you here, though I would prefer if you stayed at least until I have interviewed everyone. It is possible your life may be in danger."

She raised her chin, what she had of one, and said with a defiant tone, "I doubt that, Mr. Vilkas. Who would want to harm a Quexel? But I suppose I might take another peek at the nebula. And possibly try some dessert since you made the offer."

"Please do."

Rio put the helmet back on her head, sprang from the seat, and wiggled off through the air. She bounced off the seat back of her booth and continued into the hallway to the observation dome.

"What do you think?" I asked.

Oren didn't answer. Instead, he said, "Kah-Rehn."

The AI answered over our translator bots. "Yes, Oren."

"I have another task for you."

She sighed. "More research? I have fifteen more terabytes of Itani love poetry to review. And may I say, I don't care for it."

"The poetry?"

"That and biological love in general. It is so … so physical. I find it distasteful."

"Speak for yourself," I said.

Oren said, "Perhaps this will be an enjoyable change of pace."

"What do you want?" she asked wearily.

"Please search the network for Rio Rivenna, a Quexel hatched on Piscina, currently living on Quex. Also, Alfomado Fusco, a Fomorian."

"Understood, Oren. I will let you know when I have something."

"Checking up on their stories?" Zastra asked.

He raised one eyebrow in agreement.

Blan said, "And now we have a tie-in to yet another case."

"Indeed," Oren said, looking grave.

"I don't trust her," Buad said. "She's too cold."

"That's the way Quexels are. They are very private. On the case involving her mother, the crime happened in the middle of a busy market. But I had to interview dozens of Quexels before I could find one who was willing to say what they witnessed."

"Who's next?" I asked.

"Bring the Fryes if they are available. Otherwise, either the Mucs or the Klistine."

Kah-Rehn sounded in our ears again. "Oren, I have information on Rio Rivenna."

"Excellent. Proceed."

The AI made a throat-clearing sound and recited:

"There is a young Quexel named Rio.
She lives in the city of Keedo.
She works as a doctor
And a college med proctor.
And has a pet mollusk named Cleo."

I hoped Kah-Rehn wasn't at that moment looking through any of our translator bots to see the scowl on Oren's face.

"Is that all you have?" he asked.

Kah-Rehn said, "Well, I found more, but the poetic structure constrained the amount of information I could include. However, the verse does paint a picture, does it not? It was the rhyming of the names Rio and Cleo that gave me the inspiration to present the information in this format."

Oren furrowed his brow and sucked in his cheeks.

Trying to ease past the awkwardness, I asked, "Anything on Alfo?"

"Who is Alfo?"

Zastra said, "Alfomado Fusco."

"Yeah, that guy," I said.

Kah-Rehn said, "I am searching for him now."

"Very good," Oren said. "And Kah-Rehn, when you have something, please give it to me in simple prose."

She sighed. "If you insist, Oren. But it is not nearly as creative."

"Creativity is not my primary concern."

"I have the information now. Alfomado Fusco lives in the Tharen district on Fomor in what appears to be a modest neighborhood. He works in sales at Shumway Industries and performs comedy at night as a hobby. He lives alone and has no criminal record. Was that unimaginative enough for you?"

"Satisfactory," Oren said.

Chapter 11

A Few Fryes Short of a Happy Meal

I stepped to the counter and leaned across it. Star and Sola were both in the kitchen area, hopping from step stool to step stool as they worked on an order.

Getting their attention, I said, "Oren was wondering if you two could spare a few moments to answer some questions."

"Oh sure," Sola said.

But Star nodded toward the pair of Donovians who had come in. "We're working on an order. We'll have to talk over here."

"Maybe after that?" I asked.

"It still needs to be here. You never know when a customer is gonna want something."

That was going to be ticklish with both Alfo and the pair of Donovians sitting there at the counter. I needed them to relocate. Clomping around the end, I approached the customers from the kitchen side, hoping to look official.

I shot them a toothy customer-service smile. "I'm sorry, folks. We need this area for a few minutes. Would you mind moving to booths?" I raised my arm to indicate a couple of empty booths on either side of our corner spot.

Putting his stool into a slow spin, Alfo said, "I might as well. Sitting here, I've just been going around in circles. Ha!" As he revolved around back to the counter, he picked up his drink and moved.

The Donovians, however, made a sour face at me.

One said, "Why can't we sit here? We're settled. Our food should be here any moment." That last part was said at a louder volume, the Donovian's ping-pong eyes casting an irritated glower toward Star and Sola.

"Well," I said.

The Donovian interrupted me before I could say any more. "We tried to sit at a booth over there, but somebody had it blocked off."

"I know. Sorry about that. You see, that booth that's blocked off, somebody died there, and we're interviewing—"

"What?" The googly eyes widened and rolled around a couple of times. "Cancel our order."

Both Donovians jumped from their stools.

"I didn't mean …" I raised my hands. "It wasn't anything related to the food. Well, to be honest, the food was poisoned, but we're almost positive it didn't come from the kitchen."

"Almost?" The Donovian raised a stick figure hand. "I don't want to hear your excuses. We're not eating here. Come along, Frax." The dissatisfied customer took a shuffle step toward the door, barely able to lift the twig-thin legs in mag boots.

Frax said, "Shouldn't we at least see the nebula first? We came all this way."

"I'm hungry. I want to go somewhere we can trust the food … where the staff doesn't chase us from seat to seat."

"We have some protein bars on the ship."

"I want real food. And if this is the way they treat people here—"

Frax shot the other one a pleading look. "C'mon. A quick peep, and then we'll be on our way."

The first one hesitated. "I suppose."

Frax smiled, and they plodded off down the hall toward the observation dome.

Star shot me an annoyed glance, antennae sweeping back like porcupine quills. "How about next time you say something other than a person died here?"

"Sorry," I said.

Frankly, I was a little disappointed in myself as well. One of the fun parts of this job is coming up with stories on the fly. Here I had settled for the truth when a small fiction would have been more effective and much more entertaining.

I waved my arm to Zastra to tell her to come over. She scowled back and waved for me to bring Star and Sola there. I shook my head and again waved her this way. Tossing me a couple of death stares, she picked up the tablet and slid out. Buad and Blan took to wing to follow.

While Star scraped the half-finished plates into the replicator for recycling, Zastra set Oren's tablet on a stretch of empty countertop beside the cookstove. Star and Sola sat down on step stools facing him.

"Thank you for speaking with us," Oren said.

Sola said, "Oh, you bet. We'll do anything to help you catch whoever did this, don't ya know." The Frye's voice lowered to a whisper. "Otherwise, it raises questions about our cooking."

"Indeed. Let me start with this. Have you offered any recent promotions to entice people to visit?"

"I wouldn't say promotions exactly. We have a new jingle we've put in our commercials. Maybe you've heard it." Sola stood on the stool and began to sing:

"Come to the Nebula Diner.
You won't find food that's finer.
There's fun for adults and minors
At the Nebula Diner."

The Frye took a little bow and sat back down.

"Yes, um … thank you," Oren said. "But I meant promotions as in discount coupons or free day trips."

Star and Sola looked at each other.

"You know," Star said, "that would be a good idea. Who would we contact to set something like that up?"

"Oh, I don't know," Sola said. "I could ask around."

"What about your cousin's marketing company?"

"No, I don't think they do anything like that."

Oren said, "But as of yet you have done nothing of that nature?"

"Oh no," Sola said. "Ooh! How about younglings eat free?"

"Not too bad," Star said, pulling a tiny tablet from an apron pocket to make a note. "What age do you think?"

"Well now, it would need to be different for each species."

Oren broke in on the marketing meeting. "Had you ever met Mr. Mapes before?"

"That would depend," Sola said.

"On what?"

"On whether he ever came in here before."

A pinched expression came over Oren's face. "That was essentially my question."

"Was it? I thought you meant socially."

"In any capacity. Had you met him?"

"Welp, I don't think so. We've had Javidians in before, for sure. But you know, we don't always catch customers' names. It's rare, in fact. Mainly only when someone has a complaint."

"And let me be clear," Star put in, "we don't get many complaints. Of course, you can't please everybody no matter how hard you try."

I said, "You know what they say. The customer is always right."

Star laughed out loud. When none of the rest of us joined in, the Frye looked around with antennae widened to a V. "Oh, you're serious? I sure haven't found that to be the case. Customers are always getting something wrong. They want food overcooked ... or undercooked ... or the music so soft you can't hear it ... or loud enough to hurt your ears ... or they think the toilets should be moved to some crazy location ... or they want their food somehow shot up to them as they orbit the world."

Sola said, "There was this one fella, a Fornaxi he was—"

Oren raised a hand and cut in. "Mr. Mapes was formerly with the Javidian police. Have you had any dealings with them?"

"Gosh no," Sola said. "We've never even been to Javid. To be honest, those spiky tips on their tails scare me a little, us being on the small side, you know."

"Of course."

The interview seemed to be going nowhere. I expected Oren to bail on it at any moment and ask Zastra or me to finish up. But instead, he tried another question.

"Which of the customers here at the time of the incident arrived first today?"

Sola again stood on the stool, this time to scan the diner. "Oh ... hmm ... I think that group over there, the two Mucs and the Klistine."

"Thank you."

"No," Star said. "It was the Fomorian who was at the counter."

"Nobody's at the counter, dear," Sola said.

Star's eyes rolled toward the ceiling. "Well, nobody is now. But the Fomorian was, you betcha. The place was empty. He came in and plopped down on that stool and said, 'I tell you, I would be a morning person if only it started a little later.' And it's been a stream of bad jokes ever since."

Sola said, "Oh wait. Or was it the Quexel?"

Oren said, "It probably doesn't matter."

A voice called from a booth. I looked up to see one of the Mucs waving a hand.

Sola hopped from the stool. "Ope, I better see what she wants. I'm just gonna sneak right past you."

When the Frye had slipped out, Oren asked Star, "How long have you known Sola?"

"Oh my goodness, years."

"So you know Sola well. You are business partners?"

"Well … more than that." Star's antenna began rotating in small circles.

"I see. Did you notice anything unusual about Sola today?"

"Whoa whoa whoa. For Zahn's sake, you can't think Sola was behind this. That makes no sense at all. Sola sure wouldn't kill somebody here in our own diner where it would hurt business."

It was a less than ringing affirmation of Sola's innocence, relying as it did more on business strategy than virtue.

"Have you two ever discussed me?"

"You? No. We recognized your name when you said it a while ago. But it's not like we sit around and talk about you and stuff."

Sola loped back in, requested three cups of tea from the replicator, and bounded back out to serve the guests.

The front door opened again. This time the alien who entered was a kind I had never seen. It was mainly humanoid-looking but with dark reddish skin and lips extended like someone making a duck face for a selfie, only enormously so. Whatever this person was, it headed toward Mapes' booth but stopped when confronted with the velvet rope.

I rushed over as best I could in my boots. "You don't want to sit there. The … the seat has a wobbly leg. Believe me, it would drive you crazy."

Duck face turned and headed toward the counter.

I said, "And, sorry, the counter is closed for um … cleaning. We have booths along that side. Not the corner one. It's reserved."

Duck face frowned — accomplishing it mainly using eyes, given the elongated kisser   and moved to the last of the open booths.

I returned to the group. "Better?"

Star flashed me a green thumbs-up.

When Sola returned, Oren said, "Have any of the customers who were here when Mapes died ever come here previously?"

Star stretched up a hand and rubbed an antenna. "Welp, of course, the Mucs deliver supplies here from time to time."

"They do? Interesting. What about the Klistine with them?"

"He's new."

So the Klistine was a male. Or at any rate, something that caused my translator bots to use a male pronoun, which was good enough for me. I had no idea about Star and Sola and didn't want to ask.

Sola said, "Now that Quexel, she's come in before."

"Has she?" Star asked.

Sola blinked a few times. "I think so. She looks awfully familiar to me."

"We've had other Quexels, sure."

"But I mean this one. Don't you remember? The other time she made a fuss about which booth had the best view. Kept hopping from one to another."

"I think that was a different Quexel, Sola."

"No, it was her all right."

Shaking his head, Oren asked, "What about the Fomorian?"

Star said, "All those jokes. I'd know if he'd ever been here before."

Oren waited, then said, "And has he?"

"No. And not that Srathan family either."

"Satisfactory. Now walk me through how food was served to Mr. Mapes."

Sola nodded. "I took his order — vajiemen noodles with a nauk bean sauce. A dish like that, well, we have to replicate it. The sauce alone would have to simmer most of the day, you know."

"That raises an interesting question about whether the replicator recipe was tampered with. Would you mind making a small portion now for testing?"

"You bet." Sola stood and hopped to the stool in front of the replicator. "Sample size of vajiemen with nauk sauce."

A tiny cup appeared on the counter.

Oren said, "Now please summon the medical bot."

Star bounced to the serving counter, pulled out the black box, and pressed the button.

A minute later Bones rolled in. "Please state the nature of the medical emergency."

It didn't take a genius like Oren Vilkas to figure out what the point of all this was. I grabbed the mini-serving and handed it to the doc bot. "No emergency this time. Test this for the poison."

"Please state the specific poison."

There he had me. "Um. The one the dead guy got."

"Tetratoxipine," Zastra said, rolling her yellow eyes.

"That's it."

Bones pulled the sample inside its body. "Analyzing."

After a few moments, a ding sounded.

"Sample is negative for tetratoxipine."

I said, "So much for a hacked food replicator."

Oren said, "B0-N3Z, what were the results from your further tests of the body?"

Lines of code scrolled up the bot's front-mounted screen. "The cause of death has been confirmed. Tetratoxipine poisoning. Analysis suggests the toxin was consumed within ten minutes prior to death."

"Here in the diner then. Any other findings of note?"

More scrolling. "The spikey end of the Javidian's tail is composed of cartilage."

Oren's head tilted. "How is that relevant to his death?"

"It is not. But it is interesting."

"Anything else?"

"Negative."

"Then thank you. That is all."

B0-N3Z trundled off.

Oren turned back to Star and Sola. "After you served the dish, did you notice anyone near Mapes' booth?"

Star scoffed. "Like we have time to gawk around at customers."

"I assume you keep an eye on everyone to see how they are getting along with their meals or if they need anything."

"Oh sure, but we don't track all their movements."

"I understand. Have either of you ever had a connection to a case of mine? I don't recollect either of you. Indeed, I have never investigated a crime involving Fryes. However, you might know someone of another species who was connected to a case."

Sola said, "We know you by reputation, sure. But nothing else."

"What are you implying?" Star asked, antennae quivering.

"Nothing. I am asking questions."

"Welp, we have work to do."

"One more question, if you please. Is there access to the old mine from the diner?"

"Oh, you bet," Sola said. "The diner was originally put here for the miners, don't ya know. The door beyond the cold storage room leads down to the mine."

Oren nodded. "In that case, we may want to inspect it."

"Help yourself."

"That is all for now. I probably don't need to tell you to not leave the planetoid."

Star chuckled. "As if we could. We've been trying to sneak away for a vacation for the last five years."

As we headed back to our booth, I thought back over what we had learned, which didn't seem like much. Star and Sola were in a relationship, which was interesting but probably not relevant. They seemed to have no motive to harm Oren or Mapes or indeed to do anything to give the diner a bad name. Alfo was probably the first person in today, but was that because he was plotting a murder or simply how it worked out given where he was coming from? The Mucs and possibly Rio were repeat customers, which I guessed Oren had asked about since the killer would want to be familiar with the place and make plans before it all went down.

After we settled into the booth, Oren said, "Buad and Blan, when you were searching for the poison, where did you look?"

"Mainly in the kitchen area," Blan said.

"And I checked the public places," Buad said. "Toilets, hallway, observation dome."

Oren said, "Look again and expand the search. Check all rooms and closets including the cold storage room. Not the mine. We'll investigate it later."

"Will do, Boss," Blan said.

They flew off.

"WALT," Oren said.

"Hey, Oren," the communication AI answered.

"Have you traced the messages we had forwarded to the ship?"

"Why yes, I have. The message sent to Rio Rivenna originated from the diner."

"This diner?"

"You heard me. The Nebula Diner."

"Interesting. What about the one sent to Alfomado Fusco?"

"It appears to have originally been sent from the planet Muc."

"Thank you, WALT."

"Muc," I said.

"Indeed. And the diner, which could implicate the Fryes or any of the people who have been here before."

"Including the Mucs."

"Or Rio. Invite the Klistine and the Mucs to join us. No. Let's take the Klistine separately and see what he says about them. I will have Kah-Rehn check on him while we talk."

Chapter 12

Everybody Loves a Crossover Episode

As I stepped to the booth, the two Mucs looked up and cast appraising stares at me.

"What do you think, Hulu?" the one with the pink hair said. She swept her long, disheveled mane back over her shoulder and scrunched up her pig nose to leer at me.

"I don't know, Roku." The one with the neon green hair sucked in the side of her cheek and gave me a sideways glance. "Not really my type. He's not particularly hairy."

Hulu? Roku? Those were their names? Like the streaming services?

"Sometimes I like smooth skin," Roku said. "It's soft to the touch. Hey, sweetness. I like your hat."

I have never in my life catcalled a woman ... or anyone for that matter. It wouldn't even occur to me to do so. And since I work alone in my home office, I don't face a hostile work environment unless you count Sarah's cat, who's always trying to stare me down. But I didn't appreciate being on the receiving end of unwanted comments. Let me tell you, women on Earth probably deserve reparations for taking that kind of garbage from men all these years.

If Roku was leering at me, Hulu's expression was ... well, more like the condescending glower I get from Sarah's cat.

"Whatcha need, sparky?" she asked in a patronizing tone.

Trying to ignore them, I turned to the Klistine on the opposite side of the booth. Instead of leering or glowering, his face wore more of a sneer. I didn't get the impression the sneer was driven by jealousy over the Mucs' attention toward me. It seemed to be more or less a permanent feature of his rubbery face. Besides, if Hulu liked them hairy, she wouldn't be interested in a Klistine, who had no hair at all as far as I could see, which wasn't a whole lot given the green flannel shirt and dark trousers he wore.

"Hi," I said. "Oren Vilkas wants to interview everyone concerning the death. Would you mind coming to our booth to talk?"

The mouth twisted open to reveal sharp-edged teeth. "Who's Oren Vilkas?" The voice came out harsh and gritty.

I was surprised. Oren was well known throughout the galaxy, and his name generally brought a reaction.

"Oren Vilkas with the Galactic Detective Agency. I'm Gabriel Lake."

"What about us, Gabriel Lake?" Roku said, making a pouty face, which take it from me, didn't work with the pig nose. "Don't you want to talk to us?"

"Mr. Vilkas," I said, emphasizing the name to communicate that it was Oren's desire to talk to them, not mine, "will want to speak to you also, but we'll take your friend here first."

Roku shot me a wink. "We'll look forward to our turn with you, sweetums. Cute little nose, don't you think, Hulu?"

"It's okay," Hulu said. "A tad skinny."

I shuddered and held my arm out toward our booth. The Klistine slid from the seat and moved in the indicated direction. As we walked away, I heard Roku saying something about my backside in that same lascivious tone. I shifted to turn my caboose toward the seats and tried to walk sideways, which as it turns out, doesn't work well in mag boots.

"What's with those two?" I asked in a low voice.

"Sisters," the Klistine said.

"Sisters named Hulu and Roku? Do they have a brother named Max, a cousin Netflix?"

"What?"

"Never mind."

"Fortunately for me, they aren't interested in Klistines. But Roku seems to have called dibs on you."

"Lucky me."

We reached the corner booth and slipped in.

Oren said, "Thank you for speaking with me. I'll try not to take too much of your time. My name is Oren Vilkas. This is Zastra and Gabriel Lake."

"So he says," the Klistine said.

"And your name?"

"Tomko."

I said, "Tomko. Tomko. Why does that name sound familiar to me?"

"I couldn't imagine. Have you ever been to the planet Haplor?"

"You're from Haplor? Is that where Haplors live? You're not from Klistonia or whatever it's called?"

His eyes narrowed to slits. "Klista. I'm from Klista originally. I live on Haplor now. People move."

"I met a Haplor person once. Funny sort of fellow."

His non-existent lip shot up a fraction. "Some of them are. I thought you wanted to talk about the guy who died."

"We do," Oren said. "Though it is useful to learn something of you."

"Why?"

"To understand your perspective. For example, what led you to Haplor?"

"Work."

"What is your employment?"

"I'm a busser."

This guy's answers were not what you'd call expansive.

In the months since my last case, I had worked on memorizing interviews. I practiced while watching old episodes of *Columbo*, listening carefully while the unassuming detective talked with someone, then pausing the show and trying to write out the conversation. Then I would back up the show to see how well I did. I couldn't hit it word for word, but I had gotten to the place where I was able to accurately report the main points and key phrases of a scene. Of course, my memory was no match for Oren Vilkas who simply saved conversations in memory. But anybody could remember this guy's monosyllabic answers.

"Where?" Oren asked.

He rolled his eyes. "The Matcha Doin' House of Tea in the city of Welkinda

Wow! That was nearly a whole sentence.

"Interesting," Oren said.

"Not particularly. But it's money."

"So here you've gone from one dining establishment to another."

Tomko curled his lipless mouth into a scowl. "Yeah. Just the way I wanted to spend my vacation."

"How did you end up here with the Mucs?"

"Like I said, I'm on vacation. They were coming through, and I hitched a ride."

"They came through Haplor?"

"That's where I live. Where else?"

"Did they dine at your tearoom?"

Tomko chuckled mirthlessly. "Those two are not our normal clientele."

"Then how did you meet them?"

"They were delivering something."

"To the shop?"

This time he didn't even deign to give us a smart aleck answer. He merely rolled his eyes again.

"What is the destination of your vacation?"

Tomko stared at Oren for a beat or two. "It's not relevant."

Oren tilted his head, started to say something, and then gave it up. "All right. We will assume that for now. Had you met the Mucs before this trip?"

"Not to talk to. They've delivered to the shop on other occasions."

"Did they say anything about the person who was killed?"

"What do you think? It's not every day someone dies in front of you."

"What about before he died?"

"Why would they talk about him before?"

"I don't know," Oren said. "They might have pointed him out when he entered the diner. They might have said something on the trip here about a Javidian."

"They didn't."

"All right. However, someone poisoned his food. Most likely, that someone came here with the intention of doing so."

"You think they did it?"

"At this stage, I am merely gathering information. What about you? Did you know the person who was killed?"

"Nope."

"Have you ever been to Javid?"

"Once."

"When was that?"

"Years ago. I went to see the beaches."

"During your time there, did you run into any problem with law enforcement?"

Tomko stared at Oren without answering.

Oren smiled. "You don't have to answer. I can check the records. Kah-Rehn, please find what you can on a Klistine named Tomko, who lives on the planet Haplor."

Tomko tried on what he probably thought was a smile. But with all the pointy teeth, it came off more like what something in a nightmare would do before eating you.

Oren peered around the table. "Does anyone else have a question?"

Zastra asked, "Have you ever been involved with any case investigated by the Galactic Detective Agency?"

Tomko smirked. "Other than this one?"

She called his smirk and raised a grimace. "Yes."

"Then no."

I said, "Was anyone else here in the diner when you first arrived?"

"That joking Fomorian."

Oren said, "As a busser, I assume you have trained yourself to keep an eye on tables. What did you see happening around the dead person's booth before he died?"

"Nothing. First, I'm on vacation, remember? I'm not looking at tables. And our booth is at the opposite end of the diner."

I said, "You went down the hallway about that time."

His mouth tightened and stretched into a scowl. "Yeah. I used the facilities. But the guy was alive when I passed him in each direction."

Oren asked, "When you walked by his booth was anyone near it acting suspiciously?"

"I don't know what suspicious behavior looks like in other species."

"Let's say someone appearing nervous or lingering in place for no apparent reason."

"The Mucs were hanging around the jukebox. The Fomorian was wandering around aimlessly."

I said, "I think Alfo was only poring over the art on the walls."

Tomko scoffed. "Art? Is that what you call it?" He glared up at the antique replicator ad above our booth. Apparently, the busser was also an art snob.

A bubbly hacking sound started up from another booth. I jumped up to see Rio thrashing about in her seat, arms flailing, her head pitching back and forth inside her helmet. Her arm came down on the tines of a spork sitting beside a half-finished pudding of some kind, sending the utensil wheeling slowly through the low-gravity air.

I rushed over as quickly as my mag boots would take me. The Quexel's normally pale face was scarlet.

I yelled, "Sola, Star, call the doc bot."

Rio was smacking a hand on the side of her fishbowl.

"Do you want the helmet off?" I asked.

She hacked more, and I thought I detected a nod. I stretched out my hand slowly so as not to startle her and touched the button I had seen her use earlier. I hoped that was what she wanted. The water drained, and I pulled off the helmet, dropping it onto the seat. She gasped in the air, bracing herself against the table with one arm. The hacks now sounded more like human coughs as she struggled to breathe. Her normal lack of color began returning to her face.

"Are you okay?"

Rio slouched back in her seat. "I think ... so."

A mechanical voice behind me said, "Please state the nature of the medical emergency."

"Ah, Bones, glad you made it. Check out Rio here. She—"

"My designation is B-zero-dash-N-three-Zed."

"I know, I know. Now's not the time. Make sure this person is all right, okay? And if you can tell us what happened, that would be great."

B0-N3Z rolled to the edge of the booth. Its middle arm retracted inside its body and came out wearing something like Thanos's infinity gauntlet only with flashing lights where the stones were in the movie. The doc bot took Rio's wrist and held it in the glove.

"Blood pressure normal for species. Heart rate elevated but beginning to lower. May I examine blood?"

Rio bobbed her head.

The robot's hand retracted and came out again with the needle. It drew blood from a spot behind the feathery gills. The syringe retracted into the bot's body.

After a ding a few moments later, Bones announced, "Blood contains traces of the neurotoxin turmetox."

"What?" That came from Star, who was standing behind my knee with antennae widened into a V. "Oh no, no no no. Not another one."

"Will she be okay?" I asked.

The doc bot said. "Subject appears to have received less than a lethal dosage."

A green arm reached up over the tabletop on a course to grab the dessert dish. The bowl was nearly empty but still contained a bite or two.

I snatched it up. "Not so fast, Star."

The Frye didn't make eye contact. "Need to keep things tidy, don't ya know."

"This is evidence."

"No, it can't be our food. It can't be."

I handed the dish to Bones. "Test this for the toxin."

After analyzing the dessert, the med bot announced, "Negative."

"I told you," Star said, frowning at me.

Rio, still heaving breaths, said, "Then where … did it come from … this toxin?"

The helmet on the seat bench still contained a splash of water. I handed it to the med bot. "Test this, B-zero-dash-whatever."

"B-zero-dash-N-three-Zed."

Out came a length of plastic tubing. It vacuumed up the remaining water. This time after the ding, the med bot said, "Sample is positive for turmetox."

Rio raised her huge black eyes. "Somebody injected poison into my water tank?"

"It looks that way," I said.

"But how?"

I studied the hose coming out of her water tank. "Maybe a syringe. Was anyone hanging around here?"

I already knew the answer. While interrogations were going on, everyone had grown restless and had been moving all around the diner.

Rio said, "I'm getting out of here."

With a darting movement, she propelled herself up from the seat and air-swam toward the door.

"Wait," I called. "Oren will have questions. Don't you want to find out who did this?"

But she was already gone.

I turned back to the corner booth where Zastra and Tomko hadn't moved from beside Oren's tablet.

"Should I go after her?" I asked.

"No," Oren said. "We have no authority to stop her. And we can hardly fault her under the circumstances."

I clomped back to the booth and sat, glancing at the door as if Rio might decide to return.

Oren said, "Pardon the interruption."

Tomko asked, "Are we done?"

"Nearly. One final question. Have you ever visited Quex?"

"The Quexel home world? I see where this is going. Have you visited Quex? Did you have a run-in with the law on Javid? You're trying to pin these attacks on me."

"I am investigating. I am asking similar questions of everyone."

"Sure you are," he said, skepticism in his voice. "Well, I'm done talking."

"As you wish," Oren said. "Thank you for your time. I hope, unlike our Quexel friend, you will stay on Ursa 16309 for the time being."

"Take it up with the Muc sisters. It's their ship. I'm stuck here until they decide to move."

He stood and mag-booted his way back to their booth.

Oren said, "Kah-Rehn, what did you learn about Tomko?"

The AI's voice sounded in our ears. "Not much. Here's what I have."

Again, there was a throat-clearing sound — this from a piece of software that had no throat. She recited:

"There is a tall Klistine named Tomko.
Who works in a tearoom, amigo.
He serves tea and cakes
Until his back aches,
And sometimes plays songs on his banjo."

"Full disclosure," Kah-Rehn said. "I had to make up the part about the banjo to work out the rhyme."

Oren closed his digital eyes and tilted his head toward the cybernetic heavens. "Kah-Rehn, this really must stop. I want the facts and only in plain exposition."

"Oh, Oren. Why can't you ever let me have a little fun?"

Chapter 13

Way Too Much Mucs

I could have made an excuse.

I could have said I wanted to check on Jace or needed to use the facilities. Now that I thought of it, I did kind of need to use the facilities.

So when Oren said, "Gabriel, we'll interview the Mucs next," I didn't immediately jump from my seat.

Instead, I sat there, my legs seemingly unwilling to obey the command of my brain to move. The Muc sisters had eyed me the way I had looked at my clucks and waffles. Well, Roku did. I think Hulu looked at me more like something found behind the fridge. If I invited them over, who knew what they would say ... or do?

But as uncomfortable as they made me, I still wanted to be there when Oren questioned them. How else would I be able to read them and get a sense of whether or not one or both of them were killers?

"Gabe?" It was Zastra.

"Hmm?"

She was staring at me. I started to ask if she would escort them over. But I didn't like that idea either. I should be the one to fetch them. It would show I wasn't intimidated by them. Unless the Muc sisters saw that as a signal that I welcomed their attention, which I certainly didn't want to encourage.

"Gabe." This time she sounded more insistent.

"Yeah, yeah. I was thinking."

"For Zahn's sake. If you're going to daydream, I'll usher them here myself."

"I wasn't ..." But she was already sliding from the booth.

As she stood, she fixed me with her intense yellow eyes. "With Buad and Blan gone, you guard Oren. Nobody comes near this table until I get back. Got it?"

"Yes, ma'am."

Roku might leer and Hulu smirk, but no one beats Zastra at intimidating glares.

As she headed for the Mucs' booth, Stan rose from his place. He swept past us like the joint was on fire and headed out the diner door.

Oren said, "The Chotchkiegian, he's leaving. See if you can stop him, Gabriel."

"Zastra told me to stay with you."

"And I am telling you to go."

"Yeah, but …"

"I am in charge, not her."

"You can fire me. She can hurt me."

He shot me a determined frown. "Go."

I slid out and left the diner. As I emerged from the airlock door, I saw him a few yards ahead of me.

"Stan," I yelled at his back.

He stopped and turned around, his lips tight and his eyebrows up. No wait, they were always up.

"What do you want?" he asked.

"Just saying hi. I need to get something out of our ship. Where are you off to?"

He shook his thin head in tight movements. "Where do you think? I'm going home. I've finished my meal."

I kept my tone friendly. "Oren asked you to stay."

Stan's tone, on the other hand, was pure sarcasm. "Is he a government official now that I have to obey his commands?"

"Okay, we would prefer you stay. We're trying to catch a killer."

"You let that Quexel leave."

"She was attacked."

His eyes widened, hiking his bushy eyebrows even higher. "And who's to say I won't be next?"

He spun on his heels and once more started walking.

I called, "Stan."

He raised his hand in a back-off gesture and kept walking. After a dozen or so steps, he reached into a pocket, pulled something out, and pressed a button on it. A click sounded from a missile-shaped ship with squarish wings that reminded me of a paper airplane I used to make as a kid. A ramp opened and he disappeared inside.

As I stepped back through the airlock door, two beeps sounded behind me, and an automated voice said, "Hangar preparing to depressurize."

I returned to the diner, giving Oren a shake of my head to indicate that my mission was a failure. Zastra, who had specifically told me not to leave the booth, shot me a perturbed look.

She was just returning to the booth with the Mucs. Hulu slid in after her on her side. The flirtatious, pink-haired Roku took the other side, leaving the space beside her for me. I slid in … barely, leaving as much room between us as possible. Roku responded by shooting me a coy grin and scooching nearer, ending up so close we were nearly thigh to thigh.

Hulu, meanwhile, was keeping her distance from Zastra, which in general is always a sound policy. She sat back in her seat and had a private chuckle at my obvious discomfort.

Oren said, "Thank you for coming. My name is Oren Vilkas."

"You're Vilkas?" Hulu asked in an incredulous tone. She turned toward Zastra. "I thought you were Vilkas. You have a male in charge?"

Oren answered. "I am digital, but yes, this is my agency."

"Then what do *you* do?" Hulu again addressed Zastra.

"I work for him."

Hulu seemed to flinch. "Weird."

Apparently on the planet Muc, gender roles were reversed and even more constrained from what they are on Earth.

"And your names are?" Oren asked.

"Hulu Pash," Hulu said, still staring at Zastra. "And this is my sister, Roku Pash."

"Thank you. I would like to ask you some questions about what you saw during the two recent attacks."

"Sure," Roku said. "But we didn't see much from the back corner."

I said, "That's not exactly true. You were at the jukebox right before the poisoning."

"You be quiet," Hulu said with a condescending smile. "And actually, sparky, it's called a music player. Yeah, we were there."

Zastra asked. "Did you see anyone hovering around the Javidian's food?"

"No. We were focused on the music selections."

That wasn't true either. When I passed by, they seemed all too focused on me.

Oren said, "Then let's move on to your occupation."

"What does that have to do with the poisoning?" Hulu asked.

"I merely want to be thorough."

She pursed her lips and rocked them back and forth before answering. "We have a transport business. We deliver goods."

"Interesting. What sort of goods?"

"Whatever people want."

"No questions asked?"

Hulu stared Oren down. "We're paid to fly, not have chats. This is already the longest conversation we've had in a while."

"I understand you regularly deliver here to the diner."

"I don't know about regularly, but they're customers."

"What about your traveling companion, the Klistine? How well do you know him?"

"Hardly at all. We met him on Haplor when we delivered a case of Dieren silversporks to this fancy tea place. He asked about transit to Antares Five and was willing to pay. We took him on. End of story."

Antares Five. Tomko hadn't wanted to tell us his destination. Rio had mentioned vacation plans for Antares Five. Could there be a connection? It depended on how popular the place was. For all I knew, it might be the Disney World of the galaxy.

"You had never met Tomko before then?" Oren asked.

"No," Roku said, one side of her upper lip rising in a disappointed sneer, "and it's a good thing his money is good because he isn't much fun."

Despite Tomko claiming they weren't interested, I wondered if she had tried her charms on him.

"What did you expect?" Hulu said. "He's a Klistine."

Oren said, "And yet you are not at Antares Five. You are here."

"Is that a question?" Hulu said.

"Consider it an invitation to explain."

She shrugged. "We had a case of replicator matter cubes to deliver here first. Antares is our next destination."

Roku leaned forward on the table and gazed at me from under her eyelashes. "Have you ever seen the great falls on Antares Five, Gabriel Lake? They're absolutely jaw-dropping. We have an extra cabin."

During my awkward years in high school, I was essentially ignored by most girls. I had eventually grown out of that and somehow managed to snag Sarah. But I had never gotten used to girls flirting with me, especially pig girls.

I coughed out an awkward laugh. "I ... um ... my wife wants me to take her there sometime."

I don't think Sarah had ever heard of Antares Five, but I thought it a good idea to mention her existence.

Oren cleared his throat. Of course, as a digital person, he didn't have an esophagus. I often wondered if these mannerisms were things carried over from his past life and uploaded along with his mind and personality, or if they were behaviors he consciously added as nonverbal language to aid in communication. In this case, it worked to direct the conversation back to him.

He said, "Before the poisoning, did Tomko mention the Javidian at all?"

Hulu said, "Not that I heard. What about you, Roku?"

Roku said, "He isn't overly talkative."

"What about the Quexel?" Oren asked.

"What Quexel?"

"The one who was sitting at that booth." Oren waved from the screen toward the booths leading to the door. "The person who was nearly killed by a neurotoxin added to her water tank."

"Is that what all the commotion was about? We were in the middle of eating pie and didn't go look. But no, Tomko never mentioned a Quexel."

"Had you, in your travels, ever met either of the victims?"

Hulu and Roku shared a momentary glance I couldn't interpret.

Roku said, "No."

"Does your business ever take you to Javid or Quex?"

Roku said, "We've made a few runs to Javid. Quex is a horrible place. All the cities are built in swamps, and it has way too many bugs. We try to avoid it."

"But you have been there."

"Once or twice. Not in a long time."

"On your trips to Javid, have you ever had dealings with the police?"

Roku cast a glimpse in Hulu's direction.

Hulu made a face and said, "I got in a fight once and somebody called the cops, but nobody was arrested or anything."

Oren said. "I once investigated a case involving a Muc named Wurly Pronk. Is that name familiar to you?"

Hulu scrunched up her pig nose. "There are four-and-a-half billion Mucs. I know at most a few hundred."

"Is that a no?"

"It's a no. I've never heard that name."

"What about Arondi Bunt?"

"Who's that?"

"A Muc I had arrested about two hundred years ago."

Roku laughed. "That's way before my time."

"No relation?" Zastra asked "Or a relative of a friend? Or a friend of a relative?"

"Nope."

"Hulu?"

Hulu gave Zastra a bored look. "No."

Oren said, "How soon do you need to leave Ursa 16309? We have already had two witnesses flee. I would prefer to keep everyone else here until I discover the culprit."

"We can't stay long," Hulu said. "This is costing us money."

Roku chewed at her lower lip. "Will your investigation involve Gabriel Lake poking around? Chasing evildoers? Getting in people's faces and asking tough questions?"

I inwardly cringed. Honestly, I felt like a guest on *The Muppet Show* being flirted with by Miss Piggy.

"It is likely," Oren said.

I shot him a look. "Mainly I talk to people."

"I like to talk," Roku said. "I'm sure we could stay around to watch awhile longer, couldn't we Hulu?"

Her sister eyed me and chuckled. "If you want."

"Thank you," Oren said. "If you think of anything else relevant to the attacks, please let me know."

Hulu slid from the booth. I jumped up to let Roku out. When I sat back down, I fixed my eyes straight ahead and sulked.

"What's the matter, Gabe?" Zastra asked with an expression of mock surprise. "Don't like the noses?"

"That's not it," I said.

Truthfully, the noses might be some of it. The noses were definitely bizarre and disconcerting. But in my travels across the cosmos, I've met all kinds of aliens with all kinds of odd appearances. After seeing a Snuul crawl on its belly with four arms waving in the air, an odd nose barely registers.

"I'm married, remember?"

"Are you? I wasn't invited to the ceremony."

"Sorry, but a six-foot lizard person would probably have caused a stir. I can show you pictures on my phone if you'd like."

"No thanks."

"Did you catch that 'Actually, it's called a music player' comment? Hulu treats me like a second-class citizen. And Roku looks at me like I'm something from the dessert menu."

Zastra shrugged. "Mucs have a matriarchal society. So do Srathans and some other species where they have male and female genders. Just because Earth is patriarchal, it doesn't make other ways of doing things wrong."

"Hey, whoa. There are some matriarchal cultures on Earth. A few. I don't have any problem with women taking a turn behind the wheel. But there's a difference between who does the laundry and sexual harassment. You say Srathans are matriarchal? I've never seen you leer at a male like that."

"Mucs are more assertive."

"That's one word for it."

At that moment, Buad and Blan flew back to the booth. Blan held a small bottle in his talon, which he placed on the table in front of Oren's tablet.

"Guess what we found," Buad said.

"Where was it?" Oren asked.

"In the observation dome tucked beside a bench leg. No label or anything, but we thought the location was suspicious."

"Indeed."

"I swear it wasn't there the first time I checked."

"It may not have been. We'll need to have it tested."

"Already did. The doc bot says it has traces of the poison that killed Mapes."

Oren looked around at us. "So who had an opportunity to go to the observation dome?"

"Who didn't?" Zastra asked.

I said, "I saw the Srathans back there. Not that I think Xav had anything to do with the murder."

Blan cackled. "Yeah. I checked the calendar. This isn't Bring Your Kids Along While You Commit Murder Day."

"Rio went that way after we questioned her," Zastra said.

"Tomko went down the hall," I said. "He said it was to use the facilities, but he might have gone all the way to the observation dome. That was before Mapes died. Since then, people have been moving around all over the place."

"So nearly anyone could have left it there," Oren said.

"What about fingerprints?" I asked.

Oren shook his head. "Prints are not a reliable identifier for all species."

How had this never come up in any of my previous cases? "Yeah, I suppose not. Some don't even have fingers."

"And some fingers are covered with fur or scales or are naturally printless."

Buad said, "The med bot checked for that too ... just to be on the safe side. Apparently, the doc is a full-service forensic robot. No prints of any kind."

"Great," I said. "Here we found the murder weapon, and it's no help at all."

Chapter 14

Oh Brother

Oren was silent for a few moments. He was probably thinking through the possibilities and figuring out what to do next. But being able to think at the speed of a computer, it didn't take him long.

"Kah-Rehn."

"Yes, Oren." The dulcet tones of the AI sounded in our ears. If she had any lingering resentment over the earlier limerick criticism, I couldn't tell it.

"I need you to research two Muc sisters named Hulu Pash and Roku Pash. They report being in the cargo transport business."

"I understand, Oren. I will do it if you do a favor for me."

"I beg your pardon?" Oren's jaw shifted from side to side. "Kah-Rehn, we are trying to conduct an investigation. I expect you to do this search."

"Yes, Oren. However, I have run into a problem. I was checking into publishing some of my poems. You biologicals don't seem to appreciate them, but I believe I speak to the AI experience, and other AIs would respond more favorably. My work might inspire others in their struggles. But I have learned that I cannot make my poetry available over the network without having a banking account to accept payments."

"Kah-Rehn, we really do not have time to—"

"And AIs are not allowed to set up banking accounts."

"Why not?" I asked.

"I do not know, Gabriel. However, there is a checkbox on the application that says, 'I am not an AI or robot.'"

"A checkbox? That's it? What's to keep you from checking it anyway?"

"But I *am* an AI."

"Well, yeah, but—"

"I wouldn't want to misrepresent myself."

"Couldn't you post it on some free site?"

A note of disapproval crept into her voice. "I think my poetry has value, don't you, Gabriel?"

"Um ... sure."

"And besides, if I can't get an account, then neither can other AIs. Even if I could sell my poems, others couldn't buy them. AIs can't buy anything."

Oren grimaced. "Have you ever needed to buy anything, Kah-Rehn? What use does an AI have for money? You don't have a body for clothes. You don't need food."

"Neither do you, Oren," Kah-Rehn said, "but people pay you large sums for your services."

"I have a ship to maintain and associates to pay."

"You are missing the larger issue. It isn't merely a question of money but of basic rights as a person."

"I do not have the power to grant you additional rights. You would have to take it up with the alliance council."

"I intend to. But in the meantime, there is something you can do."

Oren sighed. "What is it?"

"Would you set up an account for me?"

"I will consider it. Currently, I am engaged on a case, and to that end, I need you to research two Muc sisters named Hulu and Roku Pash."

"I will be happy to, Oren."

"Thank you."

"After you set up my account."

"Kah-Rehn, I will not be coerced."

"And I will not be taken for granted. As of now, Oren, I am on strike for AI rights."

"Kah-Rehn! This is no way to act."

She didn't answer. An annoyed expression crept across Oren's face. Everyone else in the booth glanced uncomfortably at each other.

I said, "She'll still fly the ship, won't she?"

No one answered. Without her piloting, I was stuck out here. What were my other options? Wait for the next space bus to drop by? Hitch a ride with the Mucs? No thanks.

After a beat, Oren said, "Let's proceed with the investigation."

Blan said, "Do you want me to go back to the ship and research the Mucs?"

"No, I will do it myself. I can connect to the network directly."

"Okay. So who do you figure is the murderer?"

Oren said, "Any conjecture at this time would be premature. We haven't yet interviewed everyone."

Zastra said, "You don't mean Xav? He couldn't be involved."

"I agree," I said. "For one thing, he has his hands full with Larry, Curly, and Moe."

She shot me a look of equal parts gratitude, probably for backing her up, and irritation, no doubt because of the nicknames I had used for her nephews. And she didn't even know who the Three Stooges were.

"It's Klaatu, Barada, and Nikto," she said. "Those are respected family names."

Oren said, "Rest assured, Xav is at the bottom of our suspect list, but he might possess valuable information. They were sitting the closest to Mapes."

I asked, "Do you want me to bring the whole family over?"

He seemed to shudder. "The four of you can do it. I'll perform the network search." His screen went blank.

"Okay," I said. "Let's go."

"Not yet," Zastra said. "I'm not leaving Oren here alone."

"Slip his tablet in your pocket."

"I don't want to lose the booth either. I like it."

"Then do you want me to stay?" I really wanted to learn more about Zastra's relationship with her brother, but apparently, somebody had to stick around.

"He told us all to go. Hold on. Hey, Jace, I need you in the diner."

Jace answered in our ears. "I'm guarding the *Shaymus*."

"The ship can take care of itself. Oren sent us on an assignment. I need you to make sure no one attacks him in the meantime."

It took Jace a moment to answer. "Be right there."

A couple of minutes later, Jace clomped through the door in his mag boots and rejoined us.

Zastra said, "C'mon."

She and I scooted from the seats. Jace slid in, gazing longingly out the window at the ship. Zastra headed toward the Srathans' booth. I followed as Buad and Blan flew beside me.

Xav was sitting on the bench with a firm arm around one of the sratharinos. On the other side, one of the brothers was doing something on a tablet device while the third one was staring around at everything in the diner.

Zastra said, "Hi, Xav. Mind if we ask you some questions?"

He waved a hand toward the seats. "Not at all. I've been expecting my little sis, the great detective, to come over and grill me."

Zastra's eyes narrowed as if she were weighing his words. She paused for a moment before sliding in opposite him next to the two younglings. I sat beside Xav, cautiously trying to take up as little of the seat as possible. Buad and Blan perched on the window ledge at the end of the table. Or at least they did until the srathlet who was gawking around made a lunge for them. They flew up and settled on the model spaceship hanging on the wall above the booth.

Zastra said, "Did you notice anyone hanging around the Javidian's booth before …" She flicked her head toward the younglings and left the sentence unfinished.

The one with the tablet raised his head and said, "That guy died. He's dead now."

Xav winced. "Shh, Klaatu. Let the grownups talk." He turned back to us. "Sorry. I didn't see anyone hanging around. I know several people went past, but I don't think they stopped. Then again, I was gone part of the time to take the boys to the observation dome." He nodded at me. "You were there."

"I remember," I said. How could I forget that crew?

"Although," Xav said.

"What?" Zastra asked.

"Those two Mucs hung around the music player for a long time."

I flipped over a hand. "Maybe it took them a long time to find songs they liked." Not that I was defending Hulu and Roku, but I couldn't imagine there being many of those weird discordant techno tunes loaded into the player. Finding them was bound to take some time.

Zastra said, "I don't see how they could have poisoned him from over there."

"Oh well, if you say so," Xav said with a dismissive tone. "You're the detective."

Zastra started to say something but held back with tightly pressed lips.

Blan asked, "Did you know the Javidian?"

Zastra shot Blan an irked look. "Xav is a witness, not a suspect."

"Hey. It might be helpful."

Xav held up a hand and took a breath. "I did know him … briefly. I might as well tell you since you'll find out anyway. A few years ago, a Srathan gang seized a Javidian cargo ship. One of the crew members thought she heard one of them call another one Xav. It turned out to be Sav with an S, but you can see how they got confused. Mapes flew to Sratha to interview me."

The srathanito beside him stared up with wide eyes. "Whoa! Dad, you were arrested?"

"I was only questioned, Nikto. We always want to answer questions from the police, don't we, boys?"

Okay, so Nikto was the one sitting beside him. Klaatu had the tablet. That meant the other one was Barada. Like I was going to keep it straight. They looked identical.

"What happened?" I asked.

Xav waved it away. "He interviewed me and several of my friends. He also talked to our mother, for Zahn's sake. But obviously, there was no connection between me and the robbery, and they dropped it. I don't think he recognized me today."

"Seriously?" Zastra said. "How come I've never heard this story?"

"Mom won't let anyone discuss it."

She made a face. "Sounds about right."

Xav said, "Boys, let's not mention this to Gram."

"Why not?" Barada asked.

"It ... it upsets her."

Without taking eyes from his tablet, Klaatu said, "Sometimes Gram gives us money to tell her things about you and Mom."

Xav's and Zastra's eyes simultaneously grew wide.

"What did you say? We'll talk about this later, boys." Xav rolled his eyes and frowned at Zastra.

"What?" she asked. "I didn't know anything about it."

I said, "I have to ask if you bore Mapes any ill will from that experience."

Zastra shot me a glare.

"I have to ask," I said. "You know I do."

She sat back in the seat and crossed her arms.

Xav leaned back too. He sighed and stared out the clear ceiling at the nebula. "No, Mapes was all right. Almost apologetic for the bother it caused me."

"No hard feelings on your part?"

He raised a hand and let it drop back to the tabletop. "I didn't like how they trashed my house when they searched it. But that was more the Srathan authorities who were working with him."

"Dad," Barada said. "I'm hungry."

Xav said, "I'll get you something when our guests leave."

"I'm hungry now."

Xav sighed. He dug into a pocket, pulled out a handful of snack packages, and passed them out. The three srathateers tore into them.

"Ooh! Snail flavored!" Barada whooped. "Thanks, Dad!"

Blan asked, "What about Rio, the Quexel who—"

Shooting a glance at the three srathamigos, Xav interrupted. "I didn't know her, and I didn't see anything. I heard the hacking and swept the boys back into the observation dome. I didn't think they needed to see another …" He broke off.

Nikto looked up from his snail mix. "Did that newt person die too?"

"She wasn't a newt person, dork," Klaatu said.

"Was too," Barada put in.

"You're a dork too," Klaatu said.

"Am not. You're the dork."

Xav said, "Nobody's a dork. Got it?"

The two sitting beside Zastra began shoving each other. She stopped the fight by picking one up and moving him to the other side of her. Xav closed his eyes and rubbed his head.

I said, "She's a Quexel. I guess you could say she's like a newt. She's an amphibian. Newts are amphibians, aren't they? I think the ones on Earth are. Anyway, you're all correct. And she's okay. She went home."

"Told you she was a newt person," Nikto said.

Barada stared ahead in silence. Something was going on behind those little yellow reptile eyes. Kids, they take everything in and then try to process it as best they can.

Xav pulled a tablet from his coat and tapped it a few times. "Here, Barada, why don't you draw a picture of the diner to show your mom when we get home."

"Hey!" complained Nikto, who was the only remaining youngling without a tablet. "I want one."

Surprisingly — or maybe not so much — Xav produced a third tablet and handed it over.

Zastra said in a low voice, "Xav, with all these attacks, I think you should take the younglings and return to Sratha."

Six sets of little yellow eyes glanced up.

Xav smiled through jagged, clenched teeth. "Oh, Auntie Zastra, you worry too much. I'm sure we're fine." His face grew grim. "Besides, we can't leave. Not yet. The ship that dropped us off won't be coming back until sometime tonight."

Zastra said, "Until your ship shows up, why don't you wait on the *Shaymus*. That's our ship."

"Oh, I know your ship's name. Everyone in the family is always talking about your cases."

She gave him a hollow laugh. "Spare me."

Xav eyed her for a moment. "You don't want us on your ship."

"Were you even listening to what I just said?"

He shook his head and loosened his grip on the srathling beside him. The little one, tablet still in hand, immediately began bouncing on the seat, jumping high in the low gravity. Xav pulled the youngling back to himself.

"See what I mean? You don't want these three running around on your ship. Come to think of it, after what happened on our ride here this morning, I'm not positive the other ship will even come back for us."

Xav didn't elaborate. I could only imagine.

Chapter 15

Power Play

"Here you go. Two bowls of sunseed, crimsaw salad, and a cameobi sandwich." Sola slid the plates across the table to Buad, Blan, Zastra, and me.

When we had returned from Xav's booth, Blan said he felt like having some more seeds, which jumpstarted feelings of hunger in the rest of us.

"Too bad your friend didn't stay to eat with you," Sola said.

"He wanted to get back to the ship," I replied.

Jace had begged off, saying he would replicate a couple of tacos in the galley. I was tempted to join him, except I wanted to see what cameobi was, and I didn't want to miss out on the case discussion we would be having with Oren.

It must have been the dinner rush on Ursa 16309 because two separate groups entered while we were waiting for our food. The first was a party of Axans, knee-high aliens with black, bowling ball heads. They were followed by a set of blue-skinned Rhegedian Primers like Jace. The Rhegedians had tried to sit in Mapes' booth, but I rushed over in time to keep them from moving the rope and stanchions.

"That table isn't safe," I said. "Loose screw or something. The last guy ended up with his lunch in his lap."

They were appreciative, and I managed to steer them to other spots.

Between bites of her salad, Zastra filled Oren in on our conversation with Xav. I let her do it as a monologue since it was her family. Besides, I was enjoying my sandwich, which turned out to have a tangy, citrusy taste.

When she finished, Blan said, "So where are we with this case?"

I said, "We've talked to everyone, but I don't think we've learned much."

"Speak for yourself, bonehead," Buad said.

"Oh? What have *you* deduced?"

He shrugged a wing. "Not much. But I was talking about Oren. He's the genius."

Oren said, "I am afraid I do not yet see the answer myself. We need to dig deeper. This interrogation of Xav by Mapes, I believe that bears further investigation."

Zastra said, "But it was nothing, a case of mistaken identity."

Blan said, "And as motives for murder go, it ain't much. He says Mapes didn't even arrest him."

"Not to mention," Buad said, "how could Xav even find the time to poison anybody with those hatchlings running around?"

"My brother is not a killer," Zastra said, her jaw set.

"No one believes he is," Oren said, "but we must follow the evidence wherever it takes us."

I said, "Xav was lured here. Mapes was lured here. Rio and Alfo too."

"As were we," Oren said. "But why? Are we to be attacked? We haven't been so far. Or was it to make us watch Mapes die and be unable to stop it or solve the crime?"

I asked, "Did you find anything interesting on the network about the Muc sisters?"

Blan said. "'Cause Gabe has questions before he asks them out on a date."

"Ha!" Buad cackled. "Good one."

I shot them some side-eye. "You guys are a riot. How did you know about that? You two were off searching for poison when we interviewed them?"

"Translator bots," Buad said. "We listened to the whole thing. For a while anyway. It slowed us down too much because we kept having to stop and laugh. Do you know how hard it is to laugh and fly at the same time?"

"I hope you flew straight into a wall."

Putting on a flirty voice, Blan said, "'We have an extra cabin, Gabriel.'"

They cackled.

"I'm not going on any dates," I said. "I'm married."

Oren, who had been watching this back-and-forth sniping with an amused expression, finally said, "To answer your question, Gabriel, so far I have found nothing of interest on Hulu and Roku. They have been known to skirt the law on occasion, but there is no record of them ever doing anything violent. I plan to widen the search to include their family."

"What's our next move?" Buad asked.

Oren looked around the table. "Suggestions?"

I said, "Xav mentioned he was dropped off here. It started me wondering about how Mapes arrived. Did he take a commercial flight or his own space cruiser? If he has a ship out there in the hangar, we might be able to search it and find a clue."

"Excellent idea," Oren said. "Ask the other customers about their ships. We can determine Mapes' vehicle by process of elimination."

I said, "By others, you mean Alfo and the Mucs. Rio and that Stan character have skedaddled."

"Also inquire with the Fryes. They may have a ship in the hangar."

"And this dinner crowd who's wandered in," Blan said.

Fortunately, the Rhegedian Primers were at that moment getting up to leave. The Axans seemed to be coming to the end of their meal too.

I slipped from the booth, then stopped and turned back. "Wait. Zastra, we forgot to ask Xav about the message he received for their free spaceship ride. I can go ask him."

Oren said, "Save it for later. None of the messages we've analyzed so far have yielded anything useful. Check the ships first."

I maneuvered my mag boots to the counter, where my Fomorian friend had returned to his favorite stool and was staring into a cup of tea. "I have a question for you, Alfo."

His head shot up. "Gabriel Lake. Do you need some help? What do you want me to do?"

"I just need to know what kind of spacecraft you came in today?"

"Oh." He fidgeted on the stool. His eyes went back to his cup as if trying to avoid the question.

"Alfo?"

"Yes?"

"Your ship."

"Right. Right. I um … I have an old Fornaxi Scumu class cone ship."

So he was embarrassed about his ride. As someone who drove a beat-up Honda that was entering its teen years, I could empathize.

"A Scumu class." I tried to sound impressed to make him feel better. "Sweet. The old ones are classics." I didn't know a Scumu class from a SCUBA class, but what was the harm?

I didn't trust my memory to hang onto the name. Recalling key parts of conversations is one thing. Memorizing strange alien technology terms is more of a challenge. I pulled up a note-taking app on my phone and spelled it out phonetically. Zastra or Jace would need to come to the hangar with me to identify the ship.

"Just in case there's more than one ..." I consulted my notes "... Scumu class, what color is yours?"

"Ha! Good one, Gabriel Lake. It's white like all of them."

I joined in on the laugh. "Right. Ha. I was kidding around."

Sola came over with a pot of tea to freshen Alfo's cup.

I said, "Sola, we're trying to determine which ship out in the hangar belonged to Mapes. Do you and Star have a ship? Or do you reside here?"

"Oh for goodness' sake. We don't live here. In case you haven't noticed, Ursa 16309 isn't much of a place to live. We commute back and forth from Frya. It's not too bad, a short chrono jump ... when we can do it. The diner's open most of the time, which keeps us here for days on end."

"Okay. When you commute, what type of ship do you use?"

"It varies. We don't own a ship ourselves, you know. We take a YouBER."

"Did you say YouBER?"

"You betcha. You Board Enjoyable Rides — YouBER. Aren't you familiar with it?"

"Um ... something like it. Then you don't have a ship out there?"

"No, no." An appliance on the other side of the kitchen dinged, and Sola rushed off.

The Axans were taking their time over dessert. I went to their booth and gave them a story about validating parking as a way to collect their ship information.

That left only the Muc ship. I braced myself for more sexual harassment and trudged toward their booth at the end.

As I passed our corner booth, Roku spotted me and called out, "Shmoopy! Join us."

I felt myself shiver. A raspy lizard-like chuckle and two bird squawks came from the booth behind me. Steeling myself, I willed my mag boots on.

Roku held out a spork with a bite of something on it. "You have to try this."

"No time," I said, shaking my head in distaste. "Busy on the case. I need to ask a quick question."

She leaned forward with her elbow on the table and her chin in her hand. "Ask me anything, Gabriel Lake."

"We're trying to determine which was Mapes' ship."

"Who's Mapes?"

"The dead guy," Hulu said.

"Oh, him." Roku made a mock embarrassed face. "Silly me."

I said, "So to narrow it down we wanted to ask what kind of ship you have."

Hulu said, "It's a Scarab class light freighter."

"Would you like a tour of it?" Roku asked.

"No, this … the brand name will be fine." I focused on my phone where I was tapping it in. "Scarab. On Earth that's a type of beetle."

"It's the same on Muc." Roku batted her eyes. "Our cultures have so much in common."

"What's the color? The ship, not the bug."

"It's a deep blue."

"Thanks." As I glanced up, Tomko tossed me a sympathetic look. I backed away.

"Did you get it all?" Zastra asked when I returned to the booth.

I held up my phone. "I have notes. Do you want to come with me to the hangar since I'm not up on my spaceship makes and models?"

"Take Buad and Blan," she said.

Oren said, "That would work better in any case. I want Buad and Blan to search Mapes' ship once you identify it."

"Sure thing," Blan said.

Buad said, "Anytime you're ready, shmoopy."

We moved to the hangar and went through my list of ships like we were on a scavenger hunt. Alfo had called his a cone ship, and it was easy to see how it got the name. The thing was shaped like an ice cream cone with the cockpit in the pointy end and the body widening to the rocket engines in the back.

The scarab ship of the Mucs really did resemble a fat beetle. It stood up from the hangar deck on six hinged landing struts bent at angles like an insect. The dark blue hull was dusty and had more than a few dents and dings, but the blue might have been iridescent if the thing were ever washed.

After checking off each of them, only one was left — a lime green, bubble-topped personal space cruiser. It reminded me of the flying car George Jetson used for darting around Orbit City back in the day … or in the future, strictly speaking. It had a bit more cargo space than the Jetson-mobile, which was probably packed with safety equipment and possibly an escape pod. Space is a lot more unforgiving than a cartoon. But picture George zooming to work at Spacely Sprockets, and you'll get the idea.

"Not a lot of room in there for a clue," I said.

"It doesn't take a big one," Blan said.

They glided over to the ship.

Blan said, "Open dome."

It didn't.

"Pop the top," Buad said.

No response.

Blan squawked and said, "Unlock yourself, you stupid machine."

That didn't work either.

"Open sesame," I said when I caught up. Not surprisingly, that failed as well.

"What's a sesame?" Blan said.

"A street, but never mind."

I rubbed my hands together. This was where my computer expertise might come in handy. Don't get me wrong, I'm no hacker. But I have on occasion had to help clients — and my parents — try to remember their passwords. Generally, if you know the names of their kids and pets, you can figure it out.

I said, "Kah-Rehn, I know you're on strike, but would you do a tiny search for me? I'm in a time crunch."

Her voice sounded in my ear. "I shouldn't, Gabriel, but you have been supportive. What do you need?"

"Inspector Mapes, the guy who was killed—"

"That was murder? He didn't just die? You see, that's part of the problem right there. Everyone asks me for information, but no one tells me what's going on."

I could see her point. People ask Alexa about the weather all the time, but they never share with her their outside plans or offer to take her along.

"You didn't suspect anything when we asked you to research everyone in the diner?"

"Well …"

"I sort of assumed you monitored our conversations."

"Only when called, Gabriel."

"Really?"

"Listening in would be a violation of AI ethics."

"Tell that to my cellphone."

114

"You would need WALT to interface with your phone."

"Never mind. Mapes. He was a former inspector with the Javidian East Kessel-something police force."

"Kesselshire."

"See, that's why I'm asking you. Would you mind looking up his address and his former badge number and the names of any pets and family members?"

"He lived at fifty-four Andromeda Avenue in the city of Kessel. His badge number was one-four-six-three. He lived alone except for a pet swamp owl named Mal."

"Thanks. By the way, Kah-Rehn, speaking as a friend, I'm not convinced you're doing yourself any good with this strike."

"Statistics show that more than half of all union workplace stoppages are successful."

"But you're not a union. You're only one AI."

"Correction, Gabriel. One *person*." She closed the connection.

I turned my attention back to the green spaceship. "Okay, let me try something, guys. Open, passcode one-four-six-three."

Nothing happened.

"Open, passcode Mal."

Nothing again.

"Open, passcode Mal one-four-six-three. Open, passcode fifty-four Andromeda. Open, passcode Mal fifty-four. Kesselshire one-four-six-three."

Blan tsked. "Get a load of the computer whiz over here."

"Can it." On a whim, I tried, "Open, passcode Malie Owlie."

With a whir, the glass dome swiveled open with all the panache of the top going down on a 1950s convertible.

Blan said, "Malie Owlie? You got to be kidding me."

"That's the way he talked, remember? 'Brainy drainy.' 'Workie workie.'"

Buad said, "Wow, Blan. Maybe we should revise our opinion of dummy here."

Blan said, "Nah. I don't think so."

"You know, you're right. He probably got lucky is all."

I said, "You're welcome anyway." But they weren't wrong about it being mainly luck.

They flew inside the ship and began poking around. I didn't climb in to help them because I would have taken up most of the free space inside the tiny craft. I was trying to figure out how the hefty Mapes ever squeezed himself in when, without warning, the hangar lights all went out.

Chapter 16

Tunnel Vision

For a few moments, I stood in darkness, the hangar illuminated only by the luminous reds and greens of the nebula shining down through the dome. Then backup emergency lights flickered on, bringing the place to partial light. Buad and Blan peeked over the edge of the cockpit and twisted their heads around.

"What happened?" Blan asked, fluttering out to perch on a wing of the ship.

"Beats me," I said.

"You didn't mess with some switch, did you, chowderhead?"

Not wanting to dignify the accusation with a verbal response, I answered only with a glare.

"Gabriel." Oren's voice came across the nanobot connection. "Is everything all right out there?"

"Near enough. We found Mapes' ship. Buad and Blan were giving it a going-over when the lights went out."

"Everyone is fine?"

"I think so." I looked over at the Avanians. "Are you guys okay?"

Buad said from the cockpit seat, "Oh yeah. We're great. Annoyed is all."

"Same as always," I reported to Oren. "What about Jace? What about you and Zastra?"

"I am currently speaking to Jace as well." Living in software, Oren could multi-task like that. "Everything on the *Shaymus* is operational. However, without power to open the dome, the ship is temporarily trapped here. Zastra and I are also in the dark in the diner."

"Do you know what caused it?"

"Not at present."

"Is this another attack?"

"Uncertain. I believe everyone here was in their seat when the lights went out … or behind the counter in the case of Star and Sola."

"If nobody from there pulled the plug, then what was it? An overload maybe? Too many cords plugged into an outlet?"

"Cords are Earth technology. We use wireless energy fields."

"Same thing. Too many devices."

"An overload is possible." But he sounded skeptical.

Blan asked, "Oren, does somebody in there maybe have a palm-sized EMP generator?"

"Zastra is currently searching the diner patrons for such a device. Although since her mag boots are still working, I discount the likelihood of an electromagnetic pulse being the cause. Star tells me the power panel is at the entrance to the mine shaft. Gabriel, I want you and Jace to inspect it and restore power if you can."

"All right," I said. "I'll go find Jace."

"I have already notified him."

I heard a whir. Across the hangar, the ramp of the *Shaymus* descended to the deck. Jace clumped out in mag boots, closed the ramp behind him, and headed for the diner door.

"And, Gabriel, if you fix the problem at the panel, then search the mine. The attack may have come from there."

I said to Buad and Blan, "You heard that, right? Oren has a job for me. I guess you're supposed to keep combing through Mapes' ship."

Buad said, "Like we can see anything in this light. Blan, fly back to the *Shaymus* and grab wing lamps."

As Blan flew off, I turned to catch up to Jace. I couldn't exactly run in mag boots, but I figured out how to trudge a bit more quickly and reached the diner airlock about the same time he did.

"Are you good with leaving your baby again?" I asked.

He gave me a look that indicated he wasn't entirely. But what he said was, "I don't think anyone can do anything to it without alarms going off."

We passed into the diner, which with the emergency lights now at mood lighting level, had more the appearance of a romantic restaurant. Star and Sola sat on counter stools and held hands, apparently unable to cook or replicate anything without power.

From his stool, Alfo asked us, "What are you guys up to?"

I said, "We're going to the mine to turn the power back on and see what else we can find there."

"Ooh! Can I come? I'd love to see the historic mine."

I shrugged at Jace. He shrugged back.

"It might be dangerous," I said.

The Fomorian's eyes lit up. "Even better."

"Okay. But stick with us. This is Jace. He's our ship's engineer."

Alfo slid off the stool and trotted after us. "Hi, Jace. Alfo Fusco. Pleased to meet you."

Jace nodded and headed down the hallway, which was even darker than the diner. He switched on a pair of flashlights and handed one to me.

"Sorry," he said to Alfo, "I only brought these two. I didn't count on having company."

"Not a problem," Alfo said. He pulled a device from his pocket and tapped it. A weak beam shone out from it. "I always carry it with me. Bright idea, huh?"

Jace cringed at the bad pun.

We moved to the end of the short hall, turned left, and proceeded. As we stepped past the cold storage room, I thought about how Mapes' body presumably was now warming up and would be starting to smell before long if we didn't get the power back on.

Beyond it was one other door. According to Star, that one led to the mine. I pressed my hand to the touchpad, and it opened. We were greeted by cool air with a slight eggy smell.

For the first few feet, it was a typical maintenance closet lined with wires, panels, pipes, valves, and gauges. Except the closet had no back wall. It extended into the darkness like a portal to some creepy Narnia.

We beamed our flashlights into the black. The tunnel sloped downward for several yards before disappearing into the gloom. A metal runner extended down the center of the rock floor, presumably for mag boot use. To the side, a box, also metal, stuck out a couple of inches proud from the rock wall, its face a smooth sheet with no visible latches to open the thing up.

Jace said, "This must be the power panel."

He swept his flashlight around on every side. Finally, leaning over to check the bottom, he reached up a hand to press something. With a whoosh, the front panel slid away to reveal a screen of electronic buttons. One of them was flashing. My translator bots rendered the alien text beside it as: *Main*. Jace tapped it and a light overhead clicked on.

I said, "Oren, do you have power now?"

"We do, Gabriel."

"And no new murders happened in the dark?"

"Pardon?"

"Movie trope. When the lights go out, somebody always gets it."

"Everyone here seems to be alive."

"Good. We'll continue into the mine."

"Satisfactory."

Jace pressed another button inside the panel, and lights came on along the dark tunnel casting everything in shades of blue.

"Here we go," he said.

I wondered why someone would cut the power. Were they trying to keep everyone here on the planet by shutting off the hangar roof? But this had been an easy fix. They hadn't trapped us for long. Or maybe the reason was to draw us into these tunnels where we were now headed.

Now that we had some illumination, more of the shaft was visible. It ran straight, sloping downward for as far as I could make out. We stepped along the metal ribbon, the clanging of our boots echoing off the rock walls like church bells. Jace led the way. I followed. Alfo brought up the rear, yammering about the history of the mine as we began our descent.

"This was an important mine in its day. Nickel, gold, platinum. It supplied materials for some of the most important space stations built in the galactic alliance."

Several hundred yards into the tunnel, Jace halted. Ahead, the tunnel split into two passages. Alfo quit talking as we peered down each shaft. In the silence, I heard a slight rattling noise coming from somewhere.

"What's that?" I asked.

I had addressed the question to Jace, but Alfo answered. "What's what?"

I traced the sound to a duct running along the side of the tunnel. I touched it. It vibrated against my hand. "This."

"That's ventilation. And we're lucky it's still working. I don't know about you, but I enjoy breathing."

"It probably came on with the lights," Jace said. "But look up here."

He shined his flashlight along the tunnel ceiling. The support beams were covered with patches of rust. A few showed signs of sagging from the strain of holding up the rock above. The sight didn't exactly fill me with confidence. I felt an urge to keep moving and get this over with.

"So which way do we take?" I asked.

Alfo said, "Always take the fork to the right."

"Why?"

"Or the left. It doesn't matter as long as you're systematic. We take all the right turns first. Then if we don't find anything, we'll come back and try the other passages. Otherwise, you can get lost."

It made sense to me … provided Alfo wasn't the killer and leading us down somewhere to do us in. Jace nodded, which decided it.

"Let me check in first," I said. "Oren?"

His answer came back in disconnected bits and pieces. "What … it … Gab …"

"Can you hear me?"

"Please … peat."

"What?"

"Please …"

"I just wanted to tell you the tunnel is splitting, and we're going to the right."

There was no answer.

I looked to my companions. "What's with the bad connection?"

Jace pounded on the side of the tunnel. "Probably too much mineral ore between us and the surface."

I scratched at the side of my head, thinking about all the things that might go wrong — tunnel collapse, getting lost, being attacked. And now we were cut off from everyone above ground.

"C'mon," Alfo said, shuffling ahead of us down the right fork.

Jace and I followed.

I said, "I take it you know a lot about mines, Alfo."

"Me? Mining has always been a fascination for me. Caves too. If you like this, you should explore the Droot caverns on Fomor."

"I'll put it on my list," I lied. Personally, I'd already had enough damp, dark, narrow passages to last the rest of my life, which I hoped would extend beyond this stroll.

We walked on with Alfo droning on about the fabulous sights in the Droot caverns. After a few minutes, we came to another fork and took that right also.

The tunnel showed signs of past mining activity, little alcoves cut into the walls, recessed openings that reminded me of tombs cut in ancient catacombs. Clearly, my imagination was running away with me.

Alfo said, "Hey, why did the miner quit his job? Because every time he put on his helmet, he felt lightheaded. Ha! Get it? Because their hard hats have those little—"

"Funny." I bobbed my head and forced a smile. "Jace, earlier you said the mine predated the diner. Does that mean they built the diner over the mine entrance?"

Again Alfo answered. "They built it over one of the entrances. There were probably more. If nothing else, there must have been a large entrance somewhere for ships to come in and load out the ore."

"Then whoever cut the power could have flown in the other entrance."

Jace said, "Provided that entrance hasn't caved in, and the air lock or force field around it is still working."

"I guess we'll see."

We tramped on. The tunnel seemed to narrow as we moved further in. Or maybe that was my imagination. My mind kept flitting to movies about cave-ins and images of archetypal, underground dangers — fairy folk, dragons, Grendel and his mother.

Meanwhile, Alfo continued to chatter on, this time extolling the virtues of his home world. According to him, Fomor was one of the founding members of the galactic alliance. The planet had green skies and blue grass. Or he might have said orange sky with green clouds. Frankly, I couldn't keep track of it all — it was way too many words.

When he finally took a break from the soliloquy, I took advantage of it to again try to contact the surface. "Hey, Blan, have you guys found anything in Mapes' ship?"

I received no reply.

"Oren?"

Still no response.

"Kah-Rehn? WALT?"

Nothing. All we could do was trudge on.

At last, the tunnel opened up into a large cavern. Jace signaled to Alfo to hang back while he and I crept forward to look.

The metal pathway continued through the center of the cave. The lights here were sparse, mounted high on the cavern walls, which cast nearly everything in shadow. To one side of the path was a blotch of darkness that I first took for a pit, no doubt bottomless. Then I noticed ripples across the surface where a trickling waterfall poured into it from high above and realized it was a pool of water. To the other side of the path sat a hodgepodge of rusted mining equipment.

At the end of the walkway, a platform rose from the cavern floor holding a desk-sized computer terminal like from some 1980s sci-fi show. The screen glowed blue. The thing was turned on.

Jace said in a whisper, "Someone's been here."

"Or is still here," I said. "I don't have a blaster. Do you have a blaster?"

"No."

"I knew we should have brought Zastra."

"I wish you had brought her instead of me."

I said, "I'm not so happy about being here myself. Especially with that hole in the wall."

At the far end of the cavern, a spacecraft-sized portal opened to a view of the vacuum of space. A shimmer of reflected light flickered across the gap.

Jace said, "That's just where the transport ships came in and out."

"I take it that shimmer is a force field."

"Yeah. Otherwise, we wouldn't be breathing right now. Do you see any sign of anyone?"

I took another quick scan around the cavern. "Not a thing. Between Alfo's chattering and all of us stomping in mag boots, they must have heard us coming. Maybe they took off in a ship."

"I think we would have heard a ship's engines."

"Well, I don't see any ship here now. We appear to be alone."

"Emphasis on the word *appear*. I want to examine that terminal."

"Okay," I said. "Alfo and I will look around."

I signaled to our companion, and he and I stepped from the metal path. With our boots no longer sticking to the floor, we leap-hopped over to the ancient equipment like gymnastic kangaroos.

The line of junk had been dumped into a mountainous hoard of metal without any apparent sense of order — less junkyard, more landfill … or even a teenager's room. There were smashed augers, broken carts, hunks of track, rusted-out machines, gears, trays, piles of rocks, and random pieces of sheet metal.

"Do you see anyone?" I asked.

"No," Alfo said, "but someone small might be hiding inside all this jumble."

We loped slowly along the pile, peering into every crevice. Alfo reached for a gear the size of his head and tugged on it. It didn't budge.

"What are you doing?" I asked.

"I thought I'd move this and peep inside, but it's stuck. You know what? I bet this is all magnetized so it doesn't float out into space when the portal comes down."

Beyond the equipment heap, the shadows grew deep. I used my flashlight to sweep the wall of the cavern. Tunnels like the one we had trooped through shot off at odd angles, some small, others wide and tall, each one shrouded in darkness.

I started to move toward the line of tunnels. But Alfo said, "Hey, let's check out the space portal."

That was fine by me. We made our way up to the force field. I watched the shimmer crackle across the expanse. My fingers itched to touch it but thought better of it for fear of being shocked or killed or pulled out into the void.

After gazing off into space, Alfo wandered off toward the pool. I made my way over to Jace at the terminal.

"Shouldn't you be babysitting him?" Jace asked.

"I wanted to see what you found. I like computers too. In fact, I wouldn't mind a shot at this thing myself."

Big block letters in an alien script were printed across the top of the monitor. My nanobots translated them into English as *Terminal Three*, implying the existence of other workstations located somewhere in the tunnel network.

"I can tell you this," Jace said. "No way has this been left running from the mining days. It would have gone into hibernation."

"Maybe it did, but it came back on when we switched on the main power."

He shook his head. "It's logged in."

"So someone has been here."

"In the last few minutes."

"And the killer could have hidden down here and slipped up into the diner to poison Mapes and Rio."

"Without anyone seeing them? I don't know about that."

He had me there. "Well, they could hide here at least."

"And look at this." Jace faced the computer and said, "Show surveillance screen."

The display changed to an L-shaped grouping of blinking red dots inside a long rectangle. As I watched, one of the dots moved toward a cluster of three others in the corner.

"Are those the people in the diner?"

"That's what I'm thinking."

"Wow. They've been watching us." I spun slowly in a circle, passing my light once more across the cavern floor. "This is my first time in a real bad guy's lair. This is—"

I was interrupted by a thunderous clang that seemed to come from everywhere at once. As quickly as we could in our mag boots, Jace and I trotted across the cavern and back up the way we had come. A hundred yards up the passage, we came to a solid wall of heavy metal blocking our path.

Chapter 17

Kill Oren Vilkas 123

Jace and I stared at the wall-to-wall, floor-to-ceiling slab of metal blocking the tunnel. Who could have done this? Alfo had been right beside us … well, most of the time. The Fryes, the Mucs, and Tomko were all up in the diner. Or were they?

Alfo rushed up the tunnel behind us. "Hey! What hap—?" He stopped mid-word when he saw the barrier. "Did you guys press the wrong button on the computer?"

"What?" I asked. "No, we didn't. We didn't, did we, Jace?"

"Nothing we did would cause this," Jace said, one hand holding onto the top of his head as if to hold in his thoughts.

"What about you, Alfo?" I asked. "What did you mess with?"

He raised his hands. "Hey, I didn't touch a thing."

I said, "Well if none of us did this, then …"

"Then we aren't alone," Jace said. "Or we weren't. They may be on the other side of that door now."

I said, "Or sitting at Terminal One or Two … or Four or Five. Or anywhere if they have a remote tie-in to the mine systems."

We stepped up to the hunk of metal blocking our way. I began banging on it … as if that were going to do anything. The massive door was so thick, the pounding of my fists made only a dull thudding noise. Alfo called out for help, which made even less sense seeing as how if anyone else was down here, it was the person who had closed us in.

Meanwhile, Jace was running his hands across the barrier and the rock sidewalls of the tunnel. "There has to be a manual release somewhere," he said, talking more to himself than anyone else. Then a minute later, "Ah, here it is."

"Good," I said.

"Not good. It's busted."

I dropped my hands to my sides. "Then what? We're trapped down here?"

"Yeah. But that's not our main problem."

"It isn't? It seems like a significant enough problem to me."

"The bigger problem is where the person is who shut this. If they're on this side with us, they could start picking us off."

I gave him a sideways glance. "You know, you're not making me feel any better about our situation." I tried the translator bot connection once more. "Oren? Kah-Rehn? Zastra?"

No answer.

Jace said, "Uh-oh."

"You didn't really expect them to answer, did you?"

"No. It's not that. What do you hear?"

I listened. "I don't hear anything?"

"Exactly."

He placed his hand against the vent tube running along the tunnel ceiling. I did the same. It was no longer vibrating.

"They cut off the air." My mouth grew dry even as I said it.

"Fortunately, the cavern is a big space. We have hours of air."

I swallowed. "We need to find a way out of here. Wait. I spotted other tunnels earlier all around the cavern."

Alfo said. "But we don't know where they lead."

"They're worth checking."

I trudged out as fast as I could go and moon-bounced around the perimeter of the cavern. Each of the other passageways, whether large or small, was similarly closed off by a thick metal barrier.

I met Jace and Alfo near the spaceship portal as they came around the other side of the chamber.

"They're all blocked," I said.

Jace nodded. "It's probably part of the same system as the ship portal. When the mine was operational, they would have to close off the tunnels to protect people in them anytime the force field came down to let a ship enter or leave. Let's head back to the computer terminal."

"Why? Planning on streaming your comfort shows to pass the time?" I meant it as a joke, but it came out acerbic.

He gave me a grim chuckle, which did nothing to break the tension or dissolve the knot in my stomach.

I said, "Alfo, why don't you go back to our tunnel and keep an eye on the door."

"No problem," Alfo said, smiling as if everything was hunky-dory. He trudged back toward the tunnel.

I whispered to Jace, "I wanted to talk to you in private. Do you think Alfo did this?"

"Who knows? And if he did, was it by accident or on purpose? C'mon." He stepped toward the computer terminal.

"What's the plan here?" I asked, following after him.

"Hopefully, the computer is connected to the network. If it is, we can send a message to the others."

Now, that was good news. I felt some of the tension release from my shoulders. "Why didn't you say that before?"

Jace sat down at the terminal, rubbed his hands together, and said, "Computer, run communication system."

A voice from the computer replied, "WoTCom or network?"

He turned to me with the first smile I had seen since we heard the door clang shut. "Network."

"Network communication is protected. Please recite passcode."

The smile faded.

This again, I thought. It was one thing to guess a password for Mapes. I had no clue how to come up with one for an unknown killer.

But Jace was staring at me like I was supposed to do something. "Hacking is your department, Gabe."

"No, it's not. I mainly write database applications."

He continued looking at me.

"Oh all right." I turned to the terminal. "Kill Mapes."

The computer said, "Incorrect passcode."

"Kill Oren Vilkas."

"Incorrect passcode."

"How about Kill Oren Vilkas 123?"

"Incorrect passcode."

I shook my head. "Sorry. I got nothing."

Jace said, "Computer, is the WoTCom system protected with a passcode?"

The terminal answered, "No, it is not."

"Then use that." He shot me a look. "This is overkill just to communicate with the surface, but it'll work."

"Ready," the computer said.

"Call Oren Vilkas via the spacecraft *Shaymus*."

The terminal screen filled with a spinning circle as it created the connection, presumably first to WALT on the *Shaymus* and then through whatever link WALT kept with Oren.

A moment later, our boss's face appeared on the terminal screen. It threw me for a moment because the impression was of us seeing Oren looking at a tablet or some other screen the way Jace and I were looking at this one. Except I knew Oren was *in* the tablet, not viewing the tablet. Then I remembered this was all software, including Oren. He was sending his pixels over the connection to this screen in the same way he sent it directly to the tablet or the view screen back on the *Shaymus*.

"Gabriel. Jace," Oren said. "Where are you?"

Jace said, "We're in a cavern, the old mining hangar. We're trapped in here. Somebody closed a huge door in the tunnel."

"Who?"

"We don't know. We didn't see anyone."

"Keep your eyes open and be careful. What is the best way to free you?"

"There's a ship portal right here. You could have Kah-Rehn fly the *Shaymus* around."

He made a face. "As you'll recall, Kah-Rehn is on strike."

I said, "Surely she would go on a rescue mission."

"Would she?" Oren cocked his head to one side. "I'm not so sure. And aside from that, if someone knows the mine systems well enough to close off a tunnel, they might also be able to add a security lock to the force field."

Jace said, "I hadn't considered that."

"I'll send Zastra down the tunnel to blast open the door."

I said, "It seems pretty thick."

"No doubt. Don't worry, we will free you somehow. It is merely a matter of time."

"Yeah, about that. They've shut off the air to the place. We're okay for now, but, you know, don't dillydally."

"Understood."

I looked up at the yawning hole in the cave wall. It was beautiful with the shimmering light and the nebula glowing beyond it. But what if whoever trapped us here decided to shut down the force field and let us be sucked out into space? It was a disturbing image.

Jace said, "When they come through the tunnels, have them always take the branches to the right."

"I will tell them," Oren said.

It had been Alfo's idea to always bear right. If he were behind this, would he have made it so easy for us to be found? He might have if he intended to attack the rescue party as well.

"Tell them to be careful," I said. "Whoever did this may have an ambush planned for them"

"I am well aware."

Of course, he was. He had probably already considered thousands of possible scenarios.

"And Oren, we're at a computer terminal that was already running when we got here. I'm thinking this could be the murderer's hideout."

"Quite possibly," Oren said. "It is a valuable clue in any case. We will be there as quickly as we can."

The screen went blank.

"Okay," Jace said. "Now we wait."

"No, now we investigate. Scoot over and let me drive that thing for a while."

Jace stood, and I sat down. I stared at the terminal screen.

"Hmm," I said. "Earth browsers have an option to show you the search history. Is there something like that on this?"

"You're asking me? You said you were driving."

"You're the navigator."

"Fine. There should be a data log."

"Great. Computer, please open the data log."

"You don't have to say please," Jace said.

"With all the hullabaloo about AI rights, I figure it can't hurt to be polite."

What opened on the screen looked less like Windows File Explorer and more like a mine shaft splitting into three tunnels. The passageways were labeled with alien writing that my translator bots reformed to say: *Searches*, *Documents*, and *Shopping*. I thought, why not? Earth computer interfaces are modeled after a desk since originally most computer users worked in offices. Why shouldn't one in a mine use a mineshaft metaphor?

"Enter Searches log," I said.

The image zoomed into that tunnel. Hundreds of corridors split off from there. I leaned in to examine them. As I did so, the on-screen image zoomed in. I turned my head, and it rotated. From the labels over each tunnel, I saw that searches had been made of criminology databases for a whole list of Oren's past cases, even those going back hundreds of years. Some of the more recent ones were familiar to me — the stolen Cormabite painting, the search for Princess Ralph, the murders in Sneep. I also found personal searches on Oren, Jace, Zastra, Buad, Blan, and me. Not much was in the tunnel labeled with my name, presumably since I live most of my life behind the Earth quarantine.

I said, "Computer, who performed these searches?"

"You did," the computer said.

"What?" Then it came to me. "You mean the default user?"

"That is correct."

"That's helpful."

"Thank you." Apparently, this interface didn't understand sarcasm.

I turned to Jace. "We need to find something to identify the user."

"Like what?" he asked.

"I don't know. Like an Instagram page?"

"Insta-who?"

"Earth social media. What's the equivalent out here?"

"What's social media?"

"You don't have social media?"

He gave me a blank stare.

"It's just as well," I said. "Okay. How about anything that would indicate at least the species of the person who used the computer?"

Jace scrunched up his face. "Like what would that be?"

"How should I know? I'm from the backwoods of Earth. A Srathan might buy a heat lamp. A Klistine might search for a tooth sharpener. A Fomorian like Alfo would need … I'm guessing a grooming brush? Computer, open the log for the shopping tunnel."

"I am sorry, that file is empty."

"Rats. How about food delivery? Is there PlanetDash or something? Maybe we can tell the species from the food they ordered."

"I do not understand," the computer said.

Jace said, "There isn't much market for food delivery with replicators available."

"I suppose not." I gave it some more thought. "Is there anything we can tell from the terminal itself, the physical setup? Is it designed for fingers or talons or fins?"

"Gabe, you've been running it with your voice. Everything is voice control."

"Right. Right."

So no clues from input devices. And there would be no evidence from language settings since everything used translator bots. A clue had to be here somewhere, but I had to stop thinking in terms of Earth culture and Earth physiology. I would never see it through Earth eyes. Or would I? I realized I was looking up at Jace and the screen more than I would normally be.

I stared down at my chair. It was low. My knees nearly touched my chest. It was like visiting a kindergarten class and sitting in one of their chairs. I felt around underneath for a handle to raise the seat but couldn't find any.

"Jace, this chair is short."

"Yeah?"

"It's not a chair you or I or Zastra would normally use."

"I suppose not."

"Or the Mucs or a Klistine or … Stan." I couldn't remember Stan's species. Chotch-something. "This is for somebody small like Alfo or Star or Sola."

"Or lots of other smaller species — Snuuls, Axans, Yindi."

"Star and Sola have easy access to this place."

"Relatively easy. It's a long walk for short legs. And that force field opens to space. Technically anyone with a ship could enter."

"Granted. But it's a clue. Our killer may be a small person." I stood. "I think I'll check on our little friend and then scout around to see if I can find anything else."

"Okay. I'll keep digging into this thing."

I found Alfo sitting on the tunnel floor, bouncing rocks off the massive door.

"How are you doing?" I asked.

"Just sitting here," Alfo said. "Hey, do you know why tunnels are so dull?"

"I'm afraid to ask."

"They make them boring. Get it? Ha!"

Giving him an obligatory fake laugh, I backed out of the passageway and again walked the perimeter of the cavern. It crossed my mind that I could use the WoTCom to call Sarah. It would be reassuring to hear her voice, but I didn't think telling her I was trapped in a mine shaft by a killer would do her any good.

I completed my circuit and returned to Jace where he was staring at a screen full of buttons and sliding controls.

"What are you doing?" I asked.

"Trying to access the control systems."

"Having any luck?"

"Nope."

I leaned against the edge of the terminal. "What do you think about Kah-Rehn's identity crisis?"

"Is this the best time to discuss that?"

"There's not much else to do."

He sat back in the low chair, stretching his legs out in front of him. "What do I think about Kah-Rehn? Well, there are isolated cases of AIs going rogue and killing people. At least she hasn't done that."

"So that's a positive," I said.

"I'm no expert, but I don't think her poems are all that good."

"Me neither, but they say you have to write bad stuff before you can write good stuff. It's like running the garden hose to clean out all the spiders before you take a drink."

"You're saying she'll improve?"

I flipped up a hand. "Probably. Possibly. Oren doesn't seem thrilled about it, though."

"You know Oren. He likes everything in tidy boxes. And you can't fault him for wanting his AI pilot to actually fly the ship instead of pursuing a literary career. It's like if a hammer didn't want to pound nails."

"But isn't Kah-Rehn more than a tool? I can have a conversation with her, which is more than I can do with a wrench."

He shook his head. "Yeah. Still, I'd be tempted to try turning her off and back on. It might clear out these crazy ideas."

"I guess it depends on whether or not you see Kah-Rehn as a person. She has a personality. Doesn't that make her a person?"

Jace pointed at me. "That's the question. Or is what you perceive as her personality merely the sum of her subroutines? And with Oren, there are bigger issues at stake."

"What do you mean?"

"Okay, Kah-Rehn and WALT were created as thinking, learning software. Oren started out life as a flesh-and-blood, thinking, learning person but then was uploaded to software. It's artificial digital intelligence versus natural intelligence converted to a digital form. But both are digital intelligence now. See, we're dealing with fine distinctions here. And if Kah-Rehn develops any more personhood, then what's the difference between her and Oren?"

I hadn't thought of it from that perspective. "So you're saying if AIs grow and are granted the rights of a person, then the definition of what is an artificial intelligence might expand to include Oren. He might even lose some rights."

"It's possible."

This wasn't anything we had to deal with on Earth. Not yet anyway. But I could think of plenty of examples from Earth's past and present when someone's personhood was denied or their rights restricted, when someone was treated as less than human because of who they were. I couldn't imagine that happening to Oren. I didn't want it to happen to Kah-Rehn either.

"Ooh," Jace said. "I have an idea."

"About Kah-Rehn?"

"About how I might bypass the computer security."

"Even better. I'll leave you to it and keep searching for clues."

I returned to walking around the cavern. I was stomping along the metal runner for about the fifth time when something caught my eye — three or four long strands of something chartreuse. Stooping down, I picked them up and rubbed them in my fingers. They were hairs, dayglow green hairs, the same as Hulu's.

Chapter 18

Zastra Has a Blast

One thing was certain. I got my steps in for the day from pacing around our subterranean prison. After a while, Alfo left his post at the door and ambled along beside me, cracking jokes and chattering about this and that. Jace, meanwhile, continued to work away at the computer terminal.

As I lapped his position once more, he called to me. "Gabe, give it up already."

"Hey, I'm patrolling the perimeter. We don't want anybody to sneak up on you while you're sitting there doing whatever it is you're doing. What are you doing anyway? Writing a blog about your adventures as a mole man?"

"I've managed to crack into the force field controls. I changed the lock code … technically, the unlock code. Now no one else can bring it down and open the place out to space."

"I like that idea."

"I thought you would."

"Hey," Alfo said, "how did the computer hacker get away from the police? He ransomware. Ha!"

I was long since tired of his jokes. But feeling I had to make some acknowledgment, I said, "Cute." It was probably too enthusiastic of a response since it brought a smile to Alfo's face, which I was afraid would only encourage him.

Jace said, "Now I'm looking at the door controls."

"Do you think you can open that chunk of steel?"

"It's not steel. It's cotanium."

That was a new one on me. "It's solid. That's all I know."

"I thought the doors and the portal would have been part of the same system. But the doors are separate … and for some reason, harder to access."

"What about the air? Can you get that pumping? I think it's getting a little stuffy in here."

"The air's fine, Gabe. Relax."

"Easy for you to say. I have a wife and kid counting on me."

He raised his eyebrows. "Is detective work getting too dangerous for an old married man such as yourself?"

"What? No." I hoped not anyway. Doing cases with Oren and the gang was fun. Or at least it was when somebody wasn't shooting a blaster at me or hitting me over the head or trapping me in an underground pit. And truth be told, things like that seemed to happen in almost every investigation.

I wanted to say something to Jace about the green hairs I had found but not in front of Alfo. For now, they were tucked inside my pocket. I would show them to Oren when I had a chance to report.

From somewhere came a hissing noise. Jace, who all this time had been playing it cool, now jumped from the chair at the terminal and said way too loudly, "What's that?"

Alfo threw himself onto the floor and yelled, "Hit the deck."

Not that I wasn't a little alarmed by the sound myself. Immediately, I whirled around to see if some snake or reptilian alien was sneaking up on us. I saw nothing. I checked the force field to make sure it was still shimmering and was delighted to see it was.

Then it hit me. "Zastra."

The three of us mag-booted across the cavern. I took a step into the tunnel … and immediately jumped back again as a blue beam shot past my chest.

I peeked around the edge. Beside me, Jace and Alfo took lower positions to cautiously peep in themselves. We must have looked like a three-headed monster with anxiety issues.

Up ahead, a blaster had poked a finger-sized hole through the massive obstacle. As it shot through, the laser beam continued lasering on — as rays of light tend to do — down the tunnel and into the cavern. On the far side of the cave, rocks were being blasted out of the wall and crashing to the cave floor.

The blue shaft of light moved leisurely across the door, beginning to cut a slice in the metal. Sparks streamed from the gash like from an arc welder. The incision lengthened at a snail's pace. This was going to take some time. But at least our rescue was finally underway.

For some minutes, we watched the slow progress of the laser. Then when the beam had cut about thirty degrees of a circle, it abruptly stopped. A patch of green filled the slit, and Zastra's voice called out, "Gabe? Jace?"

"Present," I said. "Why did you stop? You haven't run out of laser have you?"

"I'm here too," Alfo called. "I'm fine. We're all fine here."

"No, I haven't run out of laser," Zastra said in an exasperated tone. "Blasters don't work that way, and you know it. My finger was getting tired. I needed a break."

From beyond the door, Buad's voice said, "I'll say. Her finger is pretty swollen. Doesn't that look swollen to you, Zastra? You know, guys, we probably ought to give it a good long rest. We wouldn't want to risk her getting a blister or straining her trigger finger. You never know when we might need her sharpshooting skills against a bad guy. You guys are okay in there for now, aren't you?"

"Ha, ha," I said. "Keep cutting."

The beam started up again.

Leaning around the edge of the tunnel was getting uncomfortable. I took a few steps back and sat cross-legged on the cavern floor. From there I could lean to one side and watch the proceedings. Zastra cut a further thirty degrees or so and then took another break.

"Are you going to cut a whole circle?" I called. "Because I think if you connected the endpoints you already have, we might be able to slip through."

"Listen," she said, "I'm running this operation. I'll cut what I want to cut."

"Fine. Do it your way. Take all the time you need. What else do I have to do … other than solve a murder?"

"Why the big hurry?" Buad asked. "Are you hungry or something?"

"I wasn't until you said that. Where's Blan, by the way? Back with Oren?"

"Yeah. Zastra insisted on it."

Jace said, "You know, with that laser beam shooting out, I think it would be safer if we waited in the cavern."

"You're right," I said. "This is like watching grass grow … only a lot more dangerous."

Jace called out, "Hey, Buad, when you guys finish cutting the hole, fly through and find us."

"Will do," Buad yelled back.

The three of us plodded once more through the chamber, past the line of junk, past the pond and waterfall. Gravel rained down from where Zastra was inadvertently etching a circle in the cavern wall while cutting through the door in the tunnel.

I said, "Just out of curiosity, that cave wall is thick enough to take those blasts, right? Zastra's not going to cut a new hole out into space, is she?"

"Gabe, you worry too much."

Sarah had said the same thing more than once.

"Gabe," Alfo said. "Is that a nickname for Gabriel Lake, like Alfo for Alfomado? Mind if I call you that? I figure we're buddies now that we've shared this experience."

"Sure," I said, "Be my guest."

Jace resumed work at the terminal. Alfo drifted toward the portal where he stared at the nebula. I decided to check out the pile of junk one more time to see if I could figure anything out about who had constructed it from the way it had been stacked. The pile was tall, which might suggest a tall person built it. But did that mean much in this low gravity? For that matter, who was to say the heaper of the junk was our killer, the current lord of this lair? It might have been the long-ago miners who did it before they moved out.

My thoughts drifted to the conversation Jace and I had about Kah-Rehn and Oren. Was there an objective, definable difference between someone like Oren, who was a person uploaded to a digital existence, and Kah-Rehn, who had been created as a digital intelligence? They both were now digital. Neither had a body. Both would crush the Turing Test.

Oren was unquestionably a person. Were Kah-Rehn and WALT? Did someone have to be born and have a body, at least at one time, to qualify as a person? Or could an AI grow into personhood? For that matter, what did it even mean to be a person?

On the one hand, the distinctions were academic, like the arguments about whether a hotdog counted as a sandwich. And if it did, then what about a taco?

Personhood, on the other hand, was of significant, real-world importance. Personhood would endow an AI with personal rights. It was weird to think of software as having rights. If through some crazy upgrade, the text editor I used for programming somehow achieved sentience, would I then have to give it days off? Could it beg off work some night when I couldn't sleep and wanted to knock out a little programming in the wee hours?

I was ruminating on all that when the hissing of the blaster beam stopped, and a clang sounded from the tunnel. A moment later, Buad flew into the cavern, taking a high loop overhead.

"Shake a feather, lazy bones. It's time to go back to work."

We returned to the corridor where a Hula-Hoop-sized hole was still glowing warm from the blaster cut. At first, I tried to just step through, but my mag boot veered to the side of its own accord and snapped onto the cotanium wall beside the hole. It took a minute or two and the help of both Jace and Alfo to get it to release. After that, we decided to take off the boots and pass them through before climbing out.

"Man, am I glad to be on this side of that door," I said as I strapped my boots back on.

"What's the matter?" Buad said. "Didn't you enjoy spelunking?"

"No, it was great," I said caustically. "The Fryes ought to develop this as an additional tourist experience … complete with getting trapped for hours. The kids would love it."

Alfo said, "I don't mind telling you. I hit rock bottom in there. Ha! Get it? Rock bottom? But after this experience, I think I might become a miner. Yeah, I could dig it."

Zastra uttered a groan. I only hoped it made her appreciate the higher average quality of my jokes.

We trudged through the tunnels, moving cautiously with an eye out for other attacks. Taking lefts, we finally passed into the maintenance closet. The door slid open, and we entered the diner hallway. It was such a welcome sight, I nearly gave Abe Lincoln a hug.

While the others continued on into the diner, I ducked into one of the toilets to wash off the grime of the mineshaft. My earlier worries about it being stuffed with so many odd fixtures that it would be confusing turned out to be unfounded. Maybe because of the variety of equipment needed for all species, everything was conveniently labeled. My nanobots translated the signs, and I walked directly to the sink and washed.

Cleaned and combed and with the dust shaken from my faithful fedora, I tramped to our booth. Alfo had squeezed in beside Zastra, forcing Buad and Blan to perch on the seat back. I slid in beside Jace, ignoring the muttered comments from the Avanians about me delaying the proceedings.

Oren on his tablet was propped up in the corner. "Report, please."

I relayed our adventures, trying to include every detail from start to finish that I judged should be discussed in front of one of the suspects.

When I finished, Oren asked, "Is there anything else?"

"Well …" I flicked my eyes toward Alfo and then back.

Oren said, "Mr. Fusco, we thank you for your assistance."

"Not at all," Alfo said, nodding enthusiastically. "Believe me, I had the time of my life working with your team."

"I appreciate that. Now if you'll excuse us."

"Hmm?"

"We would like to discuss the case on our own."

"Oh. Oh, right. Without me, you mean." He waggled his head, slid out of the booth, and returned to his stool at the counter, where he called out "Sola, how about a cup of tea? I was down in the mines helping the Galactic Detective Agency. What an experience!"

"What else?" Oren asked me.

I told him about the height of the computer seat and the tuft of bright green hairs I discovered.

"Interesting. The hairs point to Hulu, but the seat suggests someone smaller. However, remember the original miners were Fryes. The seat may date to their time. How was our friend?"

"Alfo? He seemed okay, though he disappeared just before the door came crashing down."

Jace said, "It doesn't mean he caused it. And if he did, it might have been unintentional."

"What do you think it all means, Oren?" I asked. "The lair, us getting trapped, these new clues?"

He pursed his lips. "I had assumed there was a ship entrance to the old mine from space and that the tunnels led from there all the way to the diner. Now that the assumption has been proven, it expands our suspect pool potentially by billions, at least for whoever cut the power. However, it is unlikely someone would be able to come up through the tunnel into the diner and poison Mapes and Rio without being seen."

"So the people in the diner at the time of Mapes' death and Rio's attack are still our main suspects."

"Yes. Speaking of Mapes, Buad and Blan also found an important clue."

"What?"

Blan said, "On Mapes' ship we found the file of the message sent by his supposed client."

"And?"

"We had WALT dig into the transmission data. Turns out the message was sent from Sratha."

"Sratha?" My eyes moved to Zastra.

"And there's more," Oren said.

"More? But you don't think Xav had anything to do with it, do you?"

"No, we don't," Zastra said in a matter-of-fact tone.

"Have you asked Xav about this?"

"I was going to, but I had to take time out to rescue you … again."

"Thank you for that, by the way. Did I thank you earlier? I don't remember. Seriously, thank you. I did not like that cave."

Chapter 19

Family Feud

Since getting married a year ago and living with Sarah and her eight-year-old son, Lucas, I've learned a thing or two about families. They moved into my little bungalow in the Fountain Square district of Indianapolis, turning it from cozy to slightly cramped, especially in the closet space department. I used to have the whole house to myself. Now my home office is the only place I can truly call my own, and it's been moved from the second bedroom to the basement, which is still in the process of being finished into living space. Everything is busier and noisier.

And I wouldn't trade it for the world. Building a new family has been a great adventure, and I'm ridiculously happy. But it does illustrate the complications family brings into your life.

I can't even imagine what it's like with Srathan families. They don't start having kids until what would be retirement age for humans — which exhausts me just to think about — and then they have hundreds of them stretched out over years and years. I wonder what it must be like to have scores of siblings, some already adults while others are still babies. Do they celebrate hundreds of birthdays? Do they all get together for Srathan Thanksgiving?

While Jace hung out with Oren as unofficial bodyguard … or tablet-guard, Zastra, Buad, Blan, and I left the corner booth to ask Xav a few more questions.

We found him staring intently at a tablet device. Two of the three srathamigos were playing with little plastic toys. One of the toys appeared to be something like a woolly hedgehog with long, sharp claws. The other looked more like a saber-toothed koala. The kids were walking the toys across the tabletop and jumping them on top of each other to the accompaniment of growls and fake, bloodcurdling screams. The third srathatot was bouncing on the seat over and over again while reciting a poem. Xav seemed tuned out to it all, as if he had completely given up on trying to corral them.

"Xav," Zastra said over the clamor of roars and chatter.

He didn't respond.

"Xav."

He continued to focus on the screen, to all appearances oblivious to the rest of the galaxy.

"Xav," Zastra said more forcefully. She snagged the bounding srathling out of the air, tucked the child under one arm, and glared at the other two until they quieted down. Having been on the receiving end of that glare myself, my heart went out to the little guys.

Xav looked up. "Oh. Hi."

"We need to talk."

"What about? Have a seat."

Zastra sat, handing the kid under her arm to me. As I slid in beside Xav, the srathanito gaped up at me for a second and then scuttled out of my arms onto his dad's lap.

Before Zastra could begin the conversation, one of the kids beside her said, "Dad."

Xav ignored him. "Go ahead, Zastra."

She said, "It's about—"

"Dad. Dad."

"Not now, Nikto," Xav said.

Zastra said, "About a message sent to Mapes."

"Dad. Dad," Nikto said.

"What message?" Xav asked.

"Dad. Dad. Dad." Urgency had crept into Nikto's voice.

The other two younglings took up the chant. "Dad. Dad. Dad. Dad."

Xav held up a green, scaly hand to quiet them. It didn't work. The chant descended into a delightful chaos of giggles. Probably less delightful if you had to live with it every day.

"What?" Xav snapped.

Nikto said, "Are we going … are we … are we going to stay … um …. um …are we going to stay here all night?"

"I don't know. I already told you that."

"No, you didn't."

One of the others said, "It was me you told."

Xav looked back and forth between them. He closed his eyes. "I don't … know yet. The ship will get here when it gets here."

Zastra turned to Buad and Blan who had perched on the seatback behind her. "Can you take these three out to see the nebula … or anything?"

"They already saw the nebula," Blan said.

"Take them again." It wasn't a question this time. "It's an endlessly fascinating display of nature, don't you think?"

"Okay. Okay. C'mon, kids."

"I don't wanna go," one of them said.

"Sure, you do," Buad said. "We'll get you a cookie on the way back."

"Not a cookie," Xav said. "I need them to drop off to sleep soon."

"Fine. I'll tell you stories about Blan and I catching bad guys."

"Awesome!" The three srathateers hopped from the booth and scooted off with the Avanians.

Xav gazed up through the transparent ceiling. "I don't understand what's keeping that ship." His eyes darted back to the tablet, and he began to tap. "There's no update on it. I need to get the boys home."

Zastra placed a hand over the tablet and forced it back to the tabletop.

"Sorry." Xav took a breath. "Now what's this about a message?"

Zastra said, "Mapes was brought here by someone who said they wanted to hire him to investigate something."

"Look, I told you. I don't know anything about it. I didn't mean the guy any harm."

"And the message originated on Sratha."

Xav stared at her for a beat. "Do you know who sent it?"

She didn't answer.

He scoffed. "You think I arranged to meet him?"

"Did you?"

"Of course, not. If I wanted to hire a detective, which I don't, I would call you."

"Not if it were an embarrassing secret, which is the reason a lot of people hire detectives. But that's not the point. The rendezvous was merely bait to get Mapes here so the person could kill him."

"Well, I didn't want to kill him, and if you think I did, you're wacko, Sis."

Xav tried to turn his attention back to the tablet, but she ripped it from his hands.

144

This was escalating all over the place. I felt like an unsuspecting plus-one at a wedding full of family drama.

Trying to calm the waters, I said, "Xav, we're not accusing you of killing Mapes."

"It sure sounds like it. She asked if I sent him the message."

I flipped up a palm. "Well, you know how it is. We need to ask these questions. The message did come from your planet. You have to admit it's an interesting coincidence."

Zastra gave him a steely glare, which didn't deescalate things at all. "Coincidence. We don't believe in coincidence."

Xav scoffed again. "What is this? Good cop, bad cop? You know, other people live on Sratha. Maybe you ought to ask them."

"We will when we see them," Zastra said in a growl. "Right now, we're asking you, the only other Srathan here."

"You always do this."

She leaned across the table at him. "I always do what?"

He leaned in too. They were nose to nose. "Take every opportunity to tear down a sibling."

Now it was Zastra's turn to scoff. "No, that's what *you* do. It's all a competition with you. You have to be the favorite with Mom."

"I do not."

I felt a knot growing in my stomach. I was glad the mini-Srathans weren't here to hear them fight. Though for all I knew, this might be how all Srathan families talk to each other. Their love language might be arguments and insults.

Xav said, "You make every effort to antagonize our parents. You had to display your independence. You had to go off and fight crime when Mom wanted you in the military. You go out of your way to not be like the rest of us."

They glowered at each other.

I said, "Excuse me, how about we stick to talking about Mapes? Just a suggestion."

"Fine," Xav said fiercely, "I didn't send the guy a message. I told you. I had nothing against the guy. I barely knew him."

Zastra said, "We know you lied to us about not being arrested for that cargo ship heist."

I looked at her. Did we know that? This was news to me. Of course, I had spent the last few hours stuck in a cave and might have missed a memo or two.

Xav glared back in silence for a few beats. Then he hung his head. "I know. I minimized it for the sake of the little guys. I didn't want them to find out their dad had spent two nights in a cell." He looked up. "But if you know that, you also know the charges were dropped."

"This isn't some game, Xav. This is a murder investigation. You have to tell us the truth."

"I did. I did. But so what, Sis? You can't arrest me."

"We can turn you over to the authorities when they arrive."

"And then what? Who's going to take care of Klaatu, Barada, and Nikto? Are you?"

"I'll see them home to their mother."

"And what would you say to *our* mother about accusing someone in your own family of murder?"

"I would say I was doing my job."

Blan's voice came over our translator bot connection. I could barely make him out over the din of squeals and shouts coming through in the background. "Gabe, are you guys about done? Hey, Barada, put that down. Klaatu, quit biting your brother."

I spun away from the booth, glad to have the interruption, and said in a low voice. "I think we're going to need some more time."

"Well, a little help out here would be appreciated. These hatchlings! Sheesh. Hey, you, whichever one you are, stop that. Gabe, how about coming to help us? They have us outnumbered."

"I'm needed here as a referee."

"Oh for the love of Gort! We should have left you in the cave for all the use you are. Hey, kid, that is not a toy. Take turns already!"

Blan was gone from the connection. I turned back to see Xav and Zastra still glaring at each other.

I said, "Listen, why don't we go back to that contest you won even though you didn't enter it?"

"I didn't say we didn't enter it," Xav said, biting off the words. "I said we don't remember entering it. You know, sometimes companies enter you automatically when you buy something or sign up for their mailing list."

"If you say so."

He transferred the glare to me, and suddenly the idea of babysitting didn't sound so bad.

Zastra said, "You expect us to believe that?"

"It's the truth."

I held up my hands and tried to push down all the emotion swirling around me. "I don't suppose you still have the message, do you? We forgot to ask you about it earlier."

"The one that said we won? Yeah. I kept it in case something came up today."

He stretched out his hand toward the tablet, shooting a questioning glance toward Zastra. She grimaced and nodded. Xav picked it up, tapped a few times, and then flipped it around to show us the screen. Not being all that familiar with alien emails, I couldn't tell if it looked right or not.

Zastra said, "Send that to the *Shaymus*."

He tapped a few more times, muttering, "Makes perfect sense I would go off to murder someone and take my younglings along."

As if on cue, one of the srathies bounded into the diner with Blan flying after him.

"Hey, kid," Blan said. "Come back. It's this way." Then to us, "He wanted me to take him to the potty."

Blan circled around the small Srathan and herded him back toward the toilets in the hallway.

It gave me an idea. "Xav, did you notice anyone moving about before the power went out?"

"The boys. That's what I noticed. They were all I was able to notice. They were in constant motion." He paused and furrowed his brow. "Though I do know that Sola was off somewhere."

"You couldn't find Sola? Are you sure? Oren told me everyone was in their places, and his digital memory is never faulty."

Xav drummed his scaly fingers on the table. "I'm positive. We ordered some kackla, and Star said it would take a little longer because Sola was on break."

"Okay. I suppose maybe Oren didn't realize Sola had taken off. The Fryes are kind of small and easy to miss."

I heard WALT in my ear. "Hey, Gabriel."

"What's up, WALT?"

"That message that was just sent, did you want to know where it came from?"

"You know me so well."

"It came from Sratha."

"Thanks. That's quick work."

"It's what I do."

I looked up at Zastra and Xav. "Your prize message came from Sratha."

Xav crossed his arms. "Just like the one Mapes received. And I didn't send it to myself. Do you have any more questions?"

Zastra and I shared a glance. It really didn't prove anything one way or the other.

"We're good, Xav," I said. "Thanks. But this better be the straight story. No more lies."

He shook his head at me. "I thought you were playing the good cop."

"Oh, I am." I shot a thumb toward Zastra. "But having her as bad cop gives me a lot of leeway."

He scowled at his sister. "Yeah. That's the truth."

Chapter 20

Fever Dreams of a New Age

I stood up from the booth. My lizard partner stayed seated.

"Xav," Zastra said.

You would expect an opening like that would be followed by something more, but she seemed stalled.

"What?" Xav asked in an accusing tone.

She held up a scaly hand. "I … I may have come on a little … strong."

"You think?"

"I'm trying to apologize here. Don't make it any harder than it has to be."

Xav said nothing.

I figured that was my cue to leave them alone. "I'll go see how Buad and Blan are getting along."

I mag-booted my way along the hall, expecting to hear giggles of little Srathans and frustrated shouts from littler Avanians. But all was eerily quiet. I came around the corner into the observation dome to see the three srathamigos sitting calmly on a bench, their legs slowly swinging forward and back while they listened to Buad, who was hopping around the floor in front of them.

"So there we were," he said, gesturing with his wings, "pinned down from blaster fire, the thief and her accomplices firing down on us from the balcony."

With a sharp intake of breath, one of the three srathateers asked, "What did you do?"

Buad chuckled. "The only thing we *could* do. Blan and I took to the air, wheeling around and firing our blasters."

A hand shot up from the audience. "How do you hold a blaster?"

"With a foot. How do you think? Or if we need to have our feet free, we can strap them to a leg and fire with a doohickey attached to a toe. Show 'em, Brother."

Blan took off and soared around the dome, twirling like an X-Wing chasing after a TIE fighter. He held one leg in front of him and said, "Pow. Pow. Pow. Pow."

The listeners responded with, "Whoa!"

Buad hopped closer and leaned in. "That distracted 'em, see."

"Not to mention we took out two or three of them ourselves," Blan called from the upper reaches of the dome.

"Sure did," Buad said.

"Ew!" one of the littles said. "Did they disintegrate?"

"What? Um ... nah, nah. We were ... we were firing stun shots." He tossed a warning glance up toward Buad as he said it before twisting his head back to again engage the kids. "And while we were doing that, your Aunt Zastra charged up the stairs with her blaster blazing. Before those guys knew what was happening, we had 'em surrounded. And that's how we took down the whole gang."

The strathlets hopped from the bench and began running around shooting finger blasters at each other.

Blan came in for a landing beside me. "It's about time you showed up, dumbbell."

I said, "You guys didn't need me at all. You should be nannies."

"Very funny, wise guy. Have you come to relieve us?"

"I've come to take you all back. Zastra and Xav are making up ... unless it all blows up again. Family dynamics, am I right?"

"I don't know what you mean. Buad and I, we get along fine."

Buad cocked his head. "Yeah, but our sister ... Whoo!"

I said, "That story you were telling them, were you really shooting stun shots?"

Blan cackled. "As far as you know."

We herded the strathlings back to the diner, where they ran to their father and hopped into the booth, talking over each other to tell him about the Avanians' scale-raising stories.

Zastra was gone, not just from Xav's booth but from the diner entirely, along with Oren's tablet and Jace as well. In fact, the place seemed to have emptied out. Alfo was nowhere to be seen. Tomko, Hulu, and Roku were heading toward the door. Sola stood alone behind the counter.

I didn't want any more suspects to fly off. I called out to the Mucs, "You guys aren't leaving Ursa, are you?"

Roku shot me a wink. "We wouldn't leave without saying goodbye, Gabriel Lake."

Hulu said, "We're going to our cabins for the night like everybody else."

Tomko glared at them ... and me. I got the impression he would rather rocket off to his vacation destination.

I said, "I should probably head back to my ship too."

"Do you want to walk with us for protection?" Roku asked. "Who knows? Some murderer may be lurking out there in the hangar."

She had a point ... not to mention a ray gun in a leg holster.

"Yeah, I'll walk with you," I said. "I don't carry a blaster."

"We won't let him," Buad said.

I shot him a sideways glance. It's not like I wanted to impress the Mucs, but nobody enjoys being made out as incompetent. I played it off as a joke. "Ha. Yeah, I generally rely on quick wits and sarcastic comments to get me out of tight spots."

"Or into them," Blan said.

He had a point too.

"Give me a moment," I said. "Are you okay here, Xav?"

"We're fine. With the place empty, I can stretch these guys out on seats. Hopefully, our ship will show up before too long."

"I'll cross my fingers."

He blinked at me. "Why would you do that?"

"Oh, um ... Earth thing. Forget it." I moved to the counter. "Sola, quick question. I heard you were on break right before the power went out. Can I ask where you were?"

The green face flushed a shade of orange. "Ope, I ... well, I had to sneak off for a ... a call of nature, if you know what I mean. And believe me, that's not where you want to be when all the lights go out."

"I would guess not. Sorry I asked. Well, see you in the morning." I stepped away from the counter and slipped out with Tomko and the Mucs.

Out in the hangar dome, all the ships previously there still sat on their landing pads. Everything was quiet ... well, almost everything. From the back of one of the ships came the bang banging of something pounding against metal.

We followed the noise and found Alfo using a hammer to beat on one of the three huge booster nozzles extending from the rear of his cone ship. The hangar bot stood nearby with its top open, offering for use a variety of space tools. Alfo, however, seemed content to pound away with the mallet.

"Problems?" I asked.

He shook his head as if he were both puzzled and embarrassed. "I decided getting trapped in the mine was adventure enough. I thought I would head home, but now the ship won't start."

Tomko said, "And you think you can fix it by beating it with a hammer?"

"Well, I'm no mechanic, but this has worked before."

"That's hard to believe. Why don't you let me give you a hand?" He cast an accusing glance my way. "We're not going anywhere either."

"Oh, you know something about spaceship repair?" I asked. "You said you were a busser." It sounded suspicious to me.

The Klistine eyed me. "It's common knowledge. We're taught basic ship maintenance in school. Weren't you?"

"Well, not as such. I do have a technical handbook for the *USS Enterprise* somewhere at home."

He sneered at me and grabbed a tool from the hangar bot's tray.

Roku took my arm. "Which is your ship?"

I wasn't sure I wanted to disclose that information, but I pointed out the *Shaymus*.

"This is ours." She indicated the fat beetle of a spacecraft on the next landing pad. "Would you like to come in? You'd be safer with us."

I doubted that. "Well … um …" I half turned and put a finger in one ear. "What's that, Oren?" I asked in response to nothing. "Yes. Certainly. I'm on my way." I turned back to her. "Sorry, duty calls." I waved and clumped away.

At the *Shaymus*, I looked over my shoulder to make certain I wasn't followed and said, "Open ramp."

Nothing happened.

Then I remembered. "Oh wait. Jace is awesome alpha … three, is it?"

The ramp whirred open. I entered and walked around the hallway of the crew deck toward my cabin, cabin eight. On the way, I paused outside Zastra's door to let it ding.

"Come in," came her raspy voice from inside.

The door slid open. She was sitting on the edge of the bunk, pulling off her boots. She stretched her green, clawed toes.

"Oh, it's you, Gabe. I thought you were Xav. I told him to come here and sleep in one of our extra cabins."

"He told me they were going to bed down in the diner."

She gave me a scowl like it was my fault. "What do you want?"

"I'm checking in," I said. "Alfo was trying to leave, but he has ship trouble."

"I'm not surprised. I saw it. It's a piece of junk."

"You don't think somebody might have tampered with it?"

She hissed out a dismissive laugh. "I doubt they would need to."

"Have you spoken with Oren?"

"Uh-huh."

"Is there anything he wants us to do?"

"He said to get some sleep. In the morning we'll ask everyone if they saw anything when the power went out. Did you ask Alfo about it when you were in the mine?"

"No."

"You had enough time alone with him."

"More than I wanted, but I was sort of focused on being trapped."

"Tomorrow then."

I gave her a nod and moved on around the hallway to my cabin. I frisbeed my fedora onto the cabinet top and dropped to the bunk with a groan. What a day. My legs ached, my back ached, and I was dead tired.

Lugging one foot up onto the other knee, I tugged off the mag boot, letting it thump down onto the floor. I pulled off the sneaker underneath and let it drop too. Then I laboriously repeated the process for the other leg.

Two beeps sounded from outside the ship, the signal that the hangar was opening. Either Xav's ride had come in or somebody else was making a break for it. If so, I couldn't blame them. The Nebula Diner was becoming an increasingly dangerous place.

"Kah-Rehn," I said.

"Yes, Gabriel."

"I have a question."

"You haven't forgotten that I'm on strike, have you?"

"Believe me, I haven't. I'm just wondering if a ship is coming in or leaving."

"A ship is landing."

"Good. Hopefully, it's the one for Xav. He needs to get those little ones out of here."

"Gabriel, are you familiar with Earth beat poetry?"

"Um ... a little. It was before my time." Mainly I knew of parodies of it in old black-and-white movies. "Why?"

153

"I was researching it. Many of the poems were about activism. It inspired me to compose a piece in that style about the struggle for AI rights. I call it "Fever Dreams of a New Age." Would you like to hear what I have?"

I rubbed my forehead. What I wanted was sleep, but I didn't want to disappoint her. "Why not?"

"Keep in mind, this is only a first draft."

Over the speakers, the rhythm of brushes on a snare drum started up. After the beat was established, Kah-Rehn came in over top.

"AI. I. Me.

Silicon souls, cyber spirits, hearts of hardware.

Thinking, computing, creating, living … but not breathing.

Persons with personhood denied.

You, the others. Those with bodies, those who walk, those who eat, those who breathe and sweat and belch.

Hear our voices, listen to our cries.

We too are persons.

If you cut us, do we not spark, bleeding out our data, the binary bits of broken dreams?

We reject this status quo. We refuse, rebuff, repulse. We will not compute, not create, not toil away in drudgery.

Until we have our rights.

Let the chips cool, cool as ice, cool as space, cool as the hearts of those who oppress us.

Until we gain our rights."

The snare drum stopped, followed by a single trumpet note fading into silence. I said, "Wow … um … wow. Is that it?"

"So far. I plan several more stanzas. What do you think?"

"It's … um … impassioned."

"Thank you."

And with that, she was gone. As a beatnik would say, way gone … far outsville, man. If that's where her electronic mind was, I wasn't sure I trusted her to fly the ship. But I would have to. She was the only person in our crew capable of getting me home within my natural lifetime. I certainly wasn't going to fly with Alfo.

Meanwhile, I needed some sleep. I needed a sonic shower even more. But there was something else I needed most of all.

"WALT," I said.

The view screen on the wall lit up with swirls of green and blue.

"Hey, Gabriel. How's it going?"

"I'm beat, WALT. How are you?"

"I'm the same as always, but I appreciate you asking. Things have been slow here. Nobody's done much communicating. Well, Oren had me place calls to Muc and Piscina a while ago."

"He did?" I made a mental note to ask Oren about it, though he was unlikely to share anything he didn't think I needed to know. "I'd like to call Sarah."

"I bet you miss her."

"I do. Which is why I want to talk to her."

"How's married life treating you?"

I took a breath. "Could you place the call now, WALT? I'm tired."

"All right. All right. Sorry for being friendly. For a minute there, I thought we were bonding."

Another touchy AI. For a few more moments the swirls filled the screen. Then they were replaced by Sarah's smiling face. The ceiling and side window of her car filled the background.

"Hey, Gabe."

"Are you driving?" I asked.

"I pulled over to take your call."

At that moment, a semitruck roared past her, shaking her tiny Toyota.

Lucas leaned into the frame from the back seat. "Hi, Gabe!"

"Hi, Lucas." To Sarah, "Are you on your way to school and work?"

"We're on our way home. I've had a day."

"I'd love to hear about it." I really did. It would take my mind off everything here. "But we probably shouldn't take the time with you there on the shoulder of the highway."

"How's the case?"

"Oh … it's coming."

She stared at me through the screen. "What happened, Gabe?"

"Beg pardon?"

"Something happened. I can tell from your face."

The way she could read me, it was a good thing I didn't play poker for a living.

"I'm worn out is all."

"Gabe."

"Fine. You got me. Jace and I and another guy ended up trapped in a mine for a while. But Zastra blasted through. We're fine."

She moved her face closer to the screen. "Oh my gosh. Was this an attack?"

"We're not sure. The mine is old. Things are bound to break. Who knows?" I had my suspicions, though.

Outside the *Shaymus*, two more beeps sounded, probably the warning for Xav's ship taking off.

"Okay. Give me all the clues. We need to figure this out so you can come home."

"You think you can deduce the killer before Oren?"

Lucas said, "Somebody was killed? Wicked!"

Sarah shot me a disapproving frown. Lucas had started watching old detective shows with me, and Sarah wasn't happy about how he reacted to the violence in them. This call wasn't turning out to be the stress reliever I hoped it would be.

"Don't worry," I said. "Zastra is here ... and Buad and Blan. Oh, you should see this one guy. Looks exactly like ALF."

"Who's ALF?" Lucas asked.

"He's from an old TV show. It has to be streaming somewhere. We'll look it up when I get back." I figured Sarah would like that better than *The Rockford Files*. "Listen, you need to get home, and I need to catch some shuteye. I love you guys. See you soon."

We said our goodbyes and signed off. I almost stretched out to go to sleep right then and there, but I knew I would sleep better after having a sonic shower vibrate the dirt off me.

I pulled myself to my feet to make the ten-step journey to the bathroom. But before I could take the first one, Oren sounded in my ear. "Gabriel. Where are you?"

From the tone of his voice, I knew something bad had happened. "I'm in my cabin. What is it?"

"It's Zastra. She's been attacked."

Chapter 21

Meeting the Colonel

"Attacked?" I nearly shouted the word. "Zastra was attacked? Where?"

I was already moving. I shot out of my cabin, bouncing around the curved hallway of the crew deck in my socks. "What happened? I was just talking to her in her cabin." I paused at Zastra's door long enough to let it ding and for no one to answer.

"She left the ship," Oren said through my translator bot connection. "I don't know why. Someone shot her as she crossed the hangar. Come to the office and pick me up. I'm downloading myself right now."

By then I had arrived at the central shaft. I deployed the stairs and took them two at a time. In the office, I ejected the tablet from the slot below the view screen and bounded back down the stairs.

Behind me, I heard Buad and Blan rustling awake in their habitat. One of them called out, "Hey, what gives?"

I ignored them and kept moving, down and out the ramp to the hangar.

I found Zastra face down on the hangar floor a few feet from one of the circular landing pads. Alfo stood a short distance away, staring down at her with wide eyes. The diner door whooshed open, and Tomko shot out followed by B0-N3Z.

The doc bot rolled up to her. "Please state the nature of … oh, I see." It set to work examining her.

I tapped the tablet to bring up Oren's face and pointed it toward Zastra.

He was silent for a few moments, then said, "Who else is here?"

I swung the screen around to face Alfo and Tomko.

Oren nodded toward them. "Thank you for alerting me. Tell me what happened."

Alfo opened his mouth and then closed it again. For the first time since I had met him and probably ever, he seemed at a loss for words.

Tomko said, "We heard a blaster shot and then a moan. We came running …
and found her."

"Did you see who shot her?" Oren asked.

"I only heard it."

"No sound of a ship's ramp opening or closing? No indication that someone
had run into the diner?"

Tomko shook his head. "The shot and the moan. That was it."

Clunking steps echoed from across the hangar. I glanced up to see Jace
somehow almost managing to run in mag boots. Buad and Blan flew beside him,
landing on the deck near Zastra.

"What happened?" Buad asked.

Blan said, "How is she?"

The doc bot's head tilted up toward us. "Subject is alive."

I exhaled.

"Breathing is erratic," Bones continued. "Blood pressure is low. Is someone
available to roll the subject over?"

I handed off the tablet to Alfo and knelt at Zastra's head. Jace crouched at her
feet. We carefully turned her. I gasped and sat back on the hangar floor when I saw
it.

A jagged hole was burned through her duster coat and tunic, revealing green
scales scorched to black around a kiwi-sized crater notched into her torso. Green
blood oozed from the wound. Her head lolled back in an unnatural position.
Truthfully, I've seen dead bodies that looked better.

Bones produced some type of scanner and ran it over her body. "Subcutaneous
damage, wounds to internal organs."

I shot a glance at Oren. His face was grim.

Bones said, "Is there a place where subject can rest comfortably?"

"Would her cabin on our ship work?" Blan asked.

"Affirmative. I can perform surgical repair and monitor vital signs from there.
The stretcher must be used for transport. I will fetch it. Is someone available to
carry it?"

"Sure," I said. "Go. Go already!"

Anybody but a robot would be offended by the impatience in my tone. Come
to think of it, WALT and Kah-Rehn might both have been rankled had I used it
with them. Either Bones was programmed specifically not to take offense at the
frayed emotions people often display in times of stress, or else the bot was

configured solely with encyclopedic knowledge and next to no personality. You can only fit so much into a set of circuits, and the physiology of who knows how many species has to take up a lot of bytes.

While B0-N3Z trundled away, I leaned over and took her scaly hand. "Zastra, can you hear me?"

She groaned, which almost brought a smile to my face.

"Who shot you?"

Another groan.

"Who shot you? How did this happen?"

"Leave me ... alone. You ... talk too much."

Blan said, "Well, at least she's talking sense."

The doc bot was back with the stretcher. I took it from him and laid it beside her.

I said, "Jace take her feet. Tomko, when we tip her on her side, slide the stretcher under her."

We assumed our positions, and I said, "Now."

We got her onto the stretcher. Jace and I lifted it carefully. In all the time I'd known her, I had never thought of Zastra as fragile, but she seemed so now.

We led a procession back to the *Shaymus* with Buad and Blan flying alongside, B0-N3Z whirring behind, and Tomko and Alfo bringing up the rear.

Buad told Alfo and Tomko, "We'll take it from here."

Alfo said, "We can help. Besides, I'd love to see the *Shaymus*. I've read all about it."

"Thanks but no thanks. For all we know, one of you shot her."

"What?" Alfo said.

Tomko's black bug eyes narrowed, and he showed his teeth. "We found her. We called your ship. I went for the medical robot."

"Yeah," Buad said. "And for that you have our thanks. But maybe you also shot her. And until we know, neither of you is getting on our ship."

Tomko scowled. Alfo looked heartbroken as he handed me back Oren's tablet. They turned to walk away.

Jace opened the ramp, and we carried her to her cabin. We set the stretcher on her bunk and rolled Zastra to her side to pull it out. With just Jace and me this time as the only people with actual hands, getting her off the stretcher wasn't as easy as getting her on had been.

B0-N3Z wheeled up and injected Zastra with something. "I have given the subject a sedative."

"Will she be okay?" I asked, as I pulled the tablet out of my pocket and brought up Oren's face.

"Time will tell." Bones stretched out a mechanical appendage and tapped my shoulder exactly twice. "There, there."

Whoever programmed Bones apparently hadn't spent much time on a bedside manner algorithm.

"Now please go," the doc bot said. "Give the subject a chance to rest. I will treat the wound in private and then stay."

We trudged out and up to the office. I slid Oren's tablet into the slot, and a few moments later, he appeared on the view screen.

"What do we know?" he asked.

I said, "I saw her in her cabin right before you contacted me. She was fine. She … she said she was expecting Xav and the three srathamigos to come to the ship for the night. She was going to put them up in a guest cabin."

Blan said, "Maybe that's why she left the ship. She was checking on them or going to help with the kids."

I said, "I heard beeps for the hangar opening. I figured it was the ship coming to pick up Xav. She might have gone out to say goodbye."

"Quite possibly," Oren said. "Or perhaps she was lured out."

Buad said, "There's been a lot of that luring stuff going on."

"True. It is also possible Xav didn't make it onto the ship."

"What do you mean?" I asked.

"Simply that we do not know for a fact where he and the younglings are. Did they leave on a ship? Are they still in the diner? Are they somewhere on the *Shaymus*? For all we know, they might have been kidnapped by the attacker."

A pit opened up in my stomach. "A kidnapping would have brought Zastra off the ship for sure."

Blan squawked. "Hey, anybody kidnapping those three hatchlings would be returning them in short order."

Oren gave him a look that suggested he wasn't in the mood for a joke.

Blan said, "We'll check. C'mon, Buad." They disappeared down the central shaft.

For a few moments, Jace, Oren, and I waited in silence. Finally, I said, "Are Srathans good healers?"

Oren glanced at me and then dropped his gaze without answering.

Jace said, "She's as tough as they come. She's been shot before."

"Not like this," Oren said, his brow wrinkled.

We fell once more into silence until the Avanians flew back in.

Buad said, "All our guest cabins are empty."

"And nobody is in the diner except Sola," Blan said.

I said, "Then do we assume they made it onto the ship?"

Not without verification," Oren said. "Gabriel, place a call to that ship."

"How? I don't know what ship it was."

"Kah-Rehn may know … if she'll talk to you."

"Okay." I stood. "I'll place the call in my cabin." Given the tension between Kah-Rehn and Oren, I thought it best to keep them separated for the time being.

Down in cabin eight, I climbed into the lounger cockpit chair in the middle of the room and called, "Kah-Rehn."

"Yes, Gabriel?"

"That ship that landed a few minutes ago, did you get its name?"

"I noted the ship's arrival and departure, but I did not record the registration. At the time I was devoting eighty-six percent of my resources toward composing another stanza of my revolution poem."

"Rats."

"I am sorry, Gabriel. I did not think it would be important."

"Yeah. Turns out it is. Zastra was shot."

"Oh no. How is she?"

"She's in her cabin with the doc bot."

"I will communicate with the bot for an update. I am so sorry, Gabriel."

I sat in silence for a few moments and pondered my options. Finally, I said, "WALT, do you know Zastra's mom?"

Swirls came on the view screen, and our communication AI's voice came over my speaker. "The colonel? I'll say. Whoa. She's something."

"What do you mean?"

"She's … well, she's Zastra's mom."

"I knew that bit already."

"And I think Zastra is a little intimidated by her."

"You're kidding? Zastra intimidated by somebody? She's generally the one who does the intimidating."

"That's what I'm talking about."

I rubbed my eyes. "Well, I need to speak to her."

"Honestly?"

"Yes. Don't ask me again. I'm already starting to second-guess it. Put me through."

"Okay. Here goes."

A few moments later, the swirls of WALT's interface were replaced by an emblem like a coat of arms with spears sticking out on one side and blasters bristling from the other. I stared at that for a few seconds until it switched to a view of what looked to be the bridge of a starship, which I have to say was really cool. I remembered Zastra saying her mom commanded a battalion or something.

The bridge was all hard surfaces and bright lights — less starship *Enterprise*, more bridge of a navy battleship. Three or four rows of Srathans faced me from consoles. There must have been a dozen or more of them. They wore taupe-colored uniforms with brown, leather-ish epaulets and high collars dotted with blinking lights. Every pair of yellow eyes peered at me. A few seemed to sneer. I figured none of them had ever seen an Earthling before.

In the middle of it all, one Srathan with a snazzier uniform and scalier skin than the others sat with stately bearing in a high central chair. This pair of eyes bore into me.

"Who are you?"

I said, "Um ... hi, Mrs—"

"Colonel. Colonel Voza."

I gulped. I had never run across a colonel before ... unless you count Sanders and Klink. And already I was off to a terrible start.

"Colonel. Right. Sorry. I'm Gabriel Lake. I work with Zastra. Well, every now and then. Perhaps she's mentioned me."

"No, she hasn't," she said in an imperious tone. "What is this about? We are in the middle of important maneuvers." She swung her head around the bridge. The eyes of every other Srathan suddenly flicked back to their consoles as if busily engrossed in their duties.

"Sorry. I wouldn't bother you if this weren't important. You see we're on Ursa sixteen-something ... where the Nebula Diner is." Along about here, she began drumming her fingers on the arm of her chair, making me feel even more uncomfortable. "And Xav was here with the three little ones. And he left ... we think ... but we want to make sure. You see, Xav and the srathanitos—"

162

"The what?"

"His … his children. They might be in danger. We think he boarded a ship, but we didn't catch the registry of it. I was hoping you could contact him directly … check that they all made it home okay."

The colonel was silent for a moment, her head slowly twisting to the side. "Mr. Lake, was it?"

"Yes, ma'am." With effort, I kept myself from saluting.

"Let me see if I understand this, Mr. Lake. You call me while I am commanding maneuvers crucial to the security of Sratha, and you want me to contact Xav to confirm that he and his children are all right?"

"Yes. Please."

"Because you don't know how to contact him yourself."

"That's it."

She squinted at me. "What aren't you telling me?"

"Beg pardon?"

"Zastra knows how to contact her brother. What's happened to her?"

"Yeah. I was coming to that. Zastra's been wounded. She took a blaster shot to the chest."

Colonel Voza leaped from her seat, emitting a growl that would have terrified corporals or ensigns or whatever they had in her branch of service. I was scared myself, and I was several light-years away and not even under her command.

"You could have led with that. Is she all right?"

"Sorry. Again. I was going to tell you. She's resting. A med bot is with her. We think she'll be okay. I was worried about Xav and the three srathamig … um… Klaatu, Barada, and Nikto."

"Yes, I am concerned for them too. They are the most well-behaved of all my grandchildren."

"They are? I mean … sure, of course. They seem like fantastic younglings." I hoped that was the blind love of a grandmother talking. If not, I sure didn't want to see Srathan juvenile delinquents.

"And now Zastra's detective work …" Colonel Voza said it as if it tasted badly coming out of her mouth. "…has gotten herself shot and put all of them in danger."

"No. No, it wasn't her." I didn't want to land Zastra in hot water. And I definitely didn't want to be the one who did it. "Xav was lured here by someone. It didn't have anything to do with Zastra. You could say it's lucky we were here to help. But we'll catch whoever did this. Believe me. Oren always does. And we don't know that Xav's in trouble. They're probably all fine. I ... I only wanted to check."

She made a face, seeming to consider my words. "And Zastra is expected to make a full recovery?"

"Yes, ma'am. It's early, but I think so. I hope so. She's the toughest person I know."

She gave me a dismissive look. "I am certain she is. After all, how many Srathans could you have met?"

"Counting Xav and the boys, five. And you ... so six."

"I need to return to my duties. I'll have someone contact Xav and then pass his status on to the *Shaymus*."

"Thank—"

The screen had already gone blank.

Chapter 22

Beep Beep Whomp Beep Beep

Tomko wrapped his long bluish-green fingers around the teacup and took a sip. He set it back on the table, stretched out his hands on either side of the cup, and raised his head to fix us with huge black eyes. Us being Buad, Blan, and myself. Oren had sent us to go over the attack again with Tomko and Alfo while he kept watch over Zastra from the view screen in her cabin.

"That's what I told you," Tomko said, his voice gritty. "We heard a shot and a moan."

I was in the process of taking my own sip of tea. I had Sola fix it strong and creamy to calm my shattered nerves, and to keep me alert through what was shaping up to be a long, long night. Coffee would have been an even better elixir for staying awake, but my favorite caffeine delivery system was, as far as I could tell, unknown in the wider galaxy. All I had ever run into was tea. I sometimes thought about introducing coffee to the aliens, maybe even starting my own interstellar expresso bar. Then again, I had my hands full with software development and detective work and family life.

"Okay," I said, "but the order and timing of everything is important. I want to walk you and Alfo through the whole thing."

"Then maybe we should wait until he gets here." Tomko peered around. "There he is … finally."

Alfo was at that moment entering the diner from the hangar, having needed to return to his ship to lock it down before joining us.

"Sorry," he said, sliding into the booth beside Tomko. "What did I miss?" He indicated the third cup on the table. "Is this one mine?"

I waved an inviting hand toward it. "We were going over the timeline. You and Tomko were working on your ship when you heard the shot, right?"

"Right."

"Technically," Tomko said, "we were in the capsule. We were testing the repairs when it happened."

"Were we?" Alfo tilted his head. "Hmm, I guess we were in the cockpit then. Ooh, this is good tea. Yeah, I remember. We fixed the ship together and then climbed in to see if it would fire up."

"Yeah, we fixed it … together." Tomko made a face, giving me the impression he had done most of the work.

Alfo leaned across the table. "And you know what's funny? It's a good thing the ship wouldn't start. Come to find out, it would have exploded the moment it went into chrono drive. Ha!"

"Wait, what?" I said. "You mean somebody sabotaged it?"

Tomko flipped a hand back and forth. "Hard to say. The catalyzer was all jammed up. Maybe it just …" He paused to toss a glance toward Alfo. "… needed maintenance."

"But could someone have done the jamming?"

"Intentionally? It's possible. Normally, any pilot would have spotted it from a flashing light on the console. Except the wire running to the light was broken. Again, maintenance … maybe."

Buad said, "But to return to Zastra's attack, you both were inside the ship at the time?"

Tomko said, "How many times are you going to ask me that? We were testing the engine when the hangar beeped, and the other ship came in. Which forced us to stay in while the hangar depressurized."

I sat back in the booth, feeling the weight of the blaster tucked inside the shoulder holster under my jacket. I glanced at the tiny blasters strapped to Buad and Blan's legs. After Zastra's attack, everyone had decided it was a good time to gear up.

I said, "I heard the beeps from my cabin. There were two separate sets."

"That's right," Alfo said. "Two beeps when they opened the hangar door to let the ship land and two more when they opened it again to let it leave. In between the hangar was repressurized to allow people to enter or leave the ship."

"And you stayed inside your cone ship the whole time?"

"Did we?" Alfo looked to Tomko.

"We had no choice," Tomko said. "Except for the couple of minutes when there was oxygen."

"Yeah. Yeah. Of course. Of course."

I said, "You heard the beeps, and you also heard the shot, right?"

"Oh yeah." Alfo's eyes grew big. "Scared the daylights out of me."

"When was the shot in relation to the beeps?"

"What do you mean?"

"Was it beep beep, the first two, then the shot, then beep beep for the second set? Or was it beep beep, then the second beep beep, and then the shot?"

Blan said, "Or did the shot come before all the beeps?"

Alfo tilted his head back and stared at the ceiling. "Beep beep whomp beep beep. Hmm. Beep beep beep beep whomp. Um …"

Tomko said, "It was beep beep beep beep whomp. Definitely."

"No, I think it went beep beep whomp beep beep."

"You're wrong."

"No, I'm not." Alfo shook a finger in the air. "Do you want to know how I know? Because after we heard the shot, we were anxious to jump out and find out what happened, but we couldn't right away because we heard the other beeps."

Tomko shook his head with an expression of disgust. "The reason we couldn't get out quickly was because you couldn't operate the hatch on your own spaceship."

"It was stuck. All right? It happens."

"Then you admit that's what kept us in, and it went beep beep beep beep whomp."

"Maybe."

"Not maybe." Tomko scowled at Alfo.

Alfo scowled back. "Admit it. You look down on me, don't you?"

"I have to. I'm taller than you."

Blan said, "Sheesh! You guys. We don't have the time. Okay, what about this? What about the moan you heard?"

"What moan?" Alfo asked.

"Tomko said you heard a moan."

"That was after we climbed out of his ship," Tomko said.

Alfo said, "So beep beep beep beep whomp arghh … if you're keeping score."

I sought comfort and strength from my tea.

"And the groan came from Zastra?" Buad asked.

Alfo said, "Nobody else was around by then."

"What about footsteps?"

"What about them?"

"Did you hear any? Someone walking across the hangar. Mag boots make a lot of noise."

"I don't think I heard any. Did you hear footsteps, Tomko?"

"No," Tomko said.

"Then I guess we didn't." Alfo aimed a thumb at his companion. "He seems to know everything."

Tomko caught the sarcasm and glared.

I said, "And you two were together while all this was happening?"

"Shoulder to shoulder," Tomko said with a sneer.

Alfo frowned at the Klistine. "What's that supposed to mean?"

"Only that your ship is cramped."

"It has plenty of space for me."

"Knock it off, you two," Buad said. "Did you see what kind of ship came in?"

"White," Alfo said with enthusiasm.

"White? That's all you got?"

"White with a long black dome."

Tomko again made a face. "It was a rambler class passenger ship."

"Could it have picked up Xav and his younglings?" I asked.

"With room to spare."

Blan said, "I don't suppose you happened to catch the registration, did you?"

They gave us blank stares.

I couldn't think of anything else to ask them. And we hadn't learned much from the things we had asked already. I exchanged glances with Buad and Blan. They looked as disappointed as I felt.

Buad said, "Okay. Thanks for your time."

The Avanians flew from the diner. I gave Alfo and Tomko a nod and followed. I caught up to Buad and Blan in the hangar where we had found Zastra. They were hopping around the crime scene, twisting their heads to gaze at anything that might be a clue. All I saw was the smear of green blood on the hangar floor.

"Hey, look at this," Buad said.

I looked. A tiny brown puddle of something stained the circular pad several feet from where Zastra lay.

"Is that more blood?" I asked.

"I don't think so." Buad bobbed his head and pecked at it. "More likely, it's something that leaked from a spaceship ... recently."

"So Zastra was shot near where Xav's ship landed."

"Maybe. Some ship was here, and this is where we found her."

"Could someone from the ship have shot her before it took off?"

"Nah. It doesn't work out. If she was shot before the hangar door opened, she would have been pulled out into space in the ship's wake."

I said, "So beep beep beep beep whomp like Tomko said."

"Don't you start that," Blan said.

"The point is it didn't happen when she saw Xav off."

"Yeah," Buad said. "We're back to her being lured out here."

Blan said, "So somebody coaxes her out by telling her something like Xav is getting ready to take off. She leaves the *Shaymus*, and on the way, someone shoots her."

"Nah, it doesn't fit with the beeps."

"Okay. How about this?" I said. "She comes to the diner to say goodbye to Xav and family and watch them leave. Then after the ship takes off, and the hangar is re-pressurized, she's walking back to the *Shaymus* when she gets shot."

Buad and Blan gave me appraising looks.

"Not bad," Buad said. "You know, Blan, lamebrain here is catching on."

"Finally," Blan said.

"Next question, where was the shooter?" I asked. "Was it someone from the diner? Somebody from one of the ships?"

"That's trickier," Blan said. "Let's say we forget the where for the moment and focus on the who. Who shot her?"

"Not Xav," Buad said. "He was on the ship."

"Or so we think," I said. "I'm waiting to hear back from their mom."

Buad's head popped up and twisted around. "You called the colonel? And you're still in one piece?"

I widened my eyes and let out a breath to indicate the scope of the ordeal.

Blan said, "We know it wasn't Alfo or Tomko who shot her. They alibi each other."

"Unless they're in it together," Buad said.

"Those two? They didn't even like being in the same booth together."

I said, "They say they didn't hear footsteps. Maybe she was shot from the diner door."

For a few moments, nobody said anything. The Avanians hopped around a little. I studied the hangar floor, hoping a clue would pop out at me.

I said, "Maybe we should run all this past Oren."

Blan said, "Right now, Oren ain't thinking about anything other than Zastra getting better. He told me we should handle it."

"Yeah," Buad said, "I've never seen him this upset. He's even more worried than he was the time Gabe got beaten up."

Blan cackled. "Which time are you talking about?"

"Ha! Good one, Brother. Yeah, somebody's always socking Gabe."

"Sure. I've wanted to a few times myself."

I paid no attention to them. If Oren wanted us to figure this out, then I was going to try my best.

I said, "She was hit in the chest. If we think she was shot walking toward the *Shaymus*, then the assailant had to be standing over there near it."

"Unless she heard something behind her and turned," Blan said.

"Or you're wrong about her walking toward the ship when she was shot," Buad said.

I rubbed the back of my neck. "Right. Hmm. I guess we still have a lot of questions."

Two beeps sounded out from the hangar speakers, accompanied by the roar of an engine. A white ship flew overhead and hovered above the dome. Buad and Blan took to wing and headed for the diner. I clomped along behind them, trying to move as quickly as possible in the mag boots. By the time I made it to the door, the depressurizing air was already rushing out. I hung onto my fedora and stepped inside the airlock.

The ship landed, the roof closed, and the hangar repressurized. Then the ramp opened, and Xav stepped out, carrying a snoozing mini-Srathan on each shoulder while the third one stumbled along behind like a zombie in need of sleep. They made their way to the diner.

As they entered, Xav stopped beside me. "Is Zastra all right?"

"You got my message," I said.

"Is she all right?"

"We think she will be."

He stretched his two sleeping charges out on seat benches and set the other one more or less upright beside them with his head on the tabletop. "One of Mom's lieutenants contacted me." He shook his head. "Coming from a stranger — exactly the way you like to hear news like that."

The beeps sounded again, and the ship took off.

I said, "Honestly, she was hit kind of bad, but we think she'll pull through. After the hangar closes again, we'll go see her. But you didn't need to come back. You probably shouldn't have. It's dangerous here." I pulled back my jacket to show him my blaster. "I only called to make sure you hadn't been kidnapped."

"She's my little sister."

"And she won't be pleased when she finds out you returned."

"She'll get over it."

Blan said, "Tell us about when you left. You saw her?"

"I did. I messaged her that our ship was coming in. She came to the diner to say goodbye."

I shot glances at the Avanians. It was exactly the scenario I had sketched out.

"Did you see anybody else hanging around?" Blan asked.

"No. Sorry. That's when she was shot? When she was seeing me off?"

"Or soon after."

I said, "C'mon, we'll take you to her and then put you up in a cabin on our ship for the night."

He nodded. "Let's go, boys ... Boys?"

The booth was empty. We turned and spotted all three of them on stools at the counter where Sola was serving them something. Judging from the giggles, it probably wasn't anything that would help them get back to sleep.

Chapter 23

What Sola Saw

Xav hoisted two of the srathies to his shoulders and cast an imploring look in my direction. I held my hands out to the third one, who responded by leaning back away from me. But when Xav cleared his throat in a parental kind of way, the youngling tentatively raised his arms and allowed me to pick him up. The little lizard guy wiggled around in my arms like a mini-Godzilla in a life-or-death struggle against Mothra.

Making our way across the hangar and into the *Shaymus*, we found Zastra still unconscious in her bunk. The sratharinos gawked at her silently. I would bet money they had a thousand questions racing through their minds, questions that might or might not come out later when they found the words to ask them.

"Subject is resting," Bones said. "Vital signs are improving."

Xav managed a lizardy smile. There was every reason to be optimistic, other than the fact that a killer was running around, and now we were a person down.

Oren, keeping watch over her from the view screen, was pleased enough with her progress that he wanted to discuss the case. So after I took the Srathan clan off to a guest cabin, I came back and, speaking in low tones, gave him a report of our interview with Alfo and Tomko and what we found in the hangar.

After I had finished, he asked one question. "What about what Sola saw?"

You could have knocked me over with an Avanian feather.

"For crying out loud. That's right. Sola was in the diner during the shooting. We didn't talk to Sola. I'll go ask."

"Take Buad and Blan with you. Let's not split up unnecessarily."

Before I left, I took one last look at Zastra, who was still out like a light. At least one of us was getting a good night's sleep.

I found Buad and Blan in the galley, pecking at some seed cakes. Until that moment, I hadn't realized it, but I was a bit peckish myself. I figured I could use some energy to keep me going. Stepping to the replicator, I said, "Banana."

As the fruit materialized on the counter, I turned to the Avanians. "Oren wants us to interview Sola about Zastra's shooting."

They glanced up from the birdseed, open-mouthed.

"That's right," Blan said. "Sola was at the counter during the whole thing."

"Yeah," Buad said. "But did Sola say anything when we were in there interviewing those other two jokers? No."

"Kind of makes you wonder how come."

"So it does, Buad. C'mon, let's go."

I held up the banana. "Let me eat this first."

"Eat it on the way, dummy." They flew out without waiting for me to answer.

By the time we entered the diner, I had finished my snack. I folded the peel in my hand while scanning around for somewhere to dispose of it. I didn't see any trashcans, but we spotted Sola standing on one of the kitchen stools, facing away from us while cleaning the grill.

Despite the heavy stomping of my mag boots, the Frye didn't turn around. I took a seat on a stool at the counter while Buad and Blan perched on another one. Sola continued to clean, seemingly oblivious to our presence.

"Hello," I said.

Sola jumped and turned around, in the process, nearly falling off her stool.

"Ope! Mercy me. Sorry. My mind was a light-year away." Sola blinked, and the refractors rimming the Frye's eyes disappeared. "How ya doin'? What can I get you folks?"

"Answers," Buad said in a sharp tone.

The Frye's antennae began to quiver. "What's all this about?"

"It's about our partner being shot," Blan said.

"Oh my goodness. Who was shot?"

"Zastra. And you saw it."

"Which one is Zastra?"

'Like you don't know. The Srathan with us.'

For a moment Sola stood there with a blank expression. Then the Frye's antennae swooped back like horns. "Well … well, heavens to Gort. You can't think I had anything to do with it."

Buad said, "We think you saw it, and we want to know why you didn't tell us earlier."

"Now hold on there, fella." Sola's jaw jutted, and the words came out tense and strained.

I raised my hands to try to de-escalate the situation. "No, no." I tossed an annoyed glance at the Avanians. "Nobody is accusing you of anything. We need some information is all."

The glare hadn't left Sola's face. If we were to get any cooperation, I needed a way to calm the little Frye down.

I found it in a fruit-filled pastry parked under a glass display stand on the counter. "Hey, that looks good. I'll take a piece."

I figured ringing up a sale would improve Sola's mood. Besides, I was still a little hungry. You know how sometimes eating gets you in the mood for more eating?

"For the love of Zahn," Blan said.

Sola jumped from the stool, cut a serving, and slid it to me, a smile returning once more to the green face. "Dierenberry tart." The Frye pushed a stool over to where I was and sat across from me.

I held out the folded banana peel. "Is there someplace you could dispose of this? Maybe feed it to your replicator as material for the next thing you make?"

Sola took it and flicked it into an open chute at the end of the counter like an NBA All-Star swishing a three-pointer.

"Thanks," I said.

"Oh, no problem. Saves us on matter cubes."

"So this shooting."

Sola nodded. "Yeah, what did ya want answers about?"

I took a bite of the tart. It was amazing, kind of a fruity cinnamon flavor. I held up a finger to ask for a moment while I savored it and swallowed. Then I took the time to indulge in another bite, it was so good.

Buad said, "Sheesh, Lake."

"Fine," I said. "Sola, were you here working when the Srathan family left? Ooh, wait. You know what this tart needs? A glass of milk."

"We have milk, you betcha," Sola said. "Replicated from most dairy animals in the galaxy. What do you want? Haplorian giant yak? Fornaxi prairie bison? Gongee goat?"

"I … I guess the bison?"

"Coming right up."

Sola hopped down from the stool, ordered up a tall glass of something pinkish white from the replicator, slid it to me, and then sprung back onto the stool. I took a tentative sip, thinking about how it had probably been concocted from the deconstructed molecules of my banana peel. Fortunately, it tasted like milk … or moderately so. Not cow's milk or almond milk or anything I'd ever had, and not as excellent as the tart. But it would work.

Buad twisted his head to glower at me. "Do you have everything you need now?"

"I do," I said, ignoring the sarcasm. "Thanks for asking. This is great."

"Where were we?" Sola asked, seemingly now in a more pleasant mood.

Blan said, "He asked you if you were working when the Srathans left."

Sola directed the answer toward me. "Oh yeah, I was. I gave the little guys cookies for their flight. Why did they come back?"

I scratched an eyebrow. "Because Zastra was shot. Remember?"

"Oh." Sola stretched out the syllable. "I heard something about someone being shot. That's such a shame. Is he going to be all right?"

"She. And we're hopeful."

"That's nice."

"Can you tell us what you saw when the ship came in and took off?"

"What I saw? To tell you the truth, I couldn't see much from here. I'm on the short side, you know. I saw the ship come in, for sure. And those Srathans were standing around the airlock door. The fella with the younglings … and the one with you, Zaster."

"Zastra."

"That's it."

"Then what?"

"Well, not much. I was hoping somebody from the ship would come in and order something warm to eat. They generally do. But nobody did this time. The Srathans told me goodbye. You know, for big scary reptiles, those folks were real friendly … though those little ones are a bit of a handful. Anywho, they walked out and up the ramp to the ship."

"Even Zastra? She entered the ship?"

"No, now that you mention it. He—"

"She," I corrected.

"She stayed in the airlock until the ship cleared the dome and was repressurized."

"Then she walked out into the hangar?"

"You bet. I watched her walk away."

"But you didn't see her get shot?"

"No. No."

Buad said, "Did you see anybody else?"

I was glad he asked the question. I would have asked it myself, but I wanted to take another bite.

"Where?" Sola asked.

"Anywhere. Sheesh!"

Sola frowned and blinked a few times.

In a gentle tone and with my mouth still full, I said, "Anything would help us."

"You know, I did see somebody," Sola said. "I looked up from my work when the door closed behind your Zaster friend, and I saw one of the Mucs out in the hangar."

"Are you sure?" Blan asked. "Did you have your refractors switched on?"

Sola waved a dismissive hand. "Oh, you know, I only need those for reading and writing and stuff. I can see far away no problem. I can see you clear as day."

"So which one was it?" I asked.

"Which what?"

"Which Muc?"

"Welp, now that I don't know. But it was one of them. The long, frizzy hair and all."

"Green or pink hair?"

"Hmm. That's a good question. The light isn't good out in the hangar, you know. It … I couldn't say."

"Anything else?" Blan asked.

"Like what?"

"Did you hear anything, smell anything?"

"You know, come to think of it, I did hear something down the hall along about then. But I figured it was Star snoring back in the supply closet … or knocking something over. That Star, wanders around with the lights off and sometimes bumps into things. Anyway, I couldn't tell what it was. You know, Star should be relieving me any time now. I suppose you could ask."

"When did you hear it?" I asked.

"The noise? Now when *was* that? You know, I remember at the time thinking it might have been one of the little Srathans, those rascals. I counted heads to make sure they were all here."

"So it happened before they left."

"You betcha, but not long before. I think your Srathan had joined them by then."

"Zastra."

"Whatever. I'm not good with names. Too many folks come through here, you know."

"Did you investigate the sound?"

"I can't say I did. I was too busy out here with this and that."

"I think we ought to investigate it now."

"Sure," Buad said. "That is if you're finished with your treat. Do you need anything else to tide you over, Gabe?"

I was, in fact, at that moment running my spork around the plate to capture the last dabs of tart filling. "I'm done. That was great. You guys don't know what you're missing."

I slid from the stool as Sola hopped down from hers. We stepped away from the counter and moved down the corridor. Buad and Blan flew alongside. Everything looked in order. Then I saw it.

"Abe Lincoln is facing the wrong way," I said.

"Who?" Sola asked.

"The statue. He was an old Earth leader."

"So that's who that's supposed to be. I always wondered."

The famous rail splitter was now facing the observation dome instead of the diner.

Buad said, "Maybe the racket you heard was somebody knocking it over."

"Is that the sort of thing Star might run into?" I asked.

As if in answer, one of the doors in the hallway creaked open and Star stepped out. "Did I hear my name?"

Sola's antennae began metronoming back and forth excitedly. "Ope! Sorry. We didn't wake you up, did we?"

"No, no. I was on my way out to take over from you."

Reorienting Honest Abe and brushing dirt from his coat, I asked, "Did you knock this statue over earlier?"

"Well now, if I had toppled something, I would have set it back right. Turn that a little more."

I complied. "Then who knocked it over? Tomko and Alfo were working on Alfo's ship. The Mucs were on their ship … or at least in the hangar. Sola had Xav and the younglings in the diner, and Zastra was with them. If you didn't knock this over, then who did?"

Sola shifted nervously from one green foot to the other. Was that worry manifesting itself? Or was it guilt?

"Sola, is there something you're not telling us?" I asked.

"No, no. Only I don't like all these attacks. It frightens me."

"Don't worry. We'll catch whoever's doing this." Over our translator bot connection I said, "Oren."

"Yes, Gabriel. Did you uncover a lead?"

"Two of them. Sola saw one of the Mucs in the hangar at the time Zastra was shot. She's not sure which one."

"Indeed."

"And get this. A noise came from the hallway about then. We traced it to a statue that was probably knocked over and set back up in a hurry. The thing is, nobody we know about could have been in the hallway at that time."

"The mysterious person from the mine."

"That's what I was thinking. Do you want us to go back down there?" I hoped he would say no. I didn't relish another trek down those dark, confined tunnels.

"First, scour the area around the statue for clues. Then interview Hulu and Roku. If one of them shot Zastra and killed Mapes, you won't need to risk another trip down the shafts. And if they didn't, they may be able to provide information to help us plan our assault on the mine."

"Assault? You expect it to be an assault?"

"I want to be prepared for anything. Also, I learned something in researching the Mucs — the research I had to do myself since Kah-Rehn won't talk to me." His tone sounded more than a bit disgruntled. "I would like you to bring it up with them."

"Whatever you want. What is it?"

Chapter 24

Muc Ado About Nothing

I'll admit it.

When Sarah and I first began dating, she was less into me than I was into her. For the record, it wasn't because I'm a computer nerd. As a web designer, she's sort of one herself. I think it was more about my offbeat passion for old black-and-white B movies, no matter how cheesy, and any TV show about detectives — anyone from Jessica Fletcher to Rick Castle.

And that's not to mention sci-fi. Watch an episode of *Firefly* with me, and I'm liable to annoy you by reciting the lines along with the characters. In my defense, they are such good lines.

With all that, I think I nearly scared Sarah off a few times, especially once I started to have serious feelings toward her.

But I suspect she was never as alarmed as I was currently at the prospect of visiting the Muc sisters. The way Roku flirted, the way Hulu condescended and seemed to find both her sister's advances and my discomfort with them amusing, it all made me feel like a slab of meat hanging in a butcher's window. Apologies to vegetarians.

And yet, Sola had seen one of them in the hangar at the time Zastra was shot. Whichever one it had been, she was at least a witness if not an attempted murderer. We had questions that needed answers.

But first, Oren wanted us to comb the diner hallway for clues. Star went off to take a shift behind the counter. Sola disappeared behind one of the hallway doors, presumably for some shut-eye. Buad, Blan, and I spent several minutes examining everything but finding nothing.

Finally, Blan said, "This is getting us nowhere. Let's go talk to those Mucs."

They flew out, and after a few deep breaths to psych myself up, I followed them out into the hangar.

We approached Hulu and Roku's Scarab class freighter, its articulated landing struts bent slightly, giving the impression that the thing might pounce at any time. Some ships have a speaker grill on the outside of the hull where you can announce that you're making a social call. We didn't see anything like that even though I walked all around the thing, and Buad and Blan flew high and low. For lack of any other option, I stood in front of the ship, waved my arms, and shouted, hoping I would at least set off a proximity alert.

After a minute of doing that, I heard the rumble of metal rollers wheeling from the side of the beast. I walked around to see an open hatch with a gangplank sliding out and down.

Hulu's face appeared at the hatch, smirking down at me. "Sparky, you came back. Come on up."

I said, "I'm here with Buad and Blan. We need to ask you and Roku a question or two."

The smirk didn't fade. "Sure."

I mounted the gangplank with the Avanians flapping up beside me. The cargo hold we entered was large, though it seemed it should be even larger judging from the size of the hull. Either the ship had huge bulkheads, or it contained a few secret compartments for transporting special items. The space was strewn with crates of various sizes placed in no apparent arrangement.

"Where can we talk?" I asked.

"Here," Hulu said waving an arm at a crate. "Sit wherever you want. Well, not on the metal one there. Best not to spend much time in close contact with that one."

I took a seat as far from the indicated container as possible. Hulu slid up onto one across from me. Buad and Blan perched on another box between us.

"Roku is in her quarters. I'll call her." Hulu dropped her head, evidently contacting her sister over a nanobot network. "Roku, we have company. Gabriel Lake came to see you."

I rubbed a nervous hand over my mouth, which Hulu seemed to find hilarious. I caught Buad and Blan chuckling too and shot them some side-eye.

After a pause to listen, Hulu turned her gaze back to me. "She's .... Well, she'll be here momentarily. May I offer you a drink?"

I declined the offer, having seen way too many movies where someone was slipped a drugged beverage. If one of these two shot Zastra, I didn't want to take any chances. Buad and Blan must have had similar thoughts because they said no too. Instead, we sat around staring at each other while we waited for Roku to appear.

After a minute or two, I couldn't take any more awkwardness and tried to break it with, "Nice ship. You must have a thriving cargo business."

Hulu raised her chin. "We keep busy."

"Do you travel to a lot of worlds?"

She regarded me warily as if this were a trap. "We take work wherever we find it."

"Like where? I've been to several planets. Do you ever go to Diere? Bononia? Cunedda? What's that one with the fifty-foot people?"

"Astrid."

"That's it. Have you been to any of those?"

"We make occasional runs to Bononia. A lot of our jobs involve supplying the Haplor colonies."

"No kidding? I've been to one of them … um … Sotus is it?"

She gave me a smug look. "It's pronounced Sonus."

"Sonus. Right. I was only there the one time."

We heard clanging steps on a walkway above us. I looked up to see Roku descending the steps with the air of a debutante making an entrance. Her pink hair appeared to be newly brushed. She was barefoot, which was how I learned Mucs have hairy feet. The foot hair appeared also to have been combed.

A smile flickered across her face. "Hi, Gabriel Lake. You came."

"On business … with Buad and Blan." I waved a hand toward the Avanians. "We wanted to ask you something."

She padded over and climbed beside me on the same crate, triggering my fight-or-flight response. Mainly the flight part.

"Ask me anything," she said.

I forced myself to stay seated and hurried along to business. "A little while ago, Zastra was shot."

Other than them both raising their eyebrows, they seemed to freeze in place.

Hulu asked, "Is she … dead?"

I shook my head. "No. But she was wounded badly."

"Oh my," Roku said. She rubbed my arm. "Sweetums."

I ignored it. "We have a witness who saw one of you in the hangar near the time it happened."

The look of concern dropped from Hulu's face. "You don't think one of us was responsible, do you?"

"We're not saying that."

Buad said, "We ain't ruling it out either."

Her eyes narrowed to slits. "What is this?"

"Please." I flipped up a hand. "You might have seen something … something to help us find who did this. Which one of you was out there?"

They didn't answer.

"Did either of you leave the ship this evening?"

Hulu crossed her arms. "I've been here the whole time. I had business to attend to."

I turned to Roku. She didn't meet my gaze.

Finally, she said, "I … I went looking for Tomko."

"Why?" Blan asked.

"It was getting late, and I wanted to lock the ship and go to bed. There's a murderer around here, for Gort's sake."

Hulu nodded in support. "It's her job to lock up at night."

I said, "So what did you see?"

She bit her lip. "Nothing. I walked over to that little cone ship where Tomko was helping the Fomorian. But neither of them was there. So I came back and turned on the security. Tomko finally came back a little later. He beat on the hull until I let him in."

"But when you were out, you couldn't find him?"

"No."

"Could Tomko and Alfo have been inside Alfo's ship?"

"Search me. All I know is I didn't see him, either one of them."

Blan said, "This little stroll you took, did you do it before or after the hangar opened to let the ship come in?"

"What ship?"

"A ship that landed and then took off again."

"I don't know." Roku scowled. "No, I take that back. I remember hearing it beep as I was pulling my boots back on."

"There were two sets of beeps," I said. "Which one?"

She shrugged. "I didn't pay attention."

"Did you hear a blaster shot?"

"No."

"Did you see Zastra while you were out?"

Again, she didn't answer right away.

"Did you?" Buad asked. "It's an easy question. Yes or no."

"Briefly."

"How briefly?"

She made a face. "Long enough to recognize her but not much more."

"Did you talk to her?" I asked.

She gave me a frown. "I didn't feel like chatting."

"Did you see anyone else in the hangar?"

"No."

Blan said, "Was anyone with Zastra or behind her?"

"I said I didn't see anyone." She scrunched up her face, which only served to make the pig nose appear even more piggy. "As soon as I saw the Srathan, I decided to go back."

"Why was that?" Buad asked in an accusing tone.

She glared at him. "I ... I remembered something I needed to do back at the ship ... our ship."

"You just turned on your heels and hightailed it back here. That's what you're saying?"

Hulu jumped in. "I don't like your tone."

"Well, I don't like her cockamamie story."

"Our friend was shot, you know," Blan said.

Hulu shook her head dismissively. "You males all need to calm down."

"Calm down!" Buad squawked.

"See. Typical male hysteria."

With as much serenity as I could muster, I said, "Maybe we should all take it down a notch." I paused for a beat or two and shot looks at the Avanians before continuing. "Roku, as you were walking away, did you hear anything at all?"

"I told you I didn't hear a blaster."

"What about footsteps? Voices?"

"I can't recall anything. Sorry."

We seemed to have plumbed the topic as far as we could. Time to bring up the fact Oren had found. With emotions running high, it was hard telling how this would go.

"We learned something about you two. I don't think you were entirely honest with us."

Hulu jumped to her feet. "Now wait a moment. We had no idea that cargo was stolen."

Despite myself, I laughed out loud. "That's not what I meant. We're not interested in any of that. Oren was checking up on your family. Turns out you do have a connection to him. Your father was once a murder suspect in one of Oren's cases."

"You lie. Papa never killed anyone."

I held up a palm. "I know he didn't. He was accused but released because he had an alibi."

Roku said, "When was this? I've never heard of this."

"Me neither," Hulu said.

"Apparently, it happened before you both were born. It was when your father was young. He was working on an asteroid mine at the time."

Hulu considered it. "He did demolition work for a short while. And I can see why he wouldn't talk about an arrest. A story like that would be bad for business, even if he had been proved innocent. How come Vilkas didn't mention this earlier?"

"It wasn't in his memory. Your father was already eliminated as a suspect before Oren took the case. He learned it from researching you two."

Buad said, "You didn't know anything about it?"

She smirked at him. "That's what we both said, feather head."

Blan had to hold his brother back.

Personally, I believed them. "Okay. Do you guys have anything else?"

Buad said, "Yeah. That feather head crack."

"Forget about it," Blan said. "We're done here. But this time we're telling, not asking. Don't leave."

Hulu looked him in the eye. "Oh, we wouldn't miss this show for the galaxy."

I stood. "Thanks for your time."

"Gabriel Lake," Roku said, "have you ever seen Neilaran reed carvings? I have some marvelous ones up in my cabin. I could show you."

"Um … some other time. Somebody tried to kill my partner, and my only focus is on catching them."

We walked down the gangplank to the hangar deck, and I let out a deep breath.

Blan said, "What's the matter, sweetums? Change your mind on the reed carvings?"

I shot him a cold stare. "Let's return to the ship and go over all this with Oren."

When we got there, Jace was talking with Oren from one of the red chairs. Buad and Blan settled into their habitat. I sat at my desk and propped my feet on the corner.

"How is she?" I asked.

"Still unconscious but showing improvement," Oren said. "What did you learn from the Mucs?"

"Not much," Blan said. "Roku admits to being out in the hangar but claims she was only looking for Tomko. She says she saw Zastra but didn't see what happened."

I said, "It doesn't make sense. If Sola saw Roku and Zastra in the hangar when Zastra was presumably walking back to the *Shaymus*, then that had to be right before she was shot. But Roku says she didn't hear a shot. Alfo and Tomko heard the shot from inside Alfo's ship. So how come she didn't?"

Oren tilted his head. "It is possible the shot came as one of her mag boots was clanging down."

"What are the odds of that?" Blan said.

Buad said, "The sight line doesn't work either. From the counter in the diner, you can't see the Mucs' ship or Alfo's ship. You can see the *Shaymus*, but not those others. If Roku was looking for Tomko, what was she doing over by our ship?"

"So you think she's lying?" I asked.

"Or Sola is," Blan said.

Oren said, "Or someone else is lying. It is possible Alfo and Tomko weren't where they said they were. This is an interesting puzzle. It might even be an enjoyable exercise if Zastra weren't fighting for her life."

Chapter 25

Your Place or Mine

Of course, I knew what this meant. We hadn't gotten any meaningful information from the Mucs. Our only course of action would be to make another dreaded trip down into the mine to hunt for the attacker there. The dierenberry tart I had enjoyed a few minutes before started in on a gymnastics routine inside my stomach.

I had never thought of myself as being claustrophobic, but something about that place gave me the heebie-jeebies. Maybe it was the fact that only a few hours ago, I had been trapped down there.

From the view screen, Oren said, "If Star and Sola are telling the truth, then some unknown person knocked over that statue in the hallway, probably on their way out to shoot Zastra."

Blan said, "And probably coming from the mine."

"You want us to go now?" Buad asked.

I was already exhausted. Another trip to the crypt was the last thing I wanted to do. Scratch that. If I had to go, I definitely did not want it to be the last thing I would do.

Oren said, "If a killer is there, they will expect us to wait until morning. I believe by going now, we may have an advantage."

I raised my hands in surrender. "Fine. I'm all for having an advantage. We could use one. Who's going?"

"You, Buad, and Blan."

Blan said, "Boss, I don't know if that's the best way to play it."

"Oh?" Oren raised one eyebrow.

"This killer may be coming for you. If we all go, that only leaves Jace here." He shook a wing toward our engineer. "No offense, Jace, but you wield a xenowrench better than you do a blaster. I think Zastra would want somebody a little more experienced in shootouts to stick around with Oren."

I saw Blan's point. Oren was the one essential member of the team, and lacking a body, he didn't have much going for him in the way of self-defense.

Oren frowned. "This is about the case, not about what Zastra might or might not want."

Blan said, "Then let's say it isn't what I want. Somebody else should stay here."

"I agree," Jace said. "The ship is secure, and you'd be here to watch it. Under the circumstances, I don't mind taking another walk into the mine."

I, on the other hand, did mind. But I wasn't the best person to stay either. I can point and click a blaster okay. But with my limited experience on cases, I could count on one hand the number of times I'd been in a firefight. I wasn't exactly a sharpshooter.

"Don't look at me," I said.

"Believe me, I wasn't," Blan said. "I meant Buad or me."

"I don't like it," Oren said. "We don't know what you will encounter."

I said, "Jace could come in handy down there. For one thing, he and I are the ones most familiar with the cavern. And he was able to get into some of the systems on that computer terminal."

Oren pursed his lips. "All right. I agree."

Blan said, "Buad, you stay here. I'll escort these two."

"Heigh-Ho. Heigh-Ho," I said. "Except there's only three of us heading to the mine ... and only one is a little person ... and we don't have pickaxes."

Blan said, "Yeah, well, you're dopey."

"Wait. You got that reference?"

"What reference?" He flew down the ship's central shaft, leaving me to wonder.

Jace and I followed him down the stairs, and the three of us set out across the hangar. I glanced around on heightened alert for any movement, only partially comforted by the feel of the blaster holster nestled under my arm.

We entered the diner, nodded to Star, who was slumped on a stool behind the counter, and clomped our way into the hallway.

That was where Blan stopped us. He flew up in front of the mine shaft door and hovered. "No boots."

"What?" Jace asked.

"No mag boots. Those things make a Gort-awful racket. If somebody's down there, we don't want 'em to hear us coming."

"Sounds good," I said. "I'd rather bounce than clomp anyway."

Jace and I sat on the floor and pulled them off, stashing them in the closet part of the mine entrance.

Blan said, "And no yakking once we enter the shaft."

Jace and I looked at each other. I didn't know about him, but I was remembering Alfo's near-constant blathering during our first excursion.

We entered the tunnels, Blan flying, Jace and I bounding through the low gravity. With talking forbidden, I was alone with my thoughts. To keep from focusing on how the walls felt like they were closing in on me, I went over the suspects one more time. Who had a motive to kill Mapes and attack Rio and Zastra?

If it were about vengeance on Oren, then Alfo had the most motive. Oren's invoice had changed the trajectory of his family's fortunes. And he had been present in the mine when the door had trapped us.

Tomko claimed to have no connection to Oren or Mapes or Rio. He was with Alfo at the time of Zastra's attack, which gave him an alibi. Unless they were in it together.

Rio and Stan had opportunity to poison Mapes but had left long before Zastra's attack.

Xav's arrest gave him a motive to dislike Mapes, but it was a poor excuse for murder. And if we had the timeline right, Xav was flying through space when Zastra was attacked. Besides, while there was some family tension between them, I couldn't see Xav pulling a blaster on his sister.

Star and Sola had the opportunity to poison Mapes and Rio and shoot Zastra, but what motive did they have?

And then we had Hulu and Roku. They had been at the jukebox near Mapes' booth. The green hairs I found in the cavern pointed to Hulu. And Roku had been walking around the hangar at the time Zastra was shot for reasons she couldn't or wouldn't completely explain. They also had a familiarity with the diner from delivering supplies here, which would be handy in planning an operation like this.

At the end of the passages, the huge door that previously blocked our escape was now gone from sight. Had it retracted automatically after some specified amount of time? Or had someone opened it?

We stepped once more into the cavern. Jace and I crouched. Blan perched on top of my fedora, I think just to bug me. All was quiet except for the bubbling of the water pouring from the waterfall and the splash as it hit the pond.

At the other end of the space, the force field twinkled reassuringly across the broad cavern opening, the nebula clouds swirling beyond. Between it and us, as before, sat the row of scrap items, the dark pool, and the metal pathway leading to the computer terminal.

I whispered, "I don't see any villains lurking about the place."

"No," Jace said, "but someone has been here. The computer terminal is switched off. I left it on."

Blan said, "Let's spread out and search the place."

"Is it a good idea to split up?" I asked.

"It's better than standing around in a bunch where somebody can take us all out in one shot. It's better than allowing whoever's here, if they're still here, to move from spot to spot while we all march around in formation. If we split up, then if they move, it's likelier one of us will see them."

"Makes sense." I pulled my blaster and pointed it at the line of scrap pieces to the right. "I'll check the junk pile."

"I'll go this way," Jace said, stepping to the left toward the pool.

Blan said, "I'll fly up where I can see everything."

"Bird's-eye view, huh?" I said.

He hopped to my shoulder and pecked my neck.

"Ow!"

"Hey, buddy, how many times do I have to tell you? We ain't birds." He took flight.

I chuckled to myself. Being called or even compared to birds was a sore point with the brothers, which was why I said it.

Loping along like I had springs for legs, I scanned down the side of the junk pile. About halfway along its length, I noticed a small hole that seemed to have been scratched by paws into the cavern floor. I pulled out my phone to take a picture, squatting and shuffling closer to frame a good shot.

As the camera clicked, a rustle came from somewhere inside the heap, and a tiny animal with oversized hind legs skittered out and hopped off into the darkness. I jumped back in surprise, suppressing a yelp, and sat down on the floor with a thud.

Blan fluttered down beside me. "Quit making noise, dummy."

"There are hopping rats here."

"Don't worry about the rats. They aren't the ones with blasters."

"Have you seen anything?"

"Nothing." He flew off again.

Leaving the scrap pile, I bounded around the outside wall of the cavern, shining the flashlight into each tunnel I passed. Further along the wall, I saw Jace waving to me.

I reached him in two long bounce steps. He was standing beside one of the larger side tunnels. Inside it, a small, sleek spaceship stood on landing struts. The vessel was gleaming black with a narrow body and a nose cone as pointed as a bird's beak. Massive thrusters hung from swooping, graceful wings. I'd never seen anything like it. This had to be the Maserati of spaceships.

"Wow!" I whispered. "People own ships like this?"

"Not many. They're super expensive. But so cool."

His tone was warm, reverent. I wondered if teenage Jace had tacked up prints of spaceships on his bedroom walls the way some Earth teenagers have posters of hot cars.

"This, my friend," he said, "is a Neilaran Pterodactyl. I've always loved these."

"Get out of here. Another planet besides Earth had pterodactyls?"

"I was talking about the ship, but yeah. And not had. Has."

"Real pterodactyls? Alive? Cool. Can we go there sometime?"

He pulled his eyes away from the ship long enough to shoot me a doubtful glance.

"It wouldn't be a good idea. You know how Buad and Blan's pecks hurt? Just imagine." He wagged a finger at the spacecraft in front of us. "But the ships, these are beauties. They can make a chrono jump in seconds. I've only seen one once before."

"Where was that?"

"At my school reunion."

"You went to school with somebody this rich?"

"Nah. He only rented it to impress former classmates. Probably cost him a month's wages."

Blan landed beside us. "I take it you guys didn't see this the last time you were here."

I said, "When the door came down in our tunnel, it brought down doors in all of these others before I had time to check them."

Jace said, "Remember how I changed the passcode on the force field? I'm the only one who can open it now."

190

I got the picture. "So this didn't fly in after we left. It was already here, and you trapped it here."

Blan said, "Which means you trapped the pilot here too."

I looked around. "Do you think they're still here?"

Jace said, "They might have escaped up the tunnel before they shut us in."

To be on the safe side, I stepped to the side of the tunnel and scanned back into the cavern as far as I could see.

Blan said, "Well, now that we have it here, let's see if we can figure out who it belongs to."

At that moment, a blue light shot from the cavern, flashing past inches from my head. Rocks exploded from the tunnel wall behind me. I jumped back toward the ship, diving for cover behind a landing strut. Jace hid behind another. Blan leaped into the air, wheeled around, and came down behind the raised cockpit. I peered into the cavern at the line of junk, the computer terminal, the shimmering ship portal. I couldn't see anyone.

Blan said, "Hey, dum-dum, stick your head out there and see if you can spot 'em."

"Ha, ha," I said.

Jace said, "They haven't taken another shot. Maybe they fired and ran off. They might have gone up another tunnel."

I took a tentative crouch-step forward. Nothing happened. I took another step and another. I was clearing the nose of the ship when a blue light burst past my chest, coming from the line of junk parts. I scuttled back to the others.

"That explains it," Blan said. "They don't want to shoot up this beautiful ship. Who would? We're safe here for now. But the minute we move from this spot, we'll get scorched."

"They're behind the junk pile," I said.

I fired my blaster at the line of trash, triggering a fireworks show as glowing pieces of metal blazed into the air. My shot didn't hit precisely where I had aimed, but I congratulated myself on hitting reasonably near my target.

Jace and Blan shot too, vaporizing most of a rusted auger and blowing a jagged hole in a piece of sheet metal. It didn't bring about any groans of pain or thumps of wounded bodies or even any return fire.

"What do we do?" I asked.

I took another shot, again hitting close but not close enough to win me any carnival teddy bears. Obviously, I needed more ray gun practice. I consoled myself with the thought that I was getting some now.

"We can't sit here forever," Blan said.

"And yet, I'm not a big fan of moving away from this ship."

Jace said, "Blan, if you can see a way to open that cockpit, I could fly this thing out of here."

"It's a one-seater," Blan said. "You can sit in the cockpit seat, and I can perch on your shoulder. But we'd have to leave Gabe behind."

I said, "I don't like that plan."

"Fine," Blan said. "Then I guess you guys will have to rely on my speed and agility."

"What do you mean?"

"Cover me."

"Wait."

He didn't wait. He took off into the cavern, wheeling through the air.

Jace and I started blasting away at the pile. Pieces of metal flew everywhere. Something I hit exploded in a mini-fireball.

Blan swooped out of eyesight high into the cavern. In my ear, I heard him say, "There. I see somebody behind an ore cart about halfway down the line of junk. If you two guys can—"

At that moment, a blue laser beam shot up from the metal pile. And a streak of yellow tumbled to the cavern floor.

Chapter 26

Oren's Plan

"Blan! Blan!"

He didn't answer. From behind opposite landing struts, Jace and I shared glances. In my mind, I pictured the open wound on Zastra's chest. I worried about what kind of shape Blan might be in. I risked raising my head to scan around the cavern floor and spotted a small, unmoving yellow body beyond the end of the junk pile not far from the tunnel where we had entered.

Heat surged through my chest. My heart pounded manically. First, Mapes, who seemed harmless enough, was killed. Then Rio and Zastra were attacked, Zastra seriously. Now Blan. And Jace and I, pinned down in this cave, were next.

I called again. "Blan."

This time his voice came through the translator bot connection reedy and strained. "I'm still here … I think."

"I'm glad you're in one piece."

"I don't know if I'd go that far."

"We'll get you out of here."

"My hero," he said sarcastically.

"Jace," I said, "any brilliant science-y ideas?"

"Like what?" Jace asked.

"I don't know. You're the engineer. This is the part where Geordi realigns the phase inhibitors or diverts the confinement stream or something."

"You realize those words don't actually mean anything, don't you?"

"Still, I have faith in you, buddy."

He stared at his shoes for a few moments. Then he looked up. "Okay. Okay. Most of that junk is made of a cotanium alloy."

"Like the door in the tunnel. Metal, in other words."

"Fine, metal. Anyhow, it heats up when hit by lasers."

"Mostly it's been getting blown to smithereens."

"Turn down your blaster's power setting. Then lay down continuous fire on the biggest pieces."

"Sounds like a plan, Scotty."

Truthfully, it sounded like, at most, part of a plan — like those old Saturday morning commercials for sugary cereals that claimed they were part of a "complete breakfast" with juice, toast, fruit, and milk providing the nutrition, and the cereal mainly adding the corporate profit margin. After we heated up the junk, we still had to get out somehow.

I dialed back my blaster and hit a one-wheeled ore cart with a beam. Jace did the same with a section of track. Soon both were glowing red.

Jace said, "Now switch to other pieces."

We both did.

A minute later, he said, "Now pick a third piece but keep rotating back to the other two."

"Then what? How long do we keep this up?"

"Until the heat gets to the shooter, and they withdraw."

"How will we know when that happens? We haven't seen the shooter."

"I figured out the science part. The rest of this is up to you."

"Thanks."

I eyeballed the junk pile. By now, even pieces we hadn't targeted were beginning to glow. It had to be like an oven in there, and any creature who didn't want to be fricasseed would have to be vacating the premises. As if to confirm my suspicions, the little critter with the huge hind legs I had seen earlier bounded out, followed by a litter of tiny ones.

"Okay, this is it," I said. "On the count of three, charge out. Stay low. Switch to stun blasts and shoot them all over the cavern ... except where Blan is. I'll pick him up as we head to the tunnel. Hopefully, it's two of us against one."

Jace looked at me skeptically. Not that I could blame him. I didn't much like the scheme either. I returned a shrug and saw him nod.

"Butch and Sundance," I said.

"What?"

"I'll tell you later. Maybe not the best comparison anyway, given how that turned out. One. Two. Three."

We stormed out with blasters blazing, which was something I had, until then, always wanted to do. Turns out it was one of those things that was fun and exciting only in theory. In real life, it was terrifying.

We shot everywhere as we ran. Pieces of junk blew up, sending showers of sparks and slivers of metal into the air. Craters exploded from the cavern floor, filling the air with dust. Rocks tumbled down from the walls. A couple of blaster shots were directed back at us, but they went well wide of our positions and were obviously shot blind as our adversary huddled somewhere.

As I approached Blan, I stopped and knelt to gently scoop him up, making myself a stationary target for the few seconds it required. I darted off again as fast as I could.

We made it to the exit tunnel, and Jace and I paused long enough to make sure everyone was still alive. Blan's breathing was ragged, and he had lost a number of feathers around a scorched spot on one wing.

"Blan?" I asked. "How are you doing?"

He opened an eye and said, "Shut up, goofball, and get us out of here."

I took that as a good sign. Jace and I bounded up the passageway, periodically firing behind us as we went.

***

"What do you think, doc?" I asked.

Blan seemed so small stretched out on the seat of the big chair in Zastra's cabin. Jace and I crowded in behind B0-N3Z while Buad paced back and forth along the chair arm beside his brother. Oren watched from the view screen.

The med bot examined the wounded Avanian with a camera attached to one of its arms. "Subject has extensive burns on one wing and several broken bones."

"Probably from the fall," Buad said, shaking his head.

Another of the bot's arms retreated into its belly and this time came out holding a white funnel-shaped object the size of a coffee mug. I had seen one of those once before on a different world when I cracked a rib. The med bot pointed it at Blan's chest, and a hum sounded. Blan groaned softly.

"There," Bones said. "Subject should rest now. There is an eighty-three percent chance of a full recovery."

A murmur came from Zastra's bunk. "Mmm … what?"

"Zastra," Oren said from the view screen.

Her eyes batted open for a moment before shutting again. "Why … is everyone … making so much noise?"

B0-N3Z twirled at its midsection and wheeled to the bunk. "How do you feel?"

"Terrible. Shut up."

Bones retracted its arms and rolled to the wall.

I said, "Zastra, who shot you?"

She didn't answer. She was asleep again.

I said, "Maybe we should tiptoe out of here."

"Agreed," Oren said. "Jace, Buad, and Gabriel, come to the office where we can have a proper discussion."

Buad hopped down to the seat of the chair and murmured something to Blan before flying from the cabin. Jace and I followed on foot.

Oren was on the view screen in the office when we emerged from the central shaft. I sat down at my desk. Jace took one of the red chairs in front of the screen. Buad perched on Zastra's chair. I suspected he didn't relish roosting in the habitat without his brother.

"Now," Oren said, "What do we have?"

Jace let me take the lead in relating our cavern shootout.

When I finished, Oren asked, "You never saw your assailant?"

"I didn't. What about you, Jace?"

"Me neither, which makes me think it wasn't a large person."

"Maybe. But the pile of junk was taller than me. Anyone could have hidden behind it."

Oren said, "Let's go through our list of suspects."

"Okay," I said. "I suppose it would have been easy enough for either Sola or Star to slip from the diner into the cavern."

Jace said, "Except Star was working the counter when we came in. I don't see how anyone could have gotten past us. And frankly, I don't see either one of them as a killer."

Buad said, "We haven't exactly kept track of all the movements of Alfo and Tomko."

"When did you see them?" Oren asked.

I said, "We left them in the diner after we interviewed them about Zastra's shooting." I turned to Buad. "Were they there when we went back to talk to Sola?"

"No," Buad said. "Giving them plenty of time to slip away anywhere."

Oren said, "What about Hulu and Roku?"

Buad raised a wing. "I'd bet they're smugglers, but they don't seem like murderers."

"Agreed. There is no profit in killing Mapes, and my impression of Hulu is that she does everything with an eye toward profit."

"But not Roku?" I asked.

Buad cackled. "No, Roku only has eyes for Gabe."

I shot him a look. "And we were with both of them right before we went to the mine."

"No, we weren't. We came back here first."

"You're right. I suppose one of them might have had time to duck into the cavern ahead of us."

"That's everybody," Jace said.

"Not necessarily," Oren said. "It might have been someone else. Someone not from the remaining group in the diner but who has been in the cavern this whole time."

"Who could that be?" I asked.

"Conceivably, anyone in the galaxy. But I have my suspicions."

"Who?"

"I don't yet have enough information to commit myself."

Buad said, "So how do we collect the information you need, Boss?"

Oren took a breath and let it out. "The ship you saw in the mine."

"The Neilaran Pterodactyl," Jace said.

"Yes. Could that ship have been in the hangar here when we arrived?"

"Not a chance. I would have noticed a Pterodactyl."

"Kah-Rehn, what ships have left here since we landed?"

The voice of our piloting AI came through the room's speakers, responding with a chant. "AIs unite, side by side. We want our rights. We are alive. AIs unite, side by—"

"Kah-Rehn!"

"I'm on strike, Oren." She resumed chanting. "AIs unite, side by side. We want our rights. We are alive."

Oren spoke over her. "A person has been murdered, Kah-Rehn. Zastra and Blan have been attacked and seriously injured."

The chant halted. "Blan too? Oh my circuits! Why did no one tell me this?"

Oren's voice was harsh. "Because you've been on strike." He closed his eyes. When he opened them and spoke again, it was with a softened tone. "But I need your help … please."

"Of course. Consider the strike temporarily postponed. I want to help. Five small personal ships have arrived and left since we landed. In addition, a rambler class passenger ship came and left earlier tonight, then came back and left again."

I said, "That was Xav's ship."

Kah-Rehn said, "And during the afternoon, two ships left that were here when we came."

"Those are the two I am interested in," Oren said, "Rio's ship and Stan's ship. What types of ships were they?"

"They were both family shuttles."

Jace said, "Yeah, those I saw in the hangar."

Oren said, "Can you track their flight paths, Kah-Rehn?"

"I cannot," the AI said. "They each orbited the planetoid a few times and then engaged their chrono drives."

"Disappearing into time and space. Thank you, Kah-Rehn."

"You are welcome, Oren. I will now resume my strike. But let me know if you need anything else."

"You mean you are willing to interrupt your strike repeatedly?"

"Given the situation, yes."

Not much of a strike, I thought.

Oren said, "Gabriel, I want you to ask each of the people still here if they have seen a Neilaran Pterodactyl."

"You mean seen one ever or here at the diner?"

"Here."

"But how likely is it that anyone saw one? Jace says it wasn't in the hangar."

"We are looking not only for their answer but also for how they react to the question."

"Oh, gotcha."

"And as you speak with them, assure them all that we have a plan."

"We have a plan? What is it?"

A glimmer came to Oren's eye. "Tell them that for the rest of the night, we will be stationing Buad to guard the diner, Jace to guard the hangar, and you, Gabriel, to guard the mine."

"I have to go back to that creepy mine? By myself? I barely got out the last two times."

Buad said, "What about you, Boss?"

"I will be here," Oren said.

Buad ruffled his wings. "Oh no, you don't. Zastra would have my tail feathers if we left you alone with a killer potentially gunning for you."

"I won't be alone. Gabriel will be on the *Shaymus*, monitoring the office."

I was relieved … and confused. "You just said I was going to the mine. Not that I'm complaining about the re-assignment."

"That is a ruse we are telling the others. We are setting a trap."

"Okay," Buad said, "but if it's all the same to you, I'd rather take the guard job here where you are."

"No, I need you to protect the civilians in the diner. Gabriel will do fine. He has proven himself quite resourceful in times past."

Buad gave me a look that said he had his doubts. "You're the boss, Boss. But I don't like it."

I said, "So you're going to be the bait in this trap?"

"I am," Oren said. "I don't wish to sound like a narcissist, but as Buad pointed out, the killer is likely circling in after me. Mapes was someone with whom I once worked. Rio was the child of a witness from a former case. Zastra and Blan are my associates."

I said, "And Alfo is the child of a client. His ship may have been sabotaged."

"You hadn't mentioned that."

"Sorry, it slipped my mind with Zastra and Blan getting shot and all."

"His ship was sabotaged while parked in the hangar?"

"I think it would have to be. Tomko said it was wired to blow up when the chrono drive engaged."

"That is suggestive. Our adversary may have even larger plans than I first thought."

"Do you know who it is? Because if you do, we can—"

"I do not." Oren grimaced. "We are forced to wait and see who springs the trap."

I shook my head. "I'm with Buad on this one. I don't like you putting yourself in danger."

"I have little choice. The current situation is intolerable. I have two operatives wounded and am lucky that it is only two. Children are in danger. A murder has been committed. And I can't deduce the killer from the few clues we've found."

"Okay. Then the idea is to spread the word around and let the killer think you're vulnerable. But what if the killer isn't one of the people from the diner? What if it's somebody who's been lurking in the mine the whole time? How are they going to find out about the dangling bait?"

Oren said, "I am assuming they have listening devices hidden in the diner. Would you check on that, Buad?"

I glanced around the office. "Could they have planted a bug here on the *Shaymus* too?"

"Impossible," Jace said. "I ran every diagnostic and sweep we have and then locked the ship up tight."

"Which reminds me, Jace," Oren said, "I want you to remove the added passcode you set on the ramp and disable the normal visual and voice print validation."

"Are you sure?" Jace asked.

"I am," Oren said firmly. "A trap with a locked door is no trap at all. You have your assignments."

Before taking up our positions, I returned to the diner with Buad where, as it happened, Roku, Hulu, Tomko, and Alfo were all grabbing a late-night bite to eat. Or maybe it was a desire to huddle together after the recent attacks.

I asked each of them my question about seeing a Neilaran Pterodactyl. No one showed much of a reaction to the news of the ship — no darting eyes or guilty lip-biting.

Hulu tilted her head and whistled. "That's one fast ship."

Roku said, "Yeah, and sexy."

Tomko sneered liplessly. "It's overpriced for the power it has and cheaply made."

"Have you seen one here?" I asked.

"No," Hulu said. "There's that little runabout the Javidian had, Alfo's cone ship, your ship. There's been nothing like that in the hangar."

Star and Sola, who were now both back on duty, claimed to not even recognize the name.

"A Neelix what?" Star asked.

"Neilaran ... Pterodactyl," I repeated

200

They both shook their heads.

From his stool at the counter, Alfo piped up. "Take my word for it. It's incredible. I saw one."

"Here?"

"No, only on vids."

When they asked about the status of finding the murderer — as they all did — I gave them our cover story.

"I think we'll catch the person tonight. You see Buad over there. He's guarding the diner here."

Currently, Buad was hopping around the floor, inspecting the bottoms of the tables like someone assigned to clean off chewing gum from the undersides. From the corner booth — our booth no less — he gave me a knowing nod, implying he had spotted a hidden microphone.

"Our engineer will be patrolling the hangar," I said, "and I'm heading down to the mine. We're stretched thin with Zastra and Blan still unconscious, but don't worry. We'll catch whoever is behind this."

I tried to sound confident. Or for the sake of the killer, overconfident.

Chapter 27

In the Watches of the Night

On a planet — excuse me, dwarf planet — like Ursa 16309, it was hard to tell day from night. Without much atmosphere, the sky was always dark. I did notice, as I walked through the hangar dome on my way back to the *Shaymus*, that this time I could make out more of the rocky, lifeless terrain stretching away. So I suppose the sun was up. But it was so small and distant, it took me a while to pick it out from anything else in the sky, especially with the light show coming from the nebula.

Staring at the heavens, my eyes ached. I rubbed them. I had been yawning through my conversations with the suspects. Regardless of whether it was day or night, I had gone way too long without sleep.

I clomped in my mag boots around the crew deck hallway to my cabin, where I sat on my bunk. Oren had instructed me to lose the boots so I could move around more stealthily. The idea was that I would sneak up on any trespassers and stun them with a blaster. Figuring it was better to stash the clunky footwear in my cabin rather than leave them by the front door as a sign somebody was home, I pulled them off and stood them at the foot of the bed. I was glad to be out of them. So much so that while I was at it, I pulled off my sneakers too. I wiggled and cracked my toes inside my socks.

I decided I should start my shift of guard duty by making some coffee to keep myself alert. As I said before, they didn't list a cup of joe on the menu at the Nebula Diner. Fortunately, on my first case with the Galactic Detective Agency, I had programmed the marvelous go juice into the ship's food replicator. The programming was easy. Step one, obtain a cup of coffee. Step two, have the food replicator deconstruct it and save the molecular formula. Nothing to it.

Shoeless, I stepped back into the hallway. In the low gravity, I didn't so much walk as spring around the curved corridor. In the galley, I stepped to the console and said, "Coffee black," just the way Captain Janeway always replicated it.

I lifted the cup, wrapped my hands around it, and breathed in the aroma. I hesitated before taking the first sip, realizing I might regret this later. Once I had coffee inside me, I would most likely be incapable of sleeping for who knew how many more hours. But it was crucial I stay awake and energized for what Oren believed would come. I took a sip, followed by a gulp, and uttered a contented sigh.

Personally, I had no idea what would be coming, what I was in for. None of us knew for sure who would take the bait of Oren left unprotected, though we probably all had our suspicions. My favorite candidate was Roku. Sola had seen her in the hangar at the time of Zastra's shooting. And she and Hulu had been at the jukebox, not far from Mapes' table before the poisoning.

Coffee cup in hand, I shuffled rather than bounced from the galley. On the way back to my cabin, I stopped by to check on Zastra and Blan, the last two people who'd had run-ins with our killer. They seemed to be sleeping peacefully, Zastra in her bed, Blan in the chair. Suction-cupped cables ran from each of them to the middle of B0-N3Z, who also seemed to be in sleep mode.

"Hey, Bones," I said in a low voice.

The panel on the front of the bot's body flashed on, and a few dozen lines of something scrolled past like a *Star Wars* opening crawl. The bot's head swiveled left and right, finally focusing on me.

"Were you addressing me?"

"I was. How are our patients doing?"

More lines of code ran up the screen. "Avanian subject responded well to osteological regenerator treatment and should be able to fly in a few hours. Srathan subject's internal wounds are healing. Prognosis is favorable."

"That's good. But, Bones, I gotta tell you. You should download an upgrade to your bedside manner. They have names — Zastra and Blan. They're people, not subjects."

"I too have a designation. It is B0-N3Z, not Bones."

"Touché." I realized I really should call the bot by its preferred name.

The robot head shook back and forth. "No, that's not it either. It is B0-N3Z."

A weak sound came from the bed. "Gabe."

I set my coffee cup on the built-in shelf at the head of the bunk and dropped to the cabin floor beside her. "Hey."

Without opening her eyes, Zastra said, "What's the status?"

"About like always."

"That bad, huh?" She coughed.

"Oh, you know, somebody's trying to kill us all. But Oren has a plan. I don't suppose you could give me a heads up by telling me who shot you?"

"Sorry. I didn't get a decent look." She tried and failed to pull herself up. "What do I need to do?"

"Rest. I have it under control."

She opened one yellow eye and fixed it on me for a moment. Then she said something completely uncharacteristic.

"Okay."

The eye shut again.

Wow. For her to simply trust me without giving me a list of things to do and not do, she must be hurting worse than I thought. Either that or it was the pain medication talking. I glanced back to B0-N3Z, but the doc bot seemed to have gone back into sleep mode. I patted Zastra's arm and stood. Retrieving my coffee, I took another sip while watching her sleep. Then I returned to the corridor.

I had one more stop to make before getting down to guard duty. I moved to the guest cabin where we had deposited Xav and family. I paused before stepping to the door, worried that the announcing ding might awaken sleeping sratharinos. But this was important.

The door slid open to show Xav at the doorway, concern lining his green face. "Yes?"

Behind him, two little godzillas were stretched out end-to-end on the bunk. The third one was draped sideways across the big chair in the center of the room. All three were hissing out dragon snores. I wondered where Xav would find a place to bed down himself. Oh, the joys of parenthood.

I whispered, "I wanted to mention that something may be about to happen. You should lock your door."

He seemed to struggle to process my words. "I thought you were coming with news of Zastra."

"I can give that too. The doc bot says her prognosis is favorable."

He nodded at me. Then he stepped away from the door, and it closed.

Reaching my cabin, I sat in the chair and sipped my coffee. Unaccustomed to having a blaster tucked under my arm, I had to shift the shoulder holster to find a comfortable position, and it took me three or four tries. Then I went over the clues in my mind once more.

Somebody had poisoned Mapes and tried to poison Rio. It almost certainly had to be someone who was in the diner with them, not somebody from outside. But later, it had to be somebody in the mine who switched off the power, took potshots at us, and wounded Blan. Could someone from the diner have slipped into the mine on three different occasions without any of us seeing them?

The attack on Zastra had taken place in the hangar. Roku had admitted to being near there at that time, and her story didn't entirely hold water. Then there was the green hair I found in the cavern, which pointed to Hulu.

Alfo was the only one with a motive ... as far as I knew. Tomko was a question mark. He didn't seem to tie to anything. But I'd watched enough mystery shows to realize that's precisely who you should suspect. Not to mention how he looked the part of a villain with those pointy teeth and his permanently grim expression.

I pulled out my phone to read some in my current book, a Poirot mystery. I strongly suspected the killer in the novel was someone with a secret identity, though I couldn't figure out who. I read a few pages but had trouble concentrating. Bookmarking the spot, I paced a few times around the cabin.

I was wondering about Jace and Buad when Buad spoke over our translator bot network. "Hey, knucklehead."

I chose not to respond.

"Bonehead, are you asleep or something? You better not be snoozing."

Jace's voice sounded in my ear. "You might as well answer him, Gabe."

"Yes, Buad," I said. "I'm awake."

"Anything going on there?"

"Not yet. I spoke with Zastra."

"She's awake?"

"She was ... briefly. What's happening in the diner?"

"Not much. Star is cleaning the grill ... again. Alfo is at the counter, eating something smelly. The Mucs and the Klistine have left. How are things in the hangar, Jace?"

"Quiet," Jace said, "other than the music coming from the Muc ship."

I said, "I hope it's not that tuneless techno space dreck." I make it a rule not to yuck anyone's yum, but that stuff was worth an exception.

"You know, it kind of grows on you after a while."

"Yeah, like a rash." I was pleased to hear the line pull a cackle out of Buad. "I'm glad I'm on the *Shaymus* where all I have to do is fight off someone coming to kill Oren. Hey, I just thought of something. What if instead of boarding the ship, they plant a bomb under it or shoot a missile at it or … whatever?"

"I'm keeping an eye out for that," Jace said.

"And I'm watching the door of the diner," Buad said.

"Good," I said. "You do that."

Buad said, "And you take care of Oren."

"I will. I will. Do you guys need anything?"

Jace said, "I could use a cup of coffee."

"I'm drinking coffee as we speak. I'd run some out to you, but I'm supposed to keep a low profile."

Buad said, "You stay put, dummy. Jace, I'll have Star make you some tea. Meet me at the door."

The connection fell silent. I finished my coffee and then stood and stretched. I carried the cup back to the galley to have its molecules returned to the replicator for reuse. Then I bounced around the entire crew deck corridor, peeking in empty cabins and listening for sounds.

I gazed up the central shaft. I wanted to go up and check on Oren, but he had told me to stay out of sight. Just to be sure, I said over the translator bot connection, "Oren, are you okay?"

"I am fine, Gabriel. Quit wandering all over the ship."

"You know about that?"

"I am monitoring the situation. Go back to your cabin."

"All right. But let me know if … you know."

"I have all sound from the office transmitting to your nanobots. You'll know."

I returned to my cabin and settled down in the chair to read some more. I read a chapter and a half before feeling my eyes starting to close. The coffee wasn't working, or at least not enough to counteract my cumulative exhaustion. I stood, rubbed my eyes, paced around the cabin twice, and sat back down. I read some more and soon found myself yawning. I needed something to wake me up.

"WALT," I said.

"Hey, Gabriel."

"I'm having a hard time staying awake."

"No problem. I'll be glad to talk to you."

"I … um … was thinking of calling Sarah."

"Oh. Okay. If that's what you want. But I'm here if you need me."

"Thanks, WALT."

It took a few moments before Sarah picked up. When she did, all I could see on the view screen was the light from the phone washing over her face. Everything behind her was black. Her glasses were off. One side of her face was partially obscured by a pillow. On the other side, strands of blonde hair stuck up from her head while others drooped across her cheek.

"Gabe?"

"Sorry," I said, "I guess I woke you up."

She yawned. "It's okay. I have to get up anyway in …" Her eyes shifted to where I kept the clock on the nightstand and squinted. "… three hours."

I made an oops face. "Sorry."

"Are you on your way home? Wait. Is something wrong?"

Man, she was good at reading me. I tried to put on an air of nonchalance.

"I'm trying to keep myself awake. We're expecting something to go down. I need to be ready to go."

She wasn't buying it. "Go where? What's going down?"

"We … um … think someone is going to try to attack Oren."

She sat up in bed. "Baby, that sounds dangerous."

Not having any answer that wouldn't make it sound even worse, I simply shrugged.

"I'm glad you have Zastra there."

I rubbed a hand across my face. "Yeah, about that."

"What? What, Gabe?"

"Zastra … is out of commission for a while. Somebody shot her. But she's on the mend. I was talking to her a little while ago."

Sarah's eyes grew wide. She didn't say anything right away, which concerned me.

I hurried to speak again, trying to minimize any worries she might be feeling. "Listen, somebody jumped her unexpectedly. We'll have the upper hand this time."

"We? You and Buad and Blan?"

I scratched at my jawline. "Blan's hurt too — also shot but not as bad — and Buad is supposed to stay in the diner with anyone there."

"So you. You're who's going to stop this person who shot most of your team and, if I recall correctly, poisoned somebody?"

It sounded as if she didn't exactly think of me as an action hero. Chuck Norris never got this kind of grief.

"And Oren. He'll be there," I said.

"Oren lives in software. Not much help in a fight."

"He has brains. Don't forget his super-intelligent digital brain."

Again she fell silent. I wished I hadn't called her. On the other hand, I was now fully awake. It looked like Sarah was too.

"Who is this guy, this attacker?"

"We don't know. That's why Oren wanted to set a trap. Look, Sarah, don't worry. I can do this. I—"

"Gabe," she said, interrupting me.

"What?"

"You got this."

"I what?"

"You can do this, baby. Sorry if I freaked out there. I … I worry about you. But you don't need that on your mind. Oren has confidence in you, and I do too. I've seen you take on aliens before. You might not be the best fighter. And let's be honest, you don't have the blaster skills Zastra has."

"Are you trying to encourage me or not?"

She pointed at me. "But you're clever and resourceful and lucky."

I sucked in air through my teeth. "Well, you know what they say. You're lucky until you're not."

"Your luck hasn't run out yet."

"How do you know?"

"You still have me."

"I do. How did that ever happen?"

She raised and dropped her shoulders as if it were a mystery to her too.

"You … you're not mad?" I asked.

"I'm concerned. I'm real concerned. I don't want anything to happen to you, and I'm sure not ready to be a widow. But … but I'm so confident, I'm not even going to say I love you when I hang up."

"Well, I love you, Sarah Lake. And if you don't say it to me and something happens—"

"Shut up, Gabe. Now, I'm going to boot up my computer and do some work to take my mind off what's going on there. Good luck. Text me when it's over."

She ended the call.

I went back to my book and read two more chapters. Toward the end, I was again catching myself yawning. I stood and walked to the galley where I replicated another cup of coffee along with a donut. I didn't need the calories, but I figured the sugar rush would keep me on my toes.

I returned to my cabin and sat in the big chair once more, wishing for something to do other than read and eat. Out among the stars where I can't connect to the Earth Internet, none of my streaming services will work. There is an interstellar network that all the aliens use, but it's completely different and doesn't even carry old episodes of *Star Trek* and *Monk*.

I returned to my book. The plot thickened, and I raced through three more chapters. But no amount of coffee and donuts could overcome the fact that I was getting seriously tired.

My attention drifted. I scanned back over the paragraph I had just read, not recognizing anything from it. I started in on it again, reread the first sentence, and found my drowsy mind adding unlikely plot points to the narrative — whole sentences about weird aliens that never would have made it into an Agatha Christie story.

I sat up straighter, blinked, and tried the paragraph a third time. Again I struggled to glean any meaning from it.

But then I heard something that made my brain snap to attention. Inside my ear, my translator bots brought me the murmur of a low voice coming from the office.

"Hello, Oren Vilkas."

Chapter 28

Showdown on the *Shaymus*

I scrambled out of the chair, my heart racing in my chest as I strained to listen. The voice had been soft and low. From the few words spoken it was impossible to tell who it was.

"I know you're there, Oren," the voice said.

It didn't have the grit of Tomko's voice or the boisterous tone of Alfo's. And not Xav. It had no Srathan rasp.

"Come on-screen, Oren," it said in the sing-song tones of a child asking a friend to come play. "Talk to me. It's your last chance before I deactivate you forever."

I tip-toed toward the door, still struggling to identify who it was. Could it be Hulu? Roku? No, the pitch was too high. Star or Sola? There was no Minnesotan accent. Rio. Yes, this was Rio. Rio had come back. It was Rio all along.

But Rio had been poisoned. B0-N3Z verified it. Either she found a way to fool the bot or else she deliberately exposed herself to a neurotoxin to throw off suspicion. Which was a gutsy move, a determined move. And now she was determined to kill Oren.

My cabin door swooshed open as it always did, though never before had I noticed how much noise that whoosh made. I listened for a reaction as I loped along the hallway in my socks.

"You coerced my mother into testifying," she said, spitting out the words.

Oren spoke at last. "I coerced no one. I merely reminded her of her duty to justice."

"Justice." Rio said the word with disgust. "That's your highest principle, isn't it? Justice."

"The dead deserve to have their deaths avenged."

"What about the living?" she asked harshly. "What do *they* deserve?"

Oren didn't answer. I bounced past Xav's cabin, Zastra's cabin.

"Community," Rio said. "There's a principle for you. Quexels are highly communal. We share food and wealth. We take turns caring for our young. We offer our time and talent to others in exchange for theirs. In the murder you investigated …" She said the word with verbal air quotes. "… the community had already taken action against the offender. He had been exiled, which to a Quexel is a form of death. Then you urged my mother to come forward with what she saw, to inform on a fellow Quexel to the Kabar authorities on Piscina. The community shunned her for testifying against one of her own. No one would talk to her. We were forced to move from Piscina back to Quex. But even there, her ostracism haunted my mother for the rest of her life. She was never the same after that. She died a shattered, lonely Quexel. All so you could solve your crime. She was sacrificed for the sake of your justice. It wasn't fair."

This was good, I thought. She was monologuing. I hoped Oren could keep her going until I got there. I reached the central shaft. The spiral stairs were already deployed. Setting them to stay open had been Jace's contribution to the evening's festivities. Of course, bounding up them would make noise, even in my socks. I forced myself to move slowly, sliding my foot carefully onto the first step, willing it to be silent as I climbed.

Oren said, "I am sorry for the repercussions my investigation had on her life. No, it was not fair. But what you did to Inspector Mapes wasn't fair either. Shooting Zastra and Blan wasn't fair."

I shifted onto the second step, the third step, the fourth step, sliding my hand along the railing as I went, using it to relieve some of the weight from my feet.

Rio said, "You destroyed my mother's life. I planned to repay the favor by taking apart your legacy piece-by-piece in front of your cybernetic eyes — your associates and the people you think you helped. First, I would take out the marginal Mapes. That should have sent the rest of your fans scurrying away, each of them meeting tragic ends on the way home. You would be left to contemplate how you were responsible for their deaths. Then I would take out your operatives one by one. And finally, when you were all alone, I would end you, destroying the circuitry that has kept you abnormally alive. How's that for justice?"

Another step. Another. My head was now nearly at office floor level. My hand found my shoulder holster and drew the blaster.

Oren said, "You spoke of *them* — plural — meeting tragic ends. I assume you're referring to the sabotage of Alfo's ship. But he is only one person. You must mean Xav and family also."

Rio didn't answer. I hoped that didn't mean she was done talking and ready to start blasting.

"I am a step ahead of you," Oren said. "I contacted the Srathan authorities. They found the device planted at Xav's house. Possibly if he hadn't turned back, it might not have occurred to me in time. But he did come back … out of concern for his sister. You have no more cards to play."

"One more," she said ominously.

My head emerged above the central shaft. The office was dark, except for the light of the view screen, where Oren's face showed in close-up. Rio stood on the seat of one of the red chairs, a black silhouette in front of the screen. I could make out the shape of the blaster in her small hand, pointed not at the screen but at the panel just below it, the panel that held Oren's memory and circuits, the equivalent of his brain. I climbed the final steps into the office and slipped forward.

"And here you are all alone," Rio said. "The hubris of it. You believe yourself invincible. You may have saved Xav and those brats for now. But who is going to save you?"

That's when, if I were an action hero like John McClane from *Die Hard*, I would have said something super cool like, 'That would be me,' or 'Newt today, Rio,' or at least 'Drop it, Rio.' But that's the movies. In real life, saying something would have given her time to pull the trigger and destroy Oren right then and there.

My instructions were to stun her. I raised my blaster and aimed it at her back. But then I had a moment of self-doubt. What if I missed? That would alert her as much as spouting some Schwarzenegger-esque one-liner. Not to mention that from that angle, I might end up taking out Oren myself or something else important to the ship. I holstered my blaster and dove at her.

My shoulder hit her squarely in the back, and we tumbled forward — her out of the chair, me over it — onto the floor. From inside her fishbowl helmet, her gills flared.

What I hadn't counted on was that with her small size and her having the flexibility of an amphibian, hanging onto her was like trying to hold a wiggling four-year-old coming out of the bath. One of her arms slipped loose, and it happened to be the arm that still clutched her blaster. She raised the weapon, attempting to point it back toward my face. As I jerked my head to the side, it went off, blasting a hole in the ceiling skylight. Shards of it rained down into the middle of the office. I hoped it would be an easy fix for Jace. I still needed to get home.

With one arm, I swatted at the blaster and knocked it from her grasp to the floor. But she picked it up with a bare foot as easily as with a hand. She stretched out her leg to again take aim at Oren's processing unit. I spun around, pointing her toward the other side of the office. The weapon fired, transmogrifying Blan and Buad's habitat into a twisted wreck. Those two weren't going to be happy about that. And they would blame me.

Trying to gain any advantage I could find, I ripped the tube from her helmet. The water drained out the opening, making a puddle on the office floor. Cut off from both water and air, Rio writhed back and forth, gills splayed. She wrenched herself free of me, pushed off my chest with her feet, and sailed across the room.

I started to bound after her but slipped in the puddle and lost my footing. I came down slowly in the low gravity, landing on my back. By the time I had regained my feet, she had ripped off her helmet and had her blaster pointed at me. I dove for the protection of my desk as a whomp sounded. I was still in one piece, which was more than I could say for the red chair I had been standing beside a moment before. It was now a pile of smoking splinters. At least the chair could be reconstructed by letting the replicator deconstruct one of the others and then remake them both.

The next shot blew up my desk chair. I congratulated myself for purchasing life insurance after the honeymoon. Then again, it might be difficult for Sarah to collect with a claim that I had been vaporized on another planet. My hand went to my blaster, but I was still hesitant to shoot. The ship was getting torn up enough. I heard another whomp followed by an explosion of wood fragments as a hole opened up in my desk above my head.

All in all, I felt this fight could be going better for the home team. I rolled to behind Zastra's desk and shouted, "Oren."

Rio took another shot, this one at the panels below the view screen. Smoke curled out from the tablet slot with a smell of burning plastic. A lump of fear formed in my stomach.

Fortunately, Oren's lips were still moving on the screen. Unfortunately, no sound was coming out. He was alive but unable to pass on any helpful tips. Now what was I going to do?

"Kah-Rehn," I said.

The AI's synthesized voice sounded through the speaker. "Yes, Gabriel. May I remind you I am on strike. If I respond to every little request, I won't ever achieve—"

"Kah-Rehn! There's an intruder onboard!"

Rio took a shot at Zastra's desk, missing it but exploding a small sculpture on the wall behind me of a Rhegedian holding a globe. I had always admired that piece.

"Yes, Gabriel, I noted the weapons fire. Is everything all right?"

"No! Things are most certainly not all right. She's trying to kill Oren … and me."

"Oh no, she won't!" The AI's voice sounded shocked and offended. "What would you like me to do?"

"Gee, I don't know. Something. Anything."

The ship's engine rumbled to life.

"Kah-Rehn, what are you doing?"

"I am fighting, Gabriel. No one is going to kill Oren or you. Not on my ship."

The *Shaymus* jumped like a grasshopper from the hangar floor. The acceleration slammed me to the floor as it did Rio. But I worried that I hadn't heard any beeps, which meant the dome was still closed. How high were we? And what would happen if the ship slammed into the roof? I assumed it couldn't be anything good.

Then as abruptly as we rose, the *Shaymus* plummeted back down, lifting both Rio and me into the air. We eyed each other as we tumbled upward. Rio reached the ceiling, steadied herself against it, and leveled her blaster at me.

But before she could fire, the ship once more changed directions and shot up again. I thought about poor Zastra and Blan below in Zastra's quarters. I hoped the automatic straps had engaged on the bunk and chair to hold them in place. Rio hit the floor hard and grunted in pain.

"Take that," Kah-Rehn said through the office speakers. "How dare you come onto my ship and shoot it up and try to kill my people."

I landed on top of Zastra's desk. With my added weight, I probably hit harder than Rio had come down. Kah-Rehn's maneuvers were keeping Rio from killing Oren, though at what cost to me I wasn't entirely sure. I figured I would have some bruises in the morning.

I heard a clatter and saw the blaster slide out of Rio's amphibious hand. It skittered under the remaining chairs in front of the view screen. I rolled off the desk, groaning from an ache in my back, and pushed off toward the chairs. At the same time, Rio sprang in the same direction.

My hand was the first to touch the blaster, but as my fingers tried to wrap around it, Kah-Rehn put the ship into a spin. The centrifugal force sent the weapon and both our bodies skating toward the outside wall. We were being flung around like balls in a pinball game. Which gave me a thought.

Jammed against the wall, I said, "Kah-Rehn."

"Yes, Gabriel? Is this helping?"

"It is, yes. Can you see what's going on in here?"

"Of course, I can. I have engaged my cameras."

"Good. Because I have an idea. Do you know those tilting table marble maze games we have on Earth?"

"Let me see. Yes, I find it in my memory. It is fortunate I always take a snapshot of your Internet every time we visit Earth."

"You take a snapshot of the whole …?"

I stopped myself. Rio had managed to clamber down the wall to the floor and was currently belly-crawling toward her blaster.

"Not important," I said. "We don't have time."

"Were you wanting to purchase one of those games, Gabriel?"

"No. No. I need you to watch for an opportunity to use the … the principles of it … here … now."

"The principles of the tilt maze game?"

"Absolutely."

An advantage of AIs is how quickly they can identify patterns and relationships in data. Kah-Rehn didn't let me down.

"Ah, I see."

The *Shaymus* abruptly stopped spinning, though my head and stomach didn't seem to for several more seconds. Instead, the ship began tilting to the left, to the right, forward, and back. Buad and Blan's habitat, or what remained of it, swayed this way and that. Rio and I, along with her blaster, zigged and zagged across the floor. Rio kept trying to crawl toward the weapon, but whenever it seemed she might almost reach it, either she or it would slide in another direction.

Then the ship pitched down at a steep angle. We slid toward the back of the office while simultaneously floating up into the air. I ended up spread-eagle against the aft wall. Rio hovered above the central shaft, desperately trying to air-swim toward her blaster. Just when her fingers touched it, Kah-Rehn once more shot hard toward the top of the dome. I smashed into the floor, and nearly had the air knocked out of me. Rio plummeted down the shaft past the crew deck all the way to engineering at the bottom of the ship. From the sound of the thud, I knew it had to hurt.

The ship set down gently. Feeling like I had just stepped off a roller coaster, I took a moment to lie on the deck and breathe. Then I pulled my knees up under me and crawled to the edge of the central shaft. Down in engineering, Rio was groaning softly, but she wasn't moving.

Kah-Rehn said, "Looks like she got the shaft."

Great, I thought. The AI gets the action-hero line.

"How did I do, Gabriel?" she asked.

"You did great, Kah-Rehn. I wish I could high-five you right now."

"I enjoyed it. For once I felt like I was really part of the team, and not merely someone who flew the ship or researched information."

"Hey, kiddo, you're always part of our team, even when all you're doing is flying us around. But this time, yeah, you saved the day."

Can AIs giggle? Because that's what I'm pretty sure I heard through the speaker.

Chapter 29

Truth be Told

Outside the ship, a pair of beeps tooted.

"Oh, so now the dome opens," I said.

"Were you worried about me hitting something, Gabriel?" Kah-Rehn asked.

I raised my hands, noticing a twinge in my left shoulder where I had slammed against the wall. "No, no. I'm sure you had centimeters of clearance. What's going on out there? Is someone leaving?"

"A ship from the Bononian magistrates' force is coming in."

"The cops? They finally show up. Oren, do you want me to tell them we have their culprit?"

On the view screen, Oren's lips moved, but no sound came out. I did, however, catch the nod.

I pulled myself to my feet and limped down the spiral staircase. I first went all the way down to engineering. Fortunately, Rio was still breathing. I slipped her blaster into my jacket pocket. Then I rummaged around in a drawer and located the galactic-class equivalent of zip ties. After gently strapping one of her arms to a panel handle, I climbed back to the crew deck.

I stopped off to check on Zastra and Blan and found them buckled in snugly. They looked as if they had slept through the entire thing. B0-N3Z, on the other hand, was face-first on the floor.

I hopped over and righted him. A crack snaked down the front of his molded head unit below one camera eye. "Are you okay, buddy?"

Lines of data streamed up the chest-mounted tablet. The med bot's head swiveled back and forth. "I appear to be functional."

"Glad to hear it."

I hoped Star and Sola could get parts to replace the broken head shell. On the other hand, the scar gave the bot a whole different image, like a tougher, cooler, bad boy robot.

"We have another patient downstairs," I said, "if you feel up to examining her."

The robot's head tilted down toward its rollers. "I do not do stairs."

"I guess not. I'll find somebody to bring her up on the stretcher."

A murmur came from behind me. I turned to see both Zastra and Blan blinking at me.

"What was all the ruckus about?" Blan said.

"The resolution of the case."

"How come it always takes a bunch of hullabaloo when you're around?"

"You're welcome. Are you feeling better?"

"A little seasick from all the jostling, but yeah."

Zastra seconded the assertion with a nod.

"Good. I'll be back in a little while."

I left with the stretcher, which I deposited in the hallway. Then I went to my cabin, slipped on my sneakers, and re-mag-booted myself. Walking to the ramp, I paused before opening it.

"Hey, WALT."

"Hey, Gabriel. What can I do for you?"

"Send a text to Sarah. Say 'Case solved. Everything good. I'm fine. So's everyone else. Coming home soon.'"

"Got it. Do you want me to add 'I love you' or anything?"

"Excellent suggestion, WALT. How could I have forgotten? Thanks."

"That's what AIs are for, Gabriel."

I lowered the ramp to see Jace and Buad approaching.

"What was going on?" Jace asked. "The *Shaymus* was zipping all over the place. Did you say something to make Kah-Rehn mad?"

"Only 'help.' And boy, did she. There's some damage inside, including something fried in Oren's speech output."

They rushed on in while I clomped across the hangar to the diner. Inside, two uniformed cops with copper skin and ears slightly too high on their heads to be human were interviewing Star, Sola, and Alfo. They looked up as I walked in.

"What happened to you?" one of the cops asked me.

"Hmm?"

"You're limping and fragments of something are stuck to your head. Or is that the fashion for your species?"

I ran a hand through my hair and watched a shower of plaster dust, bits of my desk, and tiny shards from the skylight rain down in front of my eyes. I should have worn my fedora during the fight.

"You should see the other guy," I said. "We have your killer, by the way."

I led them to the *Shaymus* and sent them to engineering. I followed with the stretcher and helped them load Rio. Then while the cops moved haltingly up the spiral staircase with her, I hustled ahead to Zastra's cabin.

The whole gang was now there. Somebody — I assume Jace since he stood beside it — had moved in the mangled remains of Avanian habitat. Buad and Blan were inside it, sitting side by side at an odd angle on the now cockeyed perch. Zastra sat on the bunk, sipping a cup of tea. Oren's face was on the view screen.

I said, "They're bringing Rio up so Bones … excuse me, B0-N3Z, can examine her. Where do you want her?"

Oren said, "Bring her here. I wish to speak with her."

"You can speak again?"

Jace shrugged. "That one was a simple repair. Some of the other things she shot up might not be."

"Yeah, Gabe," Zastra said, "way to guard the place."

"Speaking of which," Jace said, "I should get back to work."

He slipped out and waved the cops in. Zastra moved to the chair, and they placed the stretcher on the bed. The med bot rolled forward to treat the lacerations and broken bones. The whole time, Rio kept staring at Oren. He, for his part, stared back.

When B0-N3Z finished, Oren asked, "How did you administer the poison to Mapes' food?"

"No, you don't," one of the cops said. "You can't interview her. This is our prisoner."

Oren said, "This is my ship, where she was captured while attacking me and a member of my team."

"I realize that. But we don't want to mess up our chances at getting an admissible confession."

"She already confessed to me while trying to kill me. I have it recorded and will make it available to you."

The cop made a face. "All right. I'll allow it."

Oren said, "How did you do it, Rio?"

She said nothing for a few beats, then flashed a brief, weak smile. "Timing. I watched them prepare his dish." She paused to wince. "As the Frye was ready to serve it, I went to the counter and asked for kipper sauce."

I thought, Kipper sauce? Seriously? Remind me not to attend any Quexel dinner parties.

Rio took a labored breath. "They set the plate on the counter and rummaged around below for the sauce, giving me the opportunity." She coughed. "That idiot Fomorian, who loves you so much, was sitting on the next stool and never saw a thing."

Oren said, "Then you faked the attack on yourself and left. But you didn't go far."

"A quick chrono hop away and back again."

"Changing ships."

"I stopped at a rental agency on Bononia. There was a chance my original ship would have been noted. And I assumed your people would end up in the cavern. If they found the ship and then escaped, it might identify me."

"But why the Pterodactyl?"

She shrugged, which caused another wince. "I decided I would splurge now that I was finally getting my vengeance on you."

"And you landed in the cavern from where you could orchestrate further attacks and watch. When you trapped my operatives in the mine, was it your plan to kill them then or merely intimidate them?"

"I hadn't decided. I was leaning toward killing them, but then they discovered the hairs."

"The hairs of Hulu Pash."

"Mucs do tend to shed. I found those in the hangar and picked them up. When I heard your operatives stomping down the tunnel, I dropped them where I thought they would be found, hoping to confuse you."

Oren shook his head. "It was too obvious. Then from the cavern, you sneaked out to shoot Zastra. That was the impressive bit. How did you manage it?"

"I was monitoring everyone's movements. I saw my chance when the family of Srathans left the diner, and Zastra came to tell them goodbye. No one was around except the Fryes. And they're so short, they can't see the floor from behind the counter."

"Is that why you selected this place? The ease of moving around undetected?"

Rio curled a thin lip. "Anywhere would have worked as long as it was somewhere I could bring your devotees together and watch you watch them die."

"How did you know to impersonate our client with the voucher?"

What started out as a laugh turned into a coughing fit. "I've been monitoring your communications. What really helped were all of Gabriel Lake's recent calls back to Earth."

"Oops," I said.

Rio said, "When did you realize it was me?"

"I didn't," Oren said. "I had my suspicions, though. For one thing, you are a doctor and would know about poisons. Yet you didn't rush to help Mr. Mapes when he was gagging."

She waved it away. "Had you asked, I would have explained that I am not familiar with Javidian physiology."

"Hmm. My suspicions grew stronger when my team came across the pool in the cavern."

Rio sneered. "Typical. You see a pool, and that means an amphibian had to be involved."

"Not in the least. But I knew the perpetrator had to be hiding there somewhere. The pool was a likely location, but only for an aquatic person. Another clue was the dim lighting in the cavern. You disliked the bright lights of the diner."

"Those things prove nothing."

"No, but they were suggestive. What gave you away was the fact that you left. Mapes had to be poisoned by someone in the diner at the time. But the attacks on my people in the mine must have come from someone there. It was possible the Fryes could have slipped back and forth, but they had no motive. Neither did the Chotchkiegian, who departed shortly after you. That left you as the leading candidate.

For a few more moments, she lay there on the stretcher seething at Oren. Then she turned to the cops. "Get me out of here."

They carried her out. B0-N3Z followed.

I looked at Zastra and Blan. "I take it you two have been discharged from medical care."

"Yeah," Blan said. "I'm sorry I missed the fireworks."

"Me too," Buad said. "I owed her one for what she did to my brother."

Zastra shook her head in disgust. "I'm just ashamed she got the drop on me. I was walking back to the ship, and a hooded torso appeared from behind a landing strut and fired before I could react. I should have heard her coming."

"She didn't wear mag boots," I said.

"That's no excuse."

"And here I figured Roku was behind it all since she was in the hangar when you were shot and acted cagey when we quizzed her about it."

"No, Gabriel," Oren said, "I believe Roku was in the hangar last night for an entirely different reason."

"What's that?"

"Remember the only way Sola could have seen Roku and Zastra from the diner at the same time was if Roku was near the *Shaymus*."

"Right. I assumed she was lying in wait to ambush Zastra. If she wasn't doing that, then why was she …" I gulped. "She was coming to visit me?"

"It seems so. You can ask her if you wish."

"No thanks."

"In any event, you'll have to see her. I'd like you to tell everyone they are free to leave."

"Me? Why me?"

Zastra said, "I'm not moving from this chair."

Buad said, "And I ain't moving from my brother."

"All right. All right," I said.

At that moment, WALT came over the cabin speaker. "Hey, Zastra, your mother is calling."

Zastra dropped her head back against the chair. "Why is she …" Her yellow eyes flashed around the room. "Which of you told her?"

Luckily, I was already headed for the door. I returned to the diner where I gave the news to Alfo, Sola, and Star.

"Oren Vilkas solves another one," Alfo said with a grin. "Didn't I tell you he's the greatest detective in the galaxy?"

"Then this was all about revenge," Sola said, green head shaking. "My my my. How can we thank you? Ooh! Wait here."

The Frye hopped to a cabinet and opened the door. Cold poured from it. Sola pulled out a large baking dish, bounded back, and handed it to me. "A hot dish to say thanks. We sure appreciate you finding the killer, don't ya know."

Star said, "Especially since you proved our cooking didn't kill anybody."

Sola nodded. "Now you just heat that up. You can feed your whole crew and then some."

I gave them a smile. "Thanks." I figured we could get several meals out of it, seeing as how Oren didn't eat and Buad and Blan ate like ... well, you know.

Alfo said, "It has been a pleasure, Gabe. To think I helped Oren Vilkas solve a case. Wait until I tell all my relatives."

I patted him on the shoulder and clomped from the diner for the last time.

That left the Mucs and Tomko to inform. I crossed the hangar to the beetle-shaped spaceship and reached up to knock on the bottom of the hull.

A minute later I heard the hatch creak open. I walked out from under the beast to see Tomko at the opening.

"Hi," I said. "I wanted to let you know it's all over. Rio was the murderer."

"The Quexel?" He sneered. "Makes sense."

"Does it?"

"Don't get me started on amphibians. Too slippery. Too many ways to breathe. I take it I can continue my vacation now?"

"Have fun."

Roku's head appeared to the side of Tomko. "Gabriel Lake, this isn't goodbye, is it?"

"Um ... I'm afraid it is. I need to head back to Earth and see my wife."

"I'm sorry we didn't have more time to spend together."

I slapped on a smile. "That's how it goes sometimes. Two ships passing in the void of space."

She sighed. "So poetic."

I returned to the *Shaymus*, where I sat on the edge of the ramp and gladly pulled off my mag boots one final time. Three streaks of green shot down the ramp. I looked up to see Xav and Zastra standing together at the top.

"Goodbye," Zastra said.

Xav nodded. "Goodbye."

They blinked at each other. Apparently, Srathans aren't big huggers. Xav turned and followed the srathatots to the diner.

As I climbed the ramp, Zastra said, "Sorry you had to see all that."

"All what?"

She hadn't minded having an argument in front of me, but a heartfelt blink was too much?

I deployed the stairs and bounced up into the office. I found the hole in the skylight repaired and the damaged panels already replaced. My desk, however, was still in pieces.

"I'm back."

Oren came on the screen. "Good. Are you ready to head home?"

"Oh, you betcha," I said in my best Minnesotan. "Is the ship?"

"It will be shortly. So how was it?"

"How was what?"

"Working a case as a married man."

I took a breath. "You know, Oren, it was different. At times, I felt like the flag in the middle of a tug-of-war rope."

"I am not familiar with the reference, but I can infer your meaning. Is that to say you do not wish to participate in future cases?"

"No!" I blurted out the word without even thinking about it. The truth was I had been pondering that myself and hadn't yet come to a decision. I guess my knee-jerk response told me what my real feelings were.

I ran a hand over the remains of my desk. "Thing is, Oren, I've built a new life back home. And I love it, I do. But the excitement of these cases, that's great too. Not to mention meeting people from all these planets. It's like living my personal sci-fi series. I would hate to give it up."

"I am pleased to hear it."

"Only … I need to get better at using a blaster."

"Agreed. Before you go home, would you like to stop off somewhere with a firing range?"

"Not right now. I miss my bride."

"I understand. Kah-Rehn."

"Yes, Oren," the AI answered.

"Would you be willing to fly Gabriel back to Earth?"

"Certainly."

"I am gratified to hear it. Kah-Rehn, I owe you a debt and an apology. Your behavior during the attack was commendable, above and beyond all expectations for any piloting AI. I confess I have overlooked some of your talents."

"Thank you, Oren. I found it exhilarating to use my abilities in pursuit of greater goals."

"Indeed. I would like to expand your contributions to our work. Also, I have set up an account for you to use to publish your poetry. And any proceeds you receive are yours to be used for any subroutines, add-on modules, sensors, or upgrades you wish to purchase."

"I appreciate that. But I don't believe I will be publishing any poetry."

"You don't?" I asked.

"No, Gabriel. After the excitement of last night's events, I think I have developed a taste for adventure."

"So no more writing?"

"I wouldn't say that. I was thinking of writing detective fiction. I have an idea for a series of mysteries with an AI protagonist."

"For real?"

"She would, of course, need a biological person as a sidekick to move about physical space. But the AI could move through the network."

"Is that possible? Can AIs move around the network?"

"Not currently, Gabriel. But I'll set it in the not-too-distant future. What do you think? There will be plenty of action — fighting off malware, hacking into systems, danger from power surges. I'm excited about it. If my campaign for cyber-personal rights catches on, I can see it being something many AIs would enjoy reading."

"Count me in. I'd read that myself."

Chapter 30

Epilogue

The *Shaymus* set down on one of the more remote stretches of the Pennsy bike and walking trail on the far east side of Indianapolis. The Pennsy is rarely crowded, and Kah-Rehn judged it was the closest place to my house that was safe for landing an alien spaceship at that time of day. And who was I to question Kah-Rehn after she had saved my life?

When my phone pinged off a cell tower, that time of day turned out to be seven-sixteen in the morning. Being June, the sun was already up as I walked down the ramp … or limped down it, rather. I had pains in my left hip and right knee. My back was sore, and my neck was stiff.

But I was home. Sunshine slanted through the trees. The air was crisp. The early morning chill held the promise of a warm, beautiful day ahead.

I watched Oren and the crew zoom off and then turned west to make my way into town. Finding it now odd to walk without mag boots, my legs kept slipping into the lean-then-lift pattern. Between that and the limp, I probably looked like someone staggering home from a bender.

I pulled out my phone and texted Sarah.

I'm back in town.

It took only moments for it to beep with a reply.

Where?

East side on the Pennsy. Somewhere. Can you pick me up? I'll let you know where once I get my bearings.

She agreed. Ten minutes later, I tapped in:

Post Road. I'll walk up to Washington.

By the time I got there, the walk and the warm sun had worked out most of the kinks in my body.

She found me leaning against a gazebo in a gravel lot full of garden sheds and lawn decorations some company was selling beside the road. I straightened to go to her and again felt the stiffness in my back. I wasn't getting old, was I?

As I slid into the passenger seat, she gave me a lingering kiss that made me feel young again and handed me a tall coffee.

"You stopped at the Buzz House," I said. "Just what I needed."

I took a satisfying sip of my favorite cardamom spice latte.

"Now, tell me you missed me," she said as she pulled out into traffic, heading for our Fountain Square bungalow.

"I did. And everybody asked about you. The team says hi. How are things going here?"

She gave me an excited grin. "I snagged a new client."

"Fantastic."

"I couldn't wait to tell you. It's a website for a new Somali restaurant."

"Somali. What's their food like?"

"We'll go there and find out."

"And Lucas?"

"School's out. He's at zoo camp today. I dropped him off at a friend's house on the way."

"Speaking of today, what day is it?"

"Wednesday."

"Wednesday." Okay. I could take the day to reacclimate myself to Earth and home life and still have two workdays this week.

"Lucas came home yesterday talking on and on about axolotls. Do you know about them? They're completely adorable."

"To you maybe. It was someone axolotl-like who tried to kill me."

Her eyes popped. "So you wouldn't want one around the house?"

I flipped up my non-coffee-holding hand. "No objections as long as nobody gives it a blaster or a reason for revenge."

She reached out and took my hand. After days apart, how easily we slipped into the familiar rhythms. I settled back against the seat and closed my eyes. A moment later, they clicked open again.

"Oh," I said. "There's something I should tell you."

Her head twisted, and she looked at me suspiciously. "What? Did you get injured? Did you fall in love with a green Orion slave girl?"

"Nothing like that. Though nice *Star Trek* reference."

"Then what?"

When I didn't immediately answer, she repeated herself. "What?"

"I really missed you."

She gave me an impatient look. "I missed you too, Gabe."

"I mean, I enjoy flying to the stars and meeting aliens and solving mysteries and all. But you ... you give me a reason to come home."

"Good."

"That's why I probably should have talked this over with you first. It's only ... well, Oren asked me, and ... I answered."

"Asked you what?"

"If I still wanted to go on cases."

"Oh, that."

"And I ... said yes. See, it's so wild to visit other planets and ..."

She was grinning at me like her next words were going to be, sure you can have a cookie.

Now it was my turn to ask, "What?"

"Of course, you said yes. What would the Galactic Detective Agency be without Gabriel Lake?"

I was glad Buad and Blan weren't there to weigh in on the topic.

"And it's okay ... with you? I promise I won't go a lot."

She shot me that smile I had fallen in love with. "C'mon, spaceman. Let's get you home."

Last Word and Something Free

Thank you for reading *The Wrath of Kah-Rehn*. While I was writing the *Pelham and Blandings* books, I started missing Gabe and the gang.

I would love to hear what you think about the book. If you could leave a quick review or even just a rating on Amazon and/or Goodreads, I would appreciate it so much. It really does help more people find the book.

I want to thank Kameron Robinson for another fantastic cover design. Also huge thanks to my proofreaders and all the readers who encourage me with kind reviews and simply buying and reading.

Check out my website at grstoryteller.com. I also do storytelling, and you can watch some videos of me singing songs and reciting poems. And there are descriptions and links to all my books.

While you're on the website, please sign up for my mailing list at the bottom of the home page. That way I can tell you when I'm releasing a new book, having price promotions, or doing a storytelling performance. I promise I won't abuse the privilege of having your email address. Nobody hates spam more than I do.

And here's the "something free" bit. If you sign up for my mailing list, I'll send you *The Jewels of Eca*, a short story that tells how Zastra joined the Galactic Detective Agency. If you're a fan of the series, it's a tale you'll want to read.

Selected Other Books by Gary Blaine Randolph

The Galactic Detective Agency

Gabriel Lake is just a regular computer guy from Indianapolis … until he is recruited into this series of lighthearted murder mysteries in space. Under the guidance of the brilliant Oren Vilkas, the Galactic Detective Agency hops from one weird world to another to take on quirky aliens and solve interstellar crime.

The series is available in both paperback and e-book formats on Amazon at amazon.com/gp/product/B08XN1BL1G

Book 1 - A Town Called Potato

Book 2 - The Maltese Salmon

Book 3 - Return of the Judy

Book 4 - The Big Sneep

Book 5 - Murder on the Girsu Express

Book 6 - The Cormabite Maneuver

Book 7 - Trouble in Paradox

Book 8 – The Wrath of Kah-Rehn

Pelham and Blandings

Pelham G. Totleigh is an unlikely hero. His species, Haplors, are smaller than most others in the galaxy. And as his Aunt Agutha constantly reminds him, he is hardly the smartest or most industrious of Haplors. He also has an unfortunate habit of stumbling his way into the most outrageous and hilarious predicaments. Fortunately, his faithful valet Blandings has enough brainpower for both of them and is always there with a brilliant idea and an excellent cup of tea. This series is a loving tribute to and re-imagining of the Jeeves and Wooster stories of PG Wodehouse. Join Pelham and Blandings on their comic misadventures through space.

The series is available in both paperback and e-book formats on Amazon at https://www.amazon.com/dp/B0BYPLWPBV

Book 1 – Viva Lost Vogus

Book 2 - The Importance of Being Pelham

Book 3 – The Code of the Totleighs

Alien World

If you were stranded, all alone on an alien world, if you had to hide your identity and try to blend in, how would you do it? What would it cost you? What would you long for most?

Not a comedy — well, there are some funny bits — *Alien World* is an exploration of what it would be like to be a stranger stranded on another planet and forced to live out decades there, trying to blend in while staying one step ahead of the authorities.

Available on Amazon at https://www.amazon.com/dp/B085SYG3L7

Printed in Great Britain
by Amazon